Limerick City Library

3 0002 50028324 7

LIMERICK CITY LIBRARY

Phone: 407510
Website:
www.limerickcity.ie/library
Email: citylib@limerickcity.ie

The Granary,
Michael Street,
Limerick.

**This book is issued subject to the Rules of this Library.
The Book must be returned not later than the last date
stamped below.**

Class No. ....TF........... Acc. No. ..C 99849.

Date of Return	Date of Return	Date

... the ingredients of an
... The writing is extraordinary.'
Sarah Webb, *Irish Independent*

'It races the reader along at breathtaking speed and doesn't release
its grip until the very last page.'
International Youth Library,
on choosing *The Poison Throne* as
an outstanding new international book for young adults.

The Crowded Shadows

'Compelling and complex, romantic and suspenseful, populated
by memorable characters and intricately detailed, this impressive
middle volume will leave readers demanding the conclusion.'
US Publishers Weekly

'Excellent ... a cracking theatrical historical fantasy
set in medieval Europe.'
Irish Independent

'More than fulfils the promise of *The Poison Throne* and the completed trilogy is
likely to stand with the best of this ʃ   se,
detailed style make her parallel Eu   ʒ
creation and her mastery of storytellin   it to
leave it. This is a book tc
INIʃ

D1428738

The Rebel Prince

'An amazing conclusion to what's probably become one of my three favourite fantasy trilogies of all time, while Kiernan's thought-provoking writing has made her jump right to the top of the list of authors whose next works I'm eagerly awaiting.' *thebookbag.co.uk*

'*The Rebel Prince* is a fitting final chapter for the series. Wynter's progress from dependent young girl to insightful and self-confident woman is a carefully done, and Kiernan's world, full of mysterious wandering tribes, rich history, and the possibility, struggle, and power of change, is well worth a visit.' *bookgeeks.co.uk*

'This third in the Moorehawke Trilogy continues the fast and bloody pace, while still capable of being read as a stand-alone. Each character satisfyingly grows exponentially into his or her own potential. A must-read for any fan of the series, or of the genre.' *RT Magazine*

'Tight writing, passion and violence, plus plenty of skullduggery and intrigue combine to make this a compelling read.' *Bookfest*

'Celine Kiernan brings her Moorehawke trilogy to a gothically atmospheric ending ... the joy is in the anticipation and the depth of character formation.' *Evening Echo*

Born and raised in Dublin, **Celine Kiernan** trained at the Sullivan Bluth Studios as a classical feature character animator and worked in the film business, operating between Germany, Ireland and the USA. She is also a freelance illustrator.

Celine's Moorehawke trilogy attracted great interest from publishers worldwide and was been published in many European languages, as well as in Britain, USA and Canada, Australia and New Zealand.

Celine lives in Virginia, County Cavan.

Awards

The Poison Throne won the Reading Association of Ireland Award 2009.

It was shortlisted in two categories for the Irish Book Awards, 2009: the Dublin Airport Authority Irish Children's Book of the Year Award (Senior Selection), and the International Education Services Ltd Best Irish Newcomer of the Year Award.

It was selected by the International Youth Library for its White Ravens list of outstanding new international books for young adults.

To Mam, I love you.

To Dad, I miss you.

Acknowledgements

With many thanks to Susan Houlden who has been an absolute treasure to work with.

First published 2011 by
The O'Brien Press Ltd.
12 Terenure Road East, Rathgar,
Dublin 6, Ireland.
Tel: +353 1 4923333;
Fax: +353 1 4922777
E-mail: books@obrien.ie
Website: www.obrien.ie

ISBN 978-1-84717-164-1

Copyright for text © Celine Kiernan 2011
Copyright for typesetting, editing, layout, design © The O'Brien Press Ltd

All rights reserved.
No part of this publication may be reproduced
or utilised in any form or by any means,
electronic or mechanical, including photocopying,
recording or in any information storage
and retrieval system, without permission
in writing from the publisher.
British Library Cataloguing-in-Publication Data
A catalogue record for this title is available from the British Library.

The O'Brien Press receives assistance from

1 2 3 4 5 6 7 8
11 12 13 14 15

Author photo by Anthony Woods
Front cover image: iStockphoto

Editing, typesetting and design: The O'Brien Press Ltd
Printed and bound by Mackays of Chatham
The paper used in this book is produced using pulp from managed forests

INTO THE GREY

Celine Kiernan

THE O'BRIEN PRESS
DUBLIN

CITY OF LIMERICK
99649
PUBLIC LIBRARY

Contents

Contents

1. Nan Burns the House Down

We were watching telly the night Nan burnt the house down. It was March 1974, and I was fifteen years of age. I thought I lost everything in that fire, but what did I know about loss? Nothing, that's what. I would learn soon enough.

I think the fire changed us – me and Dom. Though I didn't feel much different at first, I think something inside of us opened up, or woke up. I think, all at once, we began to understand how easily things are broken and taken and lost. It was like walking through a door: on one side was the warm, cosy sitting room of our childhood; on the other, a burnt-out shell of ash and char.

I think that's how the goblin-boy was able to see us. Though he'd been there for every summer of our childhood – mine and Dom's – we'd only been stupid boys until then. Stupid, happy, ignorant boys. And what in hell would he have had in common with two stupid boys? But after the fire we were different. We were maybe a little bit like him. And so he saw us, at last, and he thought he'd found a home.

The night of the fire, Ma had brought chips home and we were eating them from the bags, our feet on the coffee table, our eyes glued to the TV. Looking back, it's weird to remember that we were watching *All Quiet on the Western Front*. Looking back, it seems prophetic – but at the time I just remember hating it. It didn't feel like a proper war movie at all. It was all about the Germans for one thing. Sure, they were the bad guys! Who wants to watch a war movie about the bad guys? And they weren't even acting like bad guys. They just acted like normal lads – though it had to be said they were a bloody dismal bunch. That was another thing I hated. Who needs a dismal war movie? Where were the heroics? Where was the excitement? What was it with all the mud and confusion? I flicked a glance at Dom who was lying on the floor sucking the vinegar out of the bottom of his chip bag. He was frowning uncertainly at the screen.

'Are they Nazis?' he said.

'No,' said Dad. 'They're just lads.'

Dom turned to look at him. 'But they're Germans!'

Dad went to say something but just then Nan came in from the kitchen, and he went quiet. I think he was hoping she'd just sit down and fall back asleep, but she didn't. She stood at the back of the sofa instead, staring at the TV and fluttering her hands, kind of horrified. 'Oh no!' she said. 'No, no! That's not nice! All that mud! Oh, bless him. *Bless* him! That's not *nice!*'

Ma sighed and stood up and went around to her. Nan blinked, startled, as Ma took her by the elbow.

'It's alright, Cheryl love,' said Ma. 'It's only a film.'

Dad reached behind him and touched Nan's hand. 'Tell you what, Mam,' he said quietly, 'why don't you come sit in your chair and have a nice cuppa?'

I looked away, because Nan's confusion made me angry.

I think she must have shuffled from one foot to the other for a moment; I could hear her muttering and sighing. But then that ad came on the telly – the one for Old Spice with the waves in it – and the music made her happy again, like it always did. Next I knew, she was sitting in her chair, smiling and taking a cup of tea from Dad. We all kind of relaxed a bit.

The film started again and Dad sighed. I don't think he was enjoying that movie any more than I was. The next ads came on. Nan murmured in her sleep, 'Oh, love, were you here all this time?'

Dad leapt up, rubbing his hands together. 'Right! Pee then tea.'

He kissed Ma on the way out the door and she called after him to bring in the Jaffa Cakes.

We didn't notice him backing into the room until he'd got to the end of the sofa and grabbed Ma's shoulder. She swatted him in annoyance, thinking he was messing. Then she saw his face, and her expression went all flat and ready for anything.

'What's wrong?' she said.

'Get Mam out into the front garden, Olive. Just take her out as calm as you can. Don't come back in. I'm going upstairs for Dee.'

They looked at each other and my ma's eyes got enormous. 'Dave,' she whispered, 'is that smoke?'

Dom leapt up from where he was lying. He had been drawing his comic book and was still clutching a purple marker. There were purple smudges all over his fingers, and his face was covered in purple fingerprints where he'd had his chin resting in his hand. I began to stand up. Our front room never seemed so small as when the three Finnerty men all stood up together.

I wanted to ask, *What's wrong?* As usual, Dom did it for me.

'Dad?' he said. 'Is something ...?'

'Listen!' said Dad. 'Just *listen*. Dom, help take Nan outside. Keep her calm and act like nothing's wrong.' He turned to me. 'Pat, I'm going upstairs. Once everyone's outside, don't let them come back in this house. Do you hear me? I don't care *what* happens.'

I nodded.

Dad went into the hall, glanced towards the kitchen, and motioned us to the front door.

Ma was waking Nan, a slow process at the best of times. 'Come on, Cheryl love. Get up, me old darlin'. Up you get now.'

'Where we goin'?' asked Nan, her quavery old voice fuddled with more than just sleep. 'Are we late for Mass?'

'A little bit, darlin. We need to hurry. Ups-a-daisy now. Up we go.'

Ma knew. I could tell by the way she herded Nan past Dad and didn't look back down the hall. Dom ran ahead. He already had the hall door open and was standing in the porch, his hand on the porch door latch when Dad roared, 'STOP!'

We all froze. Dad held his hand out, as if to keep us all from moving. He wasn't a broad man, but he seem to fill the entire hall right then, a living barrier between us and whatever lay hidden in the kitchen. 'Dom,' he said, 'don't open that door yet! It's very important. Let everyone into the porch *first*. *Then* shut the hall door behind you, and *then* open the porch door. Have you got that?'

Dom nodded, his brown eyes huge. Ma hustled Nan in beside him and they all stood crammed together in the porch, staring back at Dad. Nan began querulously looking for her handbag, and Ma hung onto her without speaking, her eyes glued to Dad as if afraid he'd disappear. I could smell the smoke now. I could actually hear the flames. Somewhere behind my dad, something huge was on fire. Dad pinned me down with same look he'd just given Dom, and it hit me how serious this all was.

Our house was on fire. It was on *fire*.

'Patrick,' said Dad, 'shut that porch door after everyone's outside. *It's very important*. I'm going upstairs for your sister and I don't give a shite what happens when I'm up there, you are *not* to let your ma or Dom or your nan back into this house. Do you understand?'

My eyes slid past him, and I nearly fell over with shock at the sight of the kitchen door. The cheap wood was glowing, its paint all bubbled up and hissing. Black fingers of smoke were twisting through the gaps of the doorjamb, reaching for the ceiling and spreading up the walls. I opened my mouth to yell, but before I could make a sound Dad had shoved me into the overcrowded porch and slammed the hall door in my face. I was left staring at my own reflection in the glass.

Nan was demanding to be released from this telephone box, and Ma yelled at Dom to open the porch door. He did and they all tumbled out into the coal-fire smell of the suburban night, leaving a cold space whistling at my back. I stayed where I was while Ma ran screaming four doors up to the Reid's, who had the only telephone on the road. Dom was left to corral Nan, who was trying to wander down the street to catch a bus to Galway.

I could see Dad through the rippled orange glass of the hall-door panels, lashing it up the stairs to Dee's room. I stared through the glass, willing him to come back down the stairs, Dee in his arms. I could still see that kitchen door as if it were right there in front of me. The brief glance I'd had of it had been enough to lodge every detail in my mind.

I heard Dad come barrelling down the stairs, saw his wobbly shape through the orange glass and recognised the pink bundle in his arms as my sister. As he was hitting the hall carpet, I realised I hadn't done my job. The porch door was still gaping open, and the old man was reaching for the doorhandle.

Dad. No.

My heart stuttered in my chest. I opened my mouth to warn him and lifted my hand to close the door. All late. Too late. But Jesus, Dad paused, his hand on the latch, his head bowed against the glass as if listening to the outside air. I heard him, muffled: 'Pat?'

The world slammed back full-colour and me standing there with my mouth open. 'Hang on, Dad! Hang on.' I slammed the porch door shut with a force that would have earned me a clatter at any other time, and my dad almost instantly banged open the hall door. His face was pulled down in a frightened mask, the skin under his eyes stretched thin and whiter than milk. The hall behind him was perfectly normal, apart from the huge black ball of smoke that filled the far end of it. It had rolled up the walls and was spread in a rippling fan across the ceiling, and through the smoke an eye, an evil eye, pulsed hot and red at the entrance to our kitchen. Flames were shimmering across the surface of the door, a simmering wash of heat.

At the threshold of the porch, my dad turned and looked back. Outlined against the flames and smoke, he was like some medieval hero – like something bigger than just my dad. For a moment he glared at the fire: man to dragon, mortal to elemental. Then he slammed the hall door, pushed out of the porch and shoved me ahead of him into the night.

Ma raced screaming out of the dark and grabbed Dad and Dee in a death-grip. Dee woke up and started bawling, and Ma took her in her arms, gabbling about fire brigades and phone calls while Dad pushed all of us out onto the path. Mr and Mrs Reid and their gang of girls came crowding down the road from their house, goggle-eyed and excited, as if expecting to see all of us standing in flames in the front garden. They stopped in a confused little huddle at the gate and we all stood staring at the house.

'Looks okay, Dave.' Mr Reid sounded defensive, probably beginning to suspect some kind of joke.

'Jaysus, it's bleedin' freezin'.' That was Naomi Reid's harsh nasal whine.

'Shurrup, Naomi, right?' Maureen's equally grating reply.

'*You* shurrup.'

'No, *you*.'

'Both of youse shurrup.' Sharon, skinniest and scariest of them all.

The Reid girls in all their ladylike glory.

Dom was herding Nan back up the road, and I was just beginning to think we'd all imagined it when the glass in our front door suddenly got a whole lot brighter.

'Jesus,' said Dad.

The sitting room, where we'd only just been eating chips and watching telly, was hidden behind heavy curtains. For a moment we could see no difference there. But gradually a steady, cheerful glow began to suffuse the window, as though a great big fire was burning in a great big hearth. There was no such thing as a great big hearth in these houses, no sir, just crappy, asthma-inducing central heating. I watched the jolly, orange warmth seep through the thick material of the curtains, and I imagined the dragon in there, lapping at our furniture with its seething tongue.

A thread of illumination ran along the hem of the curtain. At first it was just a thin, creeping embroidery of gold – and then *whoosh*, a window of naked flame. Just like that. One minute an innocent curtain, the next a roiling, smoke-laden landscape of fire filling the window of our front room.

The upstairs windows began to light up. First Dee's room. Then ours.

Ours.

I imagined Dom's desk. His drawings curling up and blackening – page after page of his comic books, his hard-won paintbrushes, his pencils. I imagined my notebooks, my copybooks full of short stories, my novel. All those handwritten pages being eaten one at a time, crisping, blackening, curling away from each other, the words scorching and rising up in soot, never to be read again.

We were losing it all.

My eyes were burning, but I couldn't blink. Looking up at our window, I could see the corner of our bunk bed. As I watched, the top mattress – Dom's mattress – began to smoke, and the wall behind it lit up in dancing light. I saw our Horslips poster, its edges starting to smoulder. Then suddenly it ignited, drifting up in great curls of flame. It floated away from the wall, dissolving into orange butterflies and black feathers.

'Jesus,' said Dad again.

We could hear it now – the dragon – roaring its way through

the house, eating, eating its way through our house, and leaving us nothing.

I looked over at Dom, my mirror, my reflection, my identical twin. He had sat Nan down on the garden wall and was standing behind her, his hands on her shoulders. His eyes were fixed on our bedroom window, his face a blank slate of shock.

'Dom,' I said.

He looked over to me at once. I wanted to say, *Our stuff, Dom. All our stuff.* But, as usual, I couldn't find the words. I remember his big eyes glittering then, and the beginning of realisation creeping into his expression. He looked down at his hand and took something out of his pocket. It was his purple marker. He held it up to me, a rueful expression on his face, and shrugged as if to say, *Oh well. We've got this.*

A fecking purple marker.

'I'll have butter, but no jam,' murmured Nan, complacently settling herself down to watch the show. Ma sat down beside her, Dee already asleep again in her arms.

Something huge burst inside the house with a cartoon-like *POP*.

'Jesus, Mary and Joseph,' said Dad. He backed up to sit beside Ma, and took her hand.

Mr and Mrs Reid and the girls were a row of gaping mouths and shining eyes behind them. Dom swung his legs over the wall and I went over and sat by his side. Far away, the first wails of the fire engines could be heard threading their way towards us. And as we waited, we watched, our faces all lit up with fire, as the dragon finished its complete and terminal consumption of our home.

2. The Old Biddies' Place

Every year we went to Skerries on holidays. For a whole month, sometimes longer, my ma and her sisters, Pet and Breda, would rent two old houses next to the hurdy-gurdies and we'd move down there, lock, stock and barrel. We'd spend a chaotic four weeks at the heart of those two huge families, roaming Skerries with our close-knit pack of cousins, invincible, wild and free. It was heaven.

Usually we drove down in blazing sunshine. The car windows would be open, our hair fluttering, the air vivid with fresh grass, diesel fumes and the crusty-bright smell of the sea. We'd swig Cidona from the bottle. Ma would pass back bags of iced caramels and Emerald toffees. Dom would sing. We'd all sing.

Us kids'd be stuffed into the back seat along with too many bags and blankets and all sorts of crap at our feet, we'd arrive squashed and sweaty. A tide of cousins would screech towards us across the sand-filled gardens of the adjoining houses – the swing chairs and bumper-cars and penny arcades a multicoloured, noisy blur behind them – and we'd laugh as we tumbled from the car.

This time was very different.

It rained the whole way there, and the car was a steaming claustrophobic headache. There was no warm burr of conversation from the front seats. Ma sat silently smoking, staring out the front window. Dad just drove. They'd been quiet like that since the day before, and I was beginning to get a familiar knot in my stomach about them. I told myself it was just that they were tired. Ma's brothers and sisters had done their best for us; they'd opened their arms wide and taken us in without a word. But their families were big, their houses were tiny, and we'd spent nearly a week shunting between them, sleeping on floors, crammed into narrow shared beds. We were all wrecked for want of a good night's sleep.

I shifted about a bit in the back seat, trying to get some room without waking Dee. She was sprawled between me and Dom, her feet on my lap, her head on his knee. Dom was looking out the window at the driving rain, humming to himself and absently stroking her silky hair. It looked light as feathers between his fingers, curling and dropping, curling and dropping around the ragged tops of his fingernails. He had been the usual soul of patience as she garbled her nonsense at him. He'd tolerated her tugging at his face with her fat little hands, and let her 'comb' his hair. He'd even taken her games of I-spy seriously, despite her thinking every word started with 'M' and none of us understanding half of what she said. When she'd tired of him, she'd flopped onto her back and shoved her pink sock-clad feet in my face.

''Mell, Pap,' she'd ordered. 'Mell my pongy feets.'

I'd sniffed and gone 'Paaawww!' as though they stank like old cheese. This kept her in giggles until she'd subsided into a doze, and then – thank God – a full, boneless, drooling sleep.

I watched the movement of Dom's fingers slow until his hand came to a standstill on Dee's head. His chin began to drop forward onto his chest. I turned my attention to the rain-soaked road, and listened to the silence crackle between our parents.

☠ ☠ ☠

We came up the main street of Skerries with the sky pressing down on the houses and the rain pummelling all the colour from the air. As we turned up a side street and onto the deserted beachfront, Dom and Dee were still unconscious. I was limp and heavy from the long drive, my head bobbing against the window. When we pulled up to the garden gate, I no more wanted to move than I wanted to eat my own hair.

Dad switched off the engine and sat there a moment, his hands clenched around the steering wheel. Ma said nothing. The rain hammered the roof of the car.

'I'll go in to the old biddies and get the keys,' said Dad.

Ma didn't answer him.

He sighed. There was a blast of cold as he got out of the car, then the abrupt slamming of the door. Ma sat like a stone in the front seat as he walked away. Dom and Dee's sleeping breaths filled the silence between us, and I assumed Ma thought I was asleep, too. She stabbed out her fag. As Dad ducked under the apple trees and disappeared up the side alley that led to the old biddies' house, I was shocked to hear her mutter, 'Fuck you, Finnerty.'

As if remembering us, she glanced in the rear-view mirror. Our eyes locked. Then Ma looked away. Not quickly, or shamefaced. She just looked away — cold and imperious — as if she didn't care that I had heard her.

I stared at the back of her head for a minute and swallowed something huge back down into my throat. Behind us, to the right, the swing-chairs creaked in the wind. I turned my head against the glass and watched them swaying above me. Still locked up from the winter, their chains were knotted and tied with big padlocks, their gaily coloured seats snagged upside down. Rain flowed from the ride's tent-shaped roof, down the knotted sinews of the chains, and hammered the sullied earth below. Everything was grey with rain.

Ma had just taken another fag out of the packet and was rooting for her lighter when Dad came running back down the garden, his jacket held up over his head. She sighed and slammed the fag back into the pack. Tossing it into her handbag, she gathered stray sweets and wrappers and flung them in after it. By the time Dad got to the car and opened her door in a shock of wind and rain, Ma was ready to step out. She brushed by him without a word, hoisted her handbag onto her shoulder and went around to the boot.

'Olly, get in out of the rain, love. You'll be soaked.'

She went ahead as though he hadn't spoken, pulled the boot open and yanked a big box up and onto her hip. Dad gestured in exasperation. 'Olive! I'll do that! Go in out of the rain.'

She shifted the box and walked off up the garden with it, taking her time, her head held high. The rain had already plastered her hair to her head, and soaked her trouser-suit to the skin.

Dad stood and watched her, frustration evident in every taut muscle – in his clenched fists, and the furious rise and fall of his chest. Then he moved around to the boot, grabbed a box, slammed a bag down on top of it and stamped off after her.

I glanced at Dom. His eyes were open, his head still leaning against the glass. He was following our parents' progress up the garden with an angry frown.

'They're fighting?' he said. 'I can't believe it! What the hell is wrong with them?'

And I was angry with *him* then, for not having noticed the tension earlier; for having pointed it out, instead of ignoring it; for just bloody well being there and available when I needed someone to be annoyed at. 'Jesus, Dom,' I snapped, 'what fecking planet do you live on?'

He gawped at me, a *what-did-I-say-wrong* look on his face, and that made me angry all over again. 'How can you not have seen it coming?' I said. 'Is your head that far up your arse?'

His expression ate at me. It felt as if I'd just spat on my own reflection. But instead of apologising, I grabbed Dee, hoisted her rag-doll weight into my arms and ducked out the door. I left Dom sitting in the car, a receding ghost in the rain and sloshed my way up the garden without looking back.

The house was another shock in what was becoming a litany of shocks. All these years, I'd thought I'd known it, but stepping into the kitchen and looking around me, I realised I had only known the *atmosphere* of it – the steady, nonstop rough-and-tumble of a long and boisterous holiday. The house itself had only ever been a background to the bright tapestry of summer at the beach. Now, lit by the grey spring light and empty but for us, it came into focus like a slap with a wet towel.

The two downstairs rooms – a kitchen that you stepped straight into from the garden and a sitting room immediately to your left

– were horribly drab and used-looking, threadbare and grimy. The two old biddies had obviously done their best to make the place welcoming: a jam jar of daffodils sat on the battered kitchen table and another on the deep windowsill in the sitting room; a rosy fire spat and crackled in the little sitting-room grate. It sounded like they'd lit the Aga, and the huge old kettle on the hob was just beginning to sing. But the biddies – or Mutt and Jeff as Dad called them, one being tall and grim, one small and bouncy – were old women, and their eyesight must not have been the best, because there was a soft layer of dust on everything, and every windowsill had its own brittle colony of dead flies. The floor was gritty underfoot, and the smell of the daffs did nothing but emphasise the staleness of the air.

I carried Dee into the sitting room and went to lay her on the threadbare sofa, but then hesitated, frowning down at the slightly greasy texture of the upholstery. It just didn't look *clean*. I straightened with her still in my arms and looked around me. Last year I would have flung myself blithely onto that sofa, laid my head against the mouldering cushions, and kicked my feet up onto the arms. I clearly remembered putting my food directly onto the floor at my feet, while I turned a page or watched TV. I gazed at the scarred walls and the chipped cupboards and thought, *How have I never noticed this before?* I clutched Dee tighter to me.

Nothing is the same, I thought. *It's all gone.*

The house stood around me in a way it never had before, as something real, as something sharp and focused. I wondered if it sensed us moving around inside it – this sad, angry little knot of people. It felt to me as if it did. It felt as if the house and I were suddenly *there* to each other – that we were seeing each other for the first time. The stale air seemed to close around me like a fist.

I didn't like this. I didn't like it at all.

I wanted to go home.

Dad came up behind me, then, and flung a blanket over the sofa. He snapped it open in the air like a magician, tucked it into the corners, and left to head back out into the rain. He came and went with such a surreal deftness that it left me stunned. The ratty old sofa was gone, and in its place there was now this cosy little nest of blue and cream. From somewhere behind me, either Dad or Ma threw a pillow. It landed perfectly into the crooked arm of the sofa, and I was able to lay Dee down onto it – safe and warm. She sighed and curled up like a cat without ever really waking.

I stood watching her, her tiny chest rising and falling, her yellow curls matted onto her flushed little face. I felt a sudden gush of tenderness for her – the type I only ever felt when she was asleep and not annoying the crap out of me. The world always seemed very big when I allowed myself to see her this way. It made me want to protect her forever.

Ma came back into the kitchen with another box, dumped it on the table and began unpacking with sharp angry noises. Dom shuffled in under the weight of a big suitcase and she snapped at him, 'Don't leave it *there,* for God's sake. Have a titter of wit, and take it up to the bedrooms.' I heard him labouring up the narrow stairs behind the kitchen, inching his way around the dark twists of the windowless stairwell.

Dad pushed through the door, heaving a big box of groceries and trailing rain all across the kitchen floor. Ma stuck her head around the corner and glared at me.

'*Patrick,*' she said, 'are you waiting for a bloody invitation or what?'

I slunk past her and out into the rain to help finish unloading the car.

We all traipsed around each other for well over an hour, putting things here and storing things there. It was a silent, eyes-down operation, uncomfortable and tense, but blessedly free of further confrontation. All through it, Dee slept peacefully on the sofa and the unceasing rain fell outside. Finally Ma banished me and Dom to our room to change out of our wet things and unpack the rest of our clothes.

We had the room right at the head of the stairs, the one usually claimed by the four girl cousins and their assorted friends and hangers-on. It was a good room, big, with two windows: one overlooking the apple trees, the other looking out over the fairground and onto the sea. There was a huge old-fashioned dressing table with a darkly blotched mirror against one wall, and opposite it an ancient, creaking iron-framed bunk bed.

Dom immediately and without discussion claimed the top bunk. He did this by flinging his bag into the corner, climbing the ladder and lying down with his hands crossed behind his head, staring at the ceiling.

'You've to put your clothes away!' I snapped. My heart sank at how angry I sounded. What was bloody wrong with me?

He shrugged. 'I'll unpack when you're finished,' he said. There wasn't a trace of acid in his voice. He settled deeper into the mattress and closed his eyes, really laying on the *I'm comfy* vibe.

I smiled. Okay then. He had the top bunk. He got to lie down for a while. I didn't have to say I was sorry. A hundred little knots undid themselves in the pit of my stomach. Feeling lighter than I had all evening, I started shoving my clothes into the musty drawers of the dressing table.

Every single item of clothing was brand new. Some still had the tags on them. Four days after the house had burnt down, the neighbours had done a whipround, and the whole sprawling estate had chipped in. Some families had only been able to afford a quid or two, but nevertheless, between the lot of them they'd managed to raise the unearthly sum of one hundred pounds. Stunned, my ma had simply handed us a wodge of dosh each and let us loose in the shops.

Until then, Dom and me had only ever worn our cousins' hand-me-downs. If it fit us, we wore it – the end. We had absolutely no concept of *individual style*. So when we finally got to choose our own gear, we were shocked at how different our tastes were. It turned out my brother was a bloody hippy! He even bought a shark's tooth on a piece of leather to wear around his neck. I couldn't believe it. He was all cheesecloth shirts and tie-dyed jeans and all that bleedin' Jim Morrison rubbish.

My clothes, however, were *dead* keen: poloneck jumpers, sharply creased trousers, a tweedy jacket. Steve McQueen wasn't half as suave as me. I looked like a brown-eyed, curly-headed Man from U.N.C.L.E.

I was lovingly smoothing the creases from my new pinstriped shirt when I looked up and caught Dom watching me in the mirror. He grinned. I couldn't help but smile back. He started to say something. Then the voices in the kitchen rose and the two of us went quiet.

It had been a low rumble in the background since we'd come upstairs – a lopsided conversation, just Dad mostly, his voice insistent and low. A brief reply from Ma had, eventually, led to more silence. Things were moved around, cutlery rattled, dishes snapped into place. Then Dad spoke again, a deep questioning reverberation through the floorboards, and suddenly Ma's voice rose, rapid and hard – an uninterrupted flow of anger. The words were unintelligible, but the bitterness and accusation were palpable nonetheless.

Dom and I watched each other in the mirror as her voice went on. He wasn't grinning anymore. A sudden crash made us both jump: a cup being thrown, into the sink if experience served us right. We lost a lot of cups in our house. I moved wordlessly to the door. Behind me, Dom crept down the ladder and crossed the bedroom to join me.

We stopped halfway down the stairs and sat at the first turn. At home we would have sat side by side, very close together, like children, but these stairs were too narrow for that so Dom sat behind me, his legs pressed against my shoulder, his feet on the step where I was sitting. I fastened my arms around my knees and stared at the wall, my whole being focused on the voices coming from the kitchen. The dust and smell of damp wrapped itself around us in the dark. The house listened with us – breath held.

'It's just not *possible*, Olive.'

'Why *not*? She's their bloody mother, too!'

'You know they don't see her like that, love.'

'Shut up! SHUT UP, DAVE! Why can't you take my side? Fuck them and their big bloody houses and their fucking cars and *We're too busy* and *How would we possibly?* FUCK THEM!'

'Jesus, Olive! *Stop that!*' The shock at Ma's terrible language was evident in Dad's voice. It was frightening to hear her talk like that; it didn't sound like her at all.

There was an inarticulate cry from my mother and the sound of something being flung *hard* into the other side of the wall next to our heads. Dom flinched and pressed closer to me. I hoped to God that Dee would stay asleep; the last thing we needed was for her to wake up screaming for her tea.

Ma was crying now; I could hear it in her voice and it surprised me. Anger didn't make my ma cry. Anger made her cutting – it made her scary – but it *never* made her cry. Her voice came floating up the stairs, wavery and broken, and I think it frightened me more than if she had been shouting.

'Dave, I can't have her here. How can I? *Look* at this place, look at those bloody stairs. There isn't even a proper bathroom. Dave …' She started to cry in earnest. There was a soft scuffling sound and then she yelled sharply, 'Don't *touch* me. I don't want a bloody *hug*! I want some *help*. I want them to *take* her. Just for a little while! For God's sake, is it so much to ask?'

Dad's voice spoke, so softly: 'Olly,' he said. 'Look at me.'

'You won't even be HERE! You'll be off at work!'

Again, Dad, gently: 'Ol, I *have* to go to work.'

Ma's voice, much softer: 'I think I hate her.'

'Oh Jesus, Ol. Please don't …'

'Every time I look at her now, I'm afraid I'm going to think … I'm going to think of my luh-little house and how … and how hard we worked for it. And how she buh-buh-burnt the place *dooown*.'

The last word came out in a wail and I could imagine my mother standing there, her face creased up and covered in tears. I felt sorry for her then, and I wanted to hug her. But my ma was a fierce woman. You didn't just go over and hug her – not in situations like this.

'Okay, Olive. I'll talk to Conner again. I'll ask him to try and get Maureen ...'

'*No.*' This statement came flat and decisive. 'No. I'm sick of them. Poor Cheryl. God, they're such ... poor Cheryl.' There was a scraping tinkle, shards of china being swept up. Even through the wall I could feel my mother pulling herself together. I could hear it in the tone of her voice. She was battening down the hatches. 'I'm not leaving her with them any longer than we have to.'

'Olive ...'

She interrupted him before he could finish. 'Tell them they can bring her down on Saturday, like they planned. Tell them we don't need their help. Cheryl will be no trouble to me. She's a lovely woman; their dad was lucky to find her. They didn't deserve to have her in their lives. You *tell* them that Dave.'

There were gentle sounds now: a chair scraping; my dad's voice, muffled as though he had his face pressed against her hair. 'I will,' he said. 'I'll tell them all that.'

'Okay.' Ma was barely audible. I knew he was hugging her now. She only came to his shoulder; her face would be buried in his chest. 'I'm sorry.'

'So am I, love. I wish ...'

'Go get some chips, will you?' She would have stood back now, cutting him short, scrubbing her face. 'I'm damned if I'm going to cook.'

There was a gentle laugh, a moment of stillness and then the sounds of Dad gathering up his keys and heading out the door. We could hear Ma tidying things up. Then, very softly, we heard her sobbing, the private, muffled sound of quietly desperate tears.

We slunk back to our bedroom, soundless as phantoms on the darkly attentive stairs.

For once, Dom didn't even *try* to talk about it. That was just fine by me.

3. In the Darkness

In the Darkness

It is my birthday, October 30th 1917. I am twenty years old today and running for my life. It is raining. The duckboards are slippery as ice. My feet fly out from under me and I fall. As I go down, I catch the edge of my helmet on a support stake and it is jerked from my head, wrenching my neck. I leave it swinging on the stake. Then I'm down on my back, my rifle gouging into my ribs. I try to roll over, keep running and scramble to my feet all at the same time. The other soldiers leap over me and pound past me, skidding and sliding on the treacherous boards. The rain is falling so heavy and my heart is pounding so loud that I'm deaf to anything else save my own ragged breathing. I get my feet under me and half run, half crouch, my hands supporting me on the slick wood. Someone grabs my collar and yanks me up so that I'm on my feet again. A shell bursts overhead and I'm blind but still running. That guiding hand stays on my collar, holding me up, pulling me on.

Dear God, don't let me run off the edge of the boards.

Sweet Mary, guide my feet and let me stay on the boards.

Mud is raining down on us, sloppy great clods of it, spattering the backs of our heads and our shoulders. I keep running blindly until my vision clears and my unseen saviour releases my collar. It's my pal Shamie. He looks back at me once, finds the God-given heart to grin at me, and is gone, just a black shape amongst all the other black shapes running for their lives in the night.

I turn a corner into Black Paddy's Trench and my feet go out from under me again. I go right over this time. I feel some huge bruiser go down behind me. He rams into me, sending me sliding. I reach back, feel my fingers brush his rain-slicker. But I'm unstoppable – his weight has sent me skating across the glassy wooden planks on a smooth plane of water, sliding towards the edge of the duckboards. The mud waits there, the silent glistening heave of it. Bottomless.

I scream, 'Oh Jesus! Help me! Help me!'

My voice is silent even to myself, my scream nothing against the roar of the shells and the thunder of the guns. I slide off the edge of the boards. My heart, my lungs, my stomach – all contract with fear. My eyes fill with tears at the terrible, terrible knowledge of how I am going to die.

The mud inhales me feet first. A cold gullet squeezing around my legs, my thighs, my belly, my chest, it pulls me right off the boards and into its arms. It is very fast. Men run past me, their feet a blur as my chin and mouth and nose go under.

Before the mud wraps its blindfold over me, I find myself staring up into someone's eyes. There is a boy standing above me, a solemn-eyed child of ten. Untouched by the rain and the mud and the shells, he watches me go down. I know him; I know exactly who he is. No amount of years could have erased the memory of his face.

He says my name and I am gone.

I leapt awake with my heart hammering in my throat and the taste of rain and mud on my tongue. I flailed around for a minute, making small panicked noises before I realised I was lying in bed, doing battle with my blankets. Already the dream was gone, and I found myself lying there with a racing heart and no clear idea of why I was so scared.

As the silence of the house settled around me, I became aware of a familiar sound coming from the bunk above me — a hoarse, scratching wheeze. It was Dom struggling for air, desperately gasping in a way that I hadn't heard him do in years.

'Dom!' I scrambled and half fell out of my covers. I stood on my mattress, pulling myself up to look over the edge of his bed. Dom was rigid and staring at the ceiling, his arms straight down by his sides, the blankets bunched in his fiercely clenched fists.

'Dom! Sit up!'

I tried to climb the side of the bunk and failed, scraping my belly on the battered side-rail as I slid back over the edge. Dom rolled his unfocused eyes towards me. His mouth was wide, his chest heaving, but it was obvious there was no oxygen getting to him. Just enough air to make that awful rusty-bellows heave in and out of his throat.

'Hang on, Dom! Hang on!' I took the ladder, missed the first step, took it again and scrambled to the top bunk, crawling up Dom's straining body to the head of the bed. There was nothing in this world that scared me more than Dom's asthma. I'd thought we'd seen the end of it two years ago, when the last of the really bad attacks had put him in the hospital. It was this damned house. It was this filthy, dusty house, bringing it all back again.

'Sit up!' I grabbed his shoulders, with the intention of dragging him into a sitting position, but froze when I saw his face. His eyes were all pupil, and he was searching the ceiling with horrified desperation.

'Lorry ...' he gasped, just a whistle of air meant to be a word. 'Lorry!'

He wasn't even awake. He was having an asthma attack in the middle of a nightmare.

'DOM, wake up!' I shook him so hard he'd have bruises in the morning where my fingers had dug into his shoulders. He took in a tremendous gasp of air and his head snapped up, nearly loafing me. I scurried back and the rickety bunk creaked dangerously under our combined weight as Dom bolted upright, wide awake.

'Jesus, Pat!' he yelled. 'What are you doing climbing all over me in the middle of the night?'

'You were having an asthma attack.'

'No, I wasn't.'

'Yes, you were!' But I had to admit, he didn't look like he was anymore. There was no sign of a wheeze or a cough, no difficulties breathing. Just Dom, staring at me as if I'd grown two heads, rubbing his shoulders where I'd grabbed him.

CITY OF 99649 PUBLIC LIBRARY

He pulled his feet out from under me and clutched the covers to his chest. 'Patrick,' he said, 'I believe you may have had a bad dream.' He was doing what he called his 'schoolmarm' voice, blatantly taking the piss. But damn it, I'd been bloody well awake when he was shredding the covers and gasping for air.

I gathered my dignity. 'You were the one whimpering like a big girl's blouse,' I said. 'You were dreaming about a car crash.'

He almost snorted, but seemed to think better of it halfway through and suddenly looked thoughtful, as though remembering something.

I jumped on it. 'You *were* having a dream!'

'No ... well, yeah.' He looked at me, puzzled. 'What makes you think it was about a car crash?'

'You said *Lorry*. Twice.'

Now he did snort, laughing at me, though obviously intrigued. 'Lorry?'

'Yeah! Lorry! You must have been hit by a truck or something.'

'Oookaaay. I've had enough.' He shoved my knees with his feet and pointed at the ladder. 'Goodnight, Patrick.'

I climbed back down, miffed, creeped out and mortified all at once.

I was crawling under the covers when he called down to me. 'Pat?'

Expecting more slagging, I snapped my reply. 'What?'

'Thanks for coming to my rescue ... even if you *did* nearly kill me in the process.'

I smiled. 'Shut up, you eejit. Some of us are trying to sleep.'

I bunched the covers up under my chin and settled comfortably into the pillow, but I didn't sleep. I lay listening to Dom instead; the gentle, untroubled rhythm of his breathing was reassuring, but not quite trustworthy enough for me to let go.

I found myself watching the mirror over the dressing table. Its mottled surface had little to show me of the dark room, but I could just make out the lumpy silhouette of my sleeping brother in the shadows of the bunk above mine. Car lights occasionally travelled across the walls, sending crosshatched slashes of shadow from the apple trees, and hazy rivers of reflection from the rain-soaked windows. Each intrusion of light sent a flare across the mirror glass, and the bunk would leap into focus for a moment before the car passed on.

Despite myself, I began to drift off. Just before I fell asleep, another set of beams strobed across the mirror, making me jump but not quite waking me. As I slipped under I heard Dom whisper, loud and clear as though he were calling warily into the room, hoping for but not expecting an answer.

'Lorry?' he whispered. 'Lorry? Are you still there?'

4. The Auld Drunk

The Auld Drunk

The first thing that leapt to my mind the next morning was FOOD. I went from deeply asleep to mindlessly starving all in one go. I was so thoroughly hollowed out that it felt like someone had gutted me in my sleep. I lurched out of my bed before I knew I was conscious, and was out of the room and following the smell of rashers down the stairs before my eyes had even opened.

Dom and I flanked each other into the kitchen and launched ourselves at the table like wolves. I hadn't noticed him following me and even if I had, I wouldn't have bloody cared. I was solely focused on getting something down my gullet. We paid absolutely no heed to the rest of the world, our attention centred on the six slices of batch bread that we buttered one after the other and swallowed in a compulsive, ravenous gorge. We paused at the sight of the suddenly empty bread plate and turned to scan the room, our hands opening and closing, ready to pounce on anything edible.

Dad regarded us dryly from the cooker. A grill of rashers sizzled in his hand; a pan of eggs were frying on the hob. 'Bit hungry are we, lads?' I made a move towards the rashers and he turned slightly, shielding them from me. 'Sit down,' he said, the way you would with a dog you weren't sure of.

We sat, our eyes glued to the food. Dad deposited rashers and eggs and fat, sizzling sausages onto our plates. We were barely containing ourselves, our eyes devouring the food before it left the pan. He refilled the bread plate, poured us all mugs of milky tea and, finally, sat down himself.

As soon as Dad picked up his knife and fork, Dom and I dived in. I lost track of everything but shovelling food into my gob and banging back cup after cup of tea. It was only after I had wiped up the last smear of egg yolk with the last hard-won crust of bread and was looking around hopefully for a few remaining scraps that I realised exactly how much nosh I'd packed away. I was *stuffed*. I was *crammed* with food. My belly felt like a perfectly round football straining against my pyjamas. At the same time, I wanted more.

Dom was sitting very still, his hands flat on the table, his jaw working slightly as he stared at Dad's plate. I followed his gaze and had to swallow a surge of saliva at the sight of Dad's half-eaten breakfast.

Dad hunched protectively over his food. 'Jesus, Mary and Joseph,' he muttered. 'It must be the sea air.' He pulled the plate closer to him. 'Don't suppose either of you gannets heard a word I just said to you?' We looked blankly at him and he rolled his eyes. 'I *said* your mam and Dee are still asleep, don't wake them. Dee had a bad night and your mam was walking the floor with her.'

That snapped me out of my food-induced trance long enough to ask, 'What's wrong with her? Is she sick?'

Dad shook his head and stuck a mass of fried bread and egg into his gob. Dom followed the food with his eyes. His mouth opened with Dad's, his jaw worked in little chewing movements as Dad ate. Dad eyed him as he answered me. 'I think she's just out of sorts because of the move,' he said. He swirled a bit of rasher in egg yolk and stuck a blob of brown sauce on top. 'She had bad dreams all night. Couldn't get to sleep.'

Something tickled the back of my mind, and I saw Dom frown thoughtfully. Bad dreams? I seemed to recall something about Dom having a dream … or had it been me? I couldn't quite …

'What kind of bad dream?' Dom was looking very intently at Dad; he was obviously thinking the same as me.

'Not sure. You know what Dee's like – it's hard to understand her when she's upset. Said something like, there was a bad man or something. He wanted to take her away, or' – he gestured at Dom – 'take *you* away. I don't know. Anyway, they're both knackered, so don't be galloping up and down the stairs.'

'A bad man?' The tone in Dom's voice had us both looking sharply at him.

Dad paused in the middle of cutting a sausage. 'You alright, bud? You've gone very pale.'

Dom hadn't just gone pale; he'd gone white. He was gripping the table so hard that I had visions of his fingernails popping off in bloody flakes. 'He's not taking *me* away!' he cried, his voice high and shrill – like Dee throwing a tantrum.

Dad was putting his knife and fork down. He was starting to stand up. 'Dom.'

Dom's colour scared me. I suddenly remembered something. 'Dom had an asthma attack last night, Dad!'

'Hey!' snapped Dom. 'No, I didn't!' He was perfectly normal again – normal colour, normal voice, no death-grip on the table, just righteous indignation and denial that he'd been ill the night before.

'Jesus! Why didn't you call me?' Dad was on his feet, his hand on Dom's forehead; Dom already pulling away in irritation. 'Where's your inhaler?'

'I *don't need it*. There was no bloody asthma!' He pointed at me. 'Yer man there had a bad dream. That's all!'

Dad pulled back Dom's eyelids and felt his neck like some doctor from the telly. Dom submitted to this ridiculousness with tight-lipped anger, and I knew I was in for it later. 'You … you look just fine,' said Dad, puzzled.

'I *am* fine,' gritted Dom.

And he did look fine. There were none of the lingering telltale signs of an attack, no dark rings under his eyes, no pallor – nothing to indicate that the bloody awful menace was back to haunt us.

'Alright.' Dad stepped back uncertainly, giving Dom another anxious head-to-toe examination with his eyes. 'Alright,' he said again. 'Go on upstairs and get dressed, the two of you. And don't wake the girls.'

He watched us go up the stairs, and I knew he wasn't going to let it go that easy. Dom was in for a good three days of anxious hovering – and I was in for a right bollocking as soon as we got out of earshot.

☠ ☠ ☠

We had a hissing, almost sub-audio argument as we pulled on our clothes.

'You *prawn*!'

'I'm sorry!'

Dom sat on the floor and glared up at me as he dragged on his jeans.

'He'll tell *Ma* and she'll *freak out* and the two of them will spend the next week treating me like feckin' *Helen* bleedin' *Keller.*'

'Oh, shut up. It's not *that* bad.' But I knew he was right. They were going to make a huge deal of this in their own quiet way. Why had I opened my big mouth?

'What the *hell* you were *thinking*?'

'It's your own fault anyway. What was that all about in the kitchen?'

He looked at me blankly. 'Eh?'

I paused in the middle of putting on my shoe and did a vicious impersonation: little girlie voice, clawed hands, eyes rolled into the back of my head. 'Don't let the bad man take meee. Wruuhhh!'

I laughed at myself, but Dom just squinted up at me, puzzled. 'Pat,' he said, 'I haven't a clue what you're talking about.' Something about his tone made me stop arsing around. He was studying me carefully. 'I don't remember saying *anything* in the kitchen,' he said. 'All I know is one minute I was guzzling food like a starvin' Bangladeshi and the next minute, Dad's hovering over me and you're telling him I had an asthma attack.'

I sat slowly onto the edge of the bed. 'Dad said Dee had been up all night with bad dreams,' I said. This lit a small flare of recollection in Dom's eyes. 'She thought a man was going to take her away,' I said, 'to take *you* away.'

A muscle in Dom's face twitched. He jerked forward. For a minute I thought we were going to repeat the whole kitchen scene again. But then he just sat back, his eyes thoughtful, his hand on the shark's tooth that had become a permanent fixture around his neck.

'I had a bad dream last night,' he said softly.

I nodded. 'So did I. Can you remember yours?'

He shook his head. 'Tell you what, though, what you said just now…
about the man? It scared me, Pat. Really … my heart's pounding. But
I don't know why.'

We sat deep in thought for a while. 'I think I dreamt about soldiers,'
I said quietly.

'Yeah?'

'Yeah. Soldiers in mud. Like that stupid film the night … last week.'

I couldn't bring myself to say which night we'd been watching that
film. We both went quiet.

Then Dom cleared his throat. 'Jesus,' he said, 'that film was boring
as shite, wasn't it? World War I wasn't half as good as World War II.'

He grinned and I grinned back. What else was there to do? Last
night had been freaky, one of those freaky nights where everything
seems weird and off kilter. But now? Now, the morning sun was
pouring through the window, there was a whole gansey-load of birds
singing their heads off in the bare branches of the apple trees and
everything was just so bloody *normal*.

I stood up and reached a hand out to pull Dom to his feet. 'C'mon.
Let's explore.'

As he stood, he gasped and bent double at the waist for a moment,
his face turning a delightful shade of green.

'Jesus, Pat. How much did we just *eat*?'

I groaned quietly as we crept down the stairs. 'God, I know. I'm full
as a frog. If I don't fart or burp soon I'll burst.'

Dom gawfed, and I slapped him on the back of the head with a hiss.
'Shut up, you eejit. You'll wake Ma.'

We headed out the back, through the garden filled with sand, past
Dad's car and through the shuttered amusements. We'd told Dad we

were heading up around the headland and back down the harbour. He said he wanted us back for one o'clock. 'Don't take any chances, you two. If there's trouble, just walk away. You're not with your cousins now.' As we were leaving, he gave Dom a troubled look. 'Don't get cold, Dominick.' Dom had sighed and nodded without turning around. He whacked me as soon as we were out of sight.

The day was blinding after the rain, the sun reflecting off a million puddles and hanging droplets. We cut straight onto the beach, jumped down off the grass wall and headed left towards the headland and the Martello tower. The tide was out, the great expanse of the flats stretching away in ripples of sand and water all the way to the island. The wind was wicked coming in off the sea and we huddled into our jackets, pulling the collars up to our ears and raising our voices to be heard. We had our usual conversation about taking a chance on walking out to the island: the dangers of quicksand, the possibilities of sharks and seal pups.

I don't know what it was that changed Dom's mind about the beach and made him take the harbour road. All I know is we were halfway to the rocks before it occurred to him. I was swinging a stick around, swishing it through the air, trying to make perfect 'Z's in the sand, like Zorro. Dom was doing his best Mick Jagger impersonation, all hips and lips. The two of us were singing 'Sympathy for the Devil' and were just on the eighth go-around of the chorus when Dom let a whoop out of him and took a sudden curve for the steps.

I immediately followed, his loping enthusiasm too infectious to resist. 'Where are we going?' I yelled.

He stopped at the top of the steps and turned to look back at me, his arms as wide as his grin, the wind whipping his hair and his army jacket and throwing sand into his teeth. 'Let's take the harbour!'

The town was all ours. The Easter holidays didn't start 'til next week, and all the other kids were in school. There were no summertime packs of sharp-eyed gurriers, no lounging teenagers. We were as free and unselfconscious as mutts. We tussled and ran and fenced our way up the harbour road, the fierce salty tang of the harbour itself already in our lungs. There were workmen and fishermen and auld wans out shopping, but they were on another plane of existence. They didn't impact on us at all.

Then we rounded the corner and caught them throwing the old man out of the pub.

He was very old, maybe Nan's age, but these two big men were hauling him out the door like a bundle of rags. One of them was shouting, 'Out, you old bastard. Out!' The other was silent, but his face was stony with rage and he had a grip on the auld fella vicious enough to snap his twiggy old arm.

From the smoky murk behind them, the Wolfe Tones were playing very loudly on a jukebox, and there was the general hubbub of a packed bar. A few faces were turned to the door, watching the eviction. I could just see the barman as he turned away, his mouth a firm, approving line. There were harp and shamrock flags over the bar; there was a 'Free all Irish political prisoners' poster on the wall.

The auld fella didn't seem to even notice the treatment he was getting. He was singing to himself – a gravelly, emotional waver. 'The bells of hell go ting-a-ling-a-ling,' he sang. 'For youuu but not for meeee. And awl de little devils have a sing-a-ling-a-ling, for you … but not for me.' His head bobbled about on his neck, his fine white hair a tufty cloud in the sunlight.

'Shut. UP!' yelled one of the men. 'Just *shut it!*' He shook the old man, hard, and the auld fella's feet slid out from under him so that he was suspended by one frail arm and the scruff of his neck.

'Hey!' I cried, stepping forward. 'You'll hurt him!'

Dom put his hand on my shoulder, holding me back. 'He's pissed out of his tree,' he murmured. 'Leave it.'

That became clear enough when the old man got his feet under him and tried to shrug off the two bruisers. He slurred something incomprehensible and swiped at them in the thoroughly disorganised manner of a drunk. One of the men shook his head in disgust. He gave the auld fella another shake.

'You should be ashamed of yourself, you old bollox. Coming in here, singing your British shite. Why don't you just shut up and die?'

The old man blinked up at him, his pale-blue eyes watery and unfocused. 'The ... the bells of hell ... for you. But ... not ...' He wasn't singing now, just muttering to himself. He seemed on the verge of tears and, although he was just another maudlin drunk, I couldn't help but feel sorry for him. He was swaying, and looking about him in tragic confusion. 'But not for me,' he whispered, and shuffled around in a ragged circle as though looking for something.

He saw the two bruisers, and focused on them as if for the first time. His face filled with sudden anger. He pointed a shaky, nicotine-yellowed finger and stumbled towards them, his eyes sparkling with tearful rage. 'You! Yah pups yah. What would *you* know?' He grabbed one man's coat to steady himself. 'I *fought* for my country. Yah gurrier, you ... I died ... Good men. Friends ...' He lost track and, still hanging onto the man's coat, leaned into him and started singing and crying all over again.

The other man made a wordless sound of impatience and dragged the auld fella around to face him. He violently yanked something from the old man's lapel, crushed it and threw it onto the wet ground. Then he pulled him up face to face and hissed in a low, brutal monotone, 'Fought for your country? Which country? King and Queen and rule Britannia? You listen to me, you old fart. If you come in here again, singing your old army songs and wearing your old army poppy, I will *have you disappeared*. Do you understand me?'

The auld fella looked up at the man, right into his eyes, and I saw something happen in his face. It was as though all the drink just fled from his brain and he saw everything at once, very clear and very sad. He blinked, his pale-blue eyes scanning those of the other man. Up close, their faces were so different: one a pale, slightly grubby, lined old face, thin and sagging and rough with silver stubble; the other tanned, solid, strong-featured and young, filled with sharp intelligence and uncompromising intent.

Something deflated inside the old man then; something emptied. It was as if years of pain had dissolved suddenly into tiredness and retreat. He dropped his eyes, and the younger man flung him away, turned, and disappeared back into the pub. The Wolfe Tones and the chat of the bar cut off as the door slammed shut on the daylight.

The old man sagged against the wall and stayed there, arms dangling. He seemed undecided between falling down and moving on. I shrugged off Dom's restraining hand and went to him. But when I put a hand on his shoulder, he yelled and flung his arm up. He didn't look at me – just shouted for me to leave him be, then shambled on up the road, weaving on unsteady rubber legs.

When I turned back, Dom was pushing something around with his toe, the thing from the old man's lapel. 'I thought Poppy Day was in November,' he said as the tattered silk of the red flower soaked up the mud and rain from the ground. 'What the hell was he thinking, wearing a British Army emblem in a republican bar?'

5. James

James

We walked slowly up the harbour, our hands in our pockets, a bit subdued after the incident at the pub. It didn't take long for the place to begin working its magic, though. I loved the harbour: the bell-like clang of the rigging, the gulls, the piles of fragrant netting. I loved the rows of fishing boats, their decks lined up in tempting, tilted platforms. They were three-deep at the quay today, because of the storms.

In the summer, Dad and Dom and me would often leap from boat to boat, fishing rod in one hand, tackle box in the other. We'd make our way out to the furthest boat and spend the day in the company of gulls and crab-shells, reeling in mackerel and sprat, eating cheese sandwiches with fishy fingers and drinking tea from a flask.

'We should get Dad to bring down the tackle, and we can spend the day up at the Head with him,' said Dom.

I was about to reply when I remembered there was no tackle anymore: no rods, no hooks, no lines. There was nothing but a smouldering blob of melted plastic and nylon, in the charred hole that used to be the cupboard under our stairs.

Our faces fell and we simultaneously swallowed and looked away.

'Fancy a Shandy and some crisps?' Dom ground out. He was gone before I could answer, digging in his pocket for change and heading for the little whitewashed harbour shop. I sat on the slip to wait for him, my thoughts a dark undertow to the sparkling water, the bright boats bobbing on the swell.

Dom came back. He handed me a bag of Tayto and a can of Shandy and we ate in silence, crushing the crisps into crumbs in the bag, then sucking them off our fingers, swigging the Shandy, warm and frothy from the can. We weren't going to talk about it. That was a mutual, silent decision. As we moved off again, dropping our rubbish into the bin, wiping our fingers on our trousers, Dom pucked me and grinned. 'Race yah.'

He ran. I took after him. He leapt a lobster pot and fled with a *whoop*.

It took a while, but once we'd dodged our way up the harbour and through the stone gate at the end we were well on track to regaining our good humour. By the time we'd got on the path to the lookout poles we were yelling and belting each other and making machine-gun noises and dying dramatic writhing deaths on the grass.

I leapt up from one such twitching demise and hurtled up the slope to the totem poles. Dom trailed behind me, a worried grin on his face. I always freaked him out on those poles. Sometimes I did it on purpose. In the summer, our cousin Sean and I would clamber right to the top and stand there, windmilling our arms and pretending to fall. Dom and the others would linger at the bottom in delicious fear, their hands to their mouths or covering their eyes.

Admittedly it was a bloody stupid thing to do. The totem poles were about ten feet high and hardly a foot in diameter. There was barely enough room to stand with your two feet tight together. But God, what a thrill! You could stand up there with the blue sky just in reach and look for miles out to sea.

This time I was content to stop at the top foothold and hold on, surveying the landscape. The wind was *wild*. It filled my eyes with tears and instantly snatched them away again. My nose began to run like crazy. Dom was calling to me, his voice indistinct in the blustering air, but I ignored him because something had caught my eye on the path further up the headland. I squinted against the wind. What the hell *was* that?

There came a breathless greeting in my ear. 'Hey!'

'Jesus!' I jumped and grabbed the top of the totem pole in fright. I had to grit my teeth and swallow hard just to stop my heart from flying out of my mouth. 'Dom! You lunatic!'

He had climbed the other pole and was standing on the third rung from the top, his arms wrapped around the wood. He grinned up at me, delighted at his own daring and my startled reaction. 'Woo!' he said. 'It's windy! What were you gawking at?'

Oh yeah! That guy at the top of the headland. I straightened up again craning to see. Was it the auld fella from the bar? No, this guy was taller, straighter. He looked like he was wearing a uniform. I pointed him out to Dom

'Look at him!' I said. 'What's he up to? He looks like some sort of soldier.'

Dom stretched as high as he could dare without letting go of the pole. The soldier was just at the brow of the headland, where the grass sloped out of sight and down to the sea. His long coat was whipping around him in the frenzy of wind coming up the hill and, if I hadn't known better, I would have said he was staring straight at us. His eyes were hidden beneath the brim of his military hat, but I could feel them, even at that distance. They were pinned on mine. I just knew it. As we watched, he slowly lifted his arm and pointed down towards the rocky shore that lay past him and out of our sight.

I felt the hairs prickle up on the back of my neck. I didn't like the thought that this man could see me.

'*Is* he a soldier?' asked Dom uncertainly. 'Or is he just dressed up as one? That uniform's not right.'

The soldier just stood there, calmly pointing down the hill and staring at us, his coat slapping and snapping in the wind, his unseen eyes locked on mine. I felt myself climbing down the totem pole and before I knew it I was on the path again, walking slowly up the hill towards him. He was out of sight now. But waiting. I knew it. Waiting for us to come.

Dom grabbed my arm, breathless from catching up with me. He stared into my face, pleading.

'I … I don't want to go up there,' he said.

Neither did I, but still I broke away from him, walking backwards, keeping eye contact for as long as possible before I turned back to the path. It was as if I wasn't in command of my own feet, and they were carrying me of their own accord to the place where the soldier stood. Dom followed me, begging me not to go, miserably telling me that he didn't *want* to go, but following me just the same. We quickly mounted the brow of the hill and continued on up to the spot where the soldier had been standing.

He was gone.

I looked all around us. There was nothing but empty grassland and seagulls drifting up on the breeze. I scanned the horizon, all up and down the path. There was no one there but us.

'He's gone.' Dom sounded absurdly relieved. 'Maybe he was waiting for someone and they've gone off together. Maybe …'

'He was trying to show me something,' I said. 'It was important. I could feel it …'

I looked down the slope to where the soldier had been pointing and my heart gave a startled little *bump* in my chest. The man *had* been showing me something. I grabbed Dom's arm, pointing down to the sea. 'Look!' I yelled.

Then we were running down the slope together, yelling and waving our arms. Screaming 'No! Stop it! Stop!' though there was no way the man on the shore could have heard us.

There was no doubt in my mind who it was − his unmistakable cloud of white hair whipping about in the wind, his dark, shabby coat and long twiggy arms. It was the old man from the pub, and he was trying to commit suicide in the sea.

☠ ☠ ☠

I don't know if the wind and the heavy surf drowned our voices as we got closer or if the poor old sod was just too far gone to hear us, but he never paused. His arms were up, Christ crucified, as though he was afraid to get his sleeves wet. The tails of his coat trailed behind him in the waist-high water. God knows how he kept his footing in that heavy swell. Each wave lifted him slightly and dropped him like flotsam, but he kept going, his expression calm and dreamy as the water rose above his waist.

'Mister! Hey! *Mister!*' The wind whipped great yellow curds of sea-foam into our faces as we waded into the waves. 'Mister! Come back!' We forged out into a deep, narrow channel that cut between two jagged ridges of rock. Up ahead of us, the old man was making alarming progress into deeper water. We were soon up to our chests.

'Mister!' shrieked Dom. His cry ended in a choking gurgle as a wave broke across his mouth, and he gasped, turning his head to try and catch his breath. I overtook him, both hands up to protect my mouth and eyes.

The old man had stopped, shoulder-deep in the water now, and looked up into the sky, his arms still outstretched. He lurched with each swell, but still managed to keep his feet. His eyes were fixed on the rapidly scudding clouds and he looked very peaceful, almost happy. Then he let himself fall backwards. He slid under the foam in one easy movement. His hands and the tails of his coat were the last things we saw.

'No!' I launched forward, plunged my hands under, groping for him, straining to keep my face above the waves. Dom struggled up beside me and swung his arms about under the water, his eyes scanning the foam for some sign. I was still groping blindly this way and that when Dom took a huge breath and submerged. I did the same, my eyes open. There was nothing but churning grey. Bubbles clogged my ears.

We surfaced. I went to shout 'He's gone!' but Dom just took another breath and went under again. I must confess, I hesitated. I had lost all sensation in my arms and legs. The wind was stripping the skin from my face, and my wet hair felt like stinging wire whipping at my eyes and mouth. I screamed at the empty water, my voice cracked with panic and cold, 'Dom! *Dom!*'

Dom surfaced, so close that his wake submerged me for a minute.

His face was raw and streaming. 'Can't …' There was no breath in him to finish. The next swell pushed him against me and we both nearly went down, gripping each other in a panicky realisation of the danger we were in.

We were up to our necks. Each swell hid the beach from view and filled our mouths with water. And we weren't just battling the cold anymore; our clothes were so heavy! The water sucked and tugged at our leaden jumpers and trousers, using them to drag us under and out.

I tried to say, 'We need to get back.' But my chattering teeth and repeated mouthfuls of water garbled my words. Dom understood me. He nodded and we began to drag each other to shore.

A choking gasp made us turn back. It was the old man. He'd broken the surface just a few feet from where we stood. For a moment he just lay there, looking at the sky; then he began to slip quietly under again. Without a thought, I grabbed the scruff of his neck. Dom took hold of his shoulder and we laboured to shore, the old man an unresisting weight that we towed behind us.

We staggered out of the waves like a drunken resurrection, making our way up the beach with the old man slung between us. He could hardly support himself, but with our help he managed to totter along. Dom and I were shivering uncontrollably, our clothes a tremendous, chafing weight. I'd heard people say they thought they'd *die* of cold, but until that day I'd had no concept of how that might feel. It took all my concentration to just put one foot in front of the other and when we got to the path and the wind hit us full blast I nearly stopped dead at the icy shock of it.

Dom began shouting, his voice broken and wavering. I was barely capable of taking one step, then another, but Dom was still using his noodle, trying to get the old man talking.

'Wh … where do you luh … live, mister?'

The old man didn't even lift his head. Dom's teeth began clicking like epileptic castanets. He was shaking so badly that his head wobbled, but he kept pucking the old man, yelling at him to tell us where he lived. There was no response. The old man didn't even open his eyes. But he did keep dragging one foot in front of the other, so we just kept going with him.

When we staggered and stumbled our way to the little shop on the harbour, the young wan behind the counter shrieked and ran into the back room. Her mother came tumbling out, her hands to her face. 'James!' she cried. 'Oh, James, you old fool! What happened you?' She rushed around the counter and claimed the auld fella. He stumbled into her care, his blue eyes blinking without comprehension into her face. 'Oh, you silly old *sod*,' she said.

We stood in a miserable shivering huddle in the middle of her tiny shop, water literally pouring off of us. She looked at us over the old man's shoulder. 'What happened?'

We glanced at each other and came to a mutual decision.

'He fell in the sea,' I said.

'And youse rescued him? You little angels, youse! God bless youse, lads! God bless your hearts.'

'Wuh wuh … we wanted to buh … bring him home to his fam fam family …'

'James doesn't have a fambly!' cried the girl.

I don't think Dom even heard her. He was shuddering in great jerking spasms now, his arms wrapped around himself. I began to feel sick, I was so cold. My head felt like someone had driven a metal spike from temple to temple. I started to sway on my feet.

The shop woman looked alarmed. 'Don't be worrying about James now, lads. Sure, doesn't he just live three cottages down? Sarah and I'll get him all fixed up. Have youse far to go? Will I phone someone for youse?'

'Wuh wuh … we're uh up by the huh huh huh …' I tried.

'Hurdy … guh guh … gurdies,' finished Dom. 'Nuh no phone.'

'Well, run, boys! Run!'

And we did, turning stiffly and shambling out the door on numb legs. She shouted after us as we did our best to sprint up the harbour. 'Run, boys, or youse'll catch your deaths! Run and don't stop 'til youse get home!'

6. 'Waterloo'

Our waterlogged entrance into the kitchen froze Ma and Dad into slack-jawed shock. We took full advantage of their momentary paralysis to stutter out the phrase that undoubtedly saved our skins.

'O-old man f-fell in sea … we p-p-pulled him out.'

Ma blinked, twice. Then she gripped Dad's arm.

'Get them out of those wet clothes,' she said, and bolted up the stairs.

Dee peered through the sitting-room doorway, her mouth and eyes delighted little 'O's of wonder. Dad dithered from foot to foot while we just stood there, flooding the floor and shuddering helplessly.

Finally Dee pointed and said, 'Bom 'n' Pap all wet, Daddy.'

That woke him. 'Yes. Yes. Shite.' He was over with us then, stripping us of our wet clothes, flinging them into a dribbling heap by the door.

Ma clattered down the stairs, arms full of towels. Dad pulled off our socks. We were too cold to do anything but lift our legs for him one at a time as he peeled the wet wool from our icy feet. The towels were huge, and warm and fluffy. They smelled of plastic shop-wrappers. One of them still had a tag on it. Ma ripped it off with a grimace.

As they towelled us down, Ma and Dad pushed us into the sitting room and up to the fire. All this time, Dad was giving us the third degree on what had happened.

Ma kept muttering, 'That poor old man. That poor old man. Was he a bit touched, love? Was he wandering? Is that why he fell in the sea?'

'Dunno, Ma.' Dom's head was wagging to and fro as she chaffed him dry. He was staring blankly into the fire. I knew how he felt. It was all I could manage to stay on my feet and let Dad dry my hair. I think we'd used the last of our energy just getting home.

Ma was really fretting over the old man. 'Oh, I hope he's alright. What did that woman *say*, Dom? Did she know him? Was she kind? Lift your foot, love, let me get these dry socks on you.'

Dad handed me my pyjamas. It was only half-two in the afternoon, but I didn't object. There was nothing I wanted more than to slip into warm flannel and curl up by the fire.

'Poor, poor old man,' said Ma. 'Poor old man. Do you think he's alright, Pat?'

'I think he had a bit of drink on him, Ma. I think that's why he slipped.' My words were thick and slow. My eyes kept shutting themselves. I leant on the mantelpiece, soaking up the heat. Dom was somewhere to my left, on the sofa. Dee told him to: 'Open up your eyeblibs, Bom!'

Dad spoke softly to Ma. They were standing by the door, I think. 'I'm going to check on the old man, Olive.'

'Thanks, love!'

'I think the boys should go to bed for a while.'

'I'll give them an extra blanket. Mind Dee for a minute while I get them upstairs, will you?'

I felt Ma take my hand and she led us up the stairs like sleepwalkers. It was horrible cold once we stepped away from the fire, and I started to shiver immediately. But my bed was warm because Ma had put hot-water bottles in it. She tucked an extra blanket around me as soon as I lay down. I heard her do the same for Dom, the bunks creaking as she stood on my bed to reach his. I felt the brief caress of her hand in my hair before she left.

'I'll wake you for the Eurovision.'

The door whispered shut, and Ma crept away down the stairs.

I don't think I slept; I never quite lost the sense that I was right there, in my bed. But the world seemed to drift away for a while, leaving just the sound of my breathing and Dom's breathing and the lovely heat of the hot-water bottle at my feet.

After a while, I rose to the surface just enough to know that I needed to move. I rolled on to my back, instantly comfortable again, eyes closing. The blustery wind of earlier had escalated and there was a proper storm blowing outside. Something rattled its way from one end of the garden to the other and the windows knocked rhythmically in their frames. The TV aerial on the roof creaked and groaned, and to my drowsing mind it felt like I was deep in the belly of some wooden ship. I listened contentedly, smiling. I was just beginning to wonder why things were so quiet in the kitchen, when a voice in the bunk above mine whispered, 'The bad man is here.'

I opened my eyes and stayed very still.

That wasn't Dom. That wasn't his voice!

The wind groaned through the eaves, a low monotone. A spattering of rain peppered the window. It was so quiet downstairs. No TV. No radio. I couldn't hear Ma and Dad. I couldn't hear Dee. It was just me, floating alone inside the noise of the storm – and someone who wasn't Dom, whispering.

'If we're not careful, the bad man will find us. He'll take you away and we ...' The urgent flow of words halted, as though the speaker was listening for something. The gale rushed past the windows in a sudden irritated *shhh*.

I tried to make no noise.

I tried not to breathe.

If I turned my head, I would be able to see the dressing-table mirror. I would be able to look. There was no night-time gloom now – the top bunk would be lit up, clear as the rainy grey twilight that filled the room. All I had to do was look.

But I didn't turn my head. I just couldn't.

And then it came again. That whisper: a sharp, fearful hiss: 'Do you hear him?'

The bunk above me creaked: the distinctive sound of Dom sitting up.

My eyes got so big it felt as though they might roll out of their sockets. My hands cramped into fists in the blankets. I was staring, staring, staring at the bunk above me. Waiting.

Then I heard my brother's voice: quiet, inquisitive, uncertain.

'I don't hear anything,' he said.

Dom! Oh God! Dom! Who are you talking to?

I opened my mouth to say something when that stranger's whisper came again. 'But he's *here*. He's here all the time. He wants us. He'll hurt us! We must be careful.'

Dom answered, his voice low now, nothing but a whisper: 'Is he here now?'

'Oh yes. I think so.'

Right above my head, Dom shifted. I could imagine him drawing his knees up and hugging them to his chest: the classic pose for Dom when he was frightened. 'You're scaring me,' he said softly.

'Don't be frightened. I'll take a look, shall I?'

More creaking. But not above my head! No. Not where Dom was sitting. This creaking was at the *foot* of Dom's bed. Something was sitting at the end of Dom's bed!

I shifted my terrified gaze in that direction. I could hear something up there, crawling towards the ladder. Something was going to look over the edge. It was going to look over the edge of Dom's bunk.

My fear was panting its way up my chest, into my throat – was building itself up into a scream.

I was going to scream. I was going to scream *right now*.

A small, pale hand grabbed the edge of Dom's bunk. Little fingers curled around the mattress. I could see the indents in the fabric where they gripped tight. There was a pause, as though it was frightened to look and then a small, pale, dark-eyed face cleared the edge.

It was a boy. Maybe ten years old. White face. Dark, *dark* eyes, underscored with deep lines, surrounded with purple shadows. His cheeks were hollow and filled with shadows. He scanned the gloom of my bunk with fear, his white lips compressed. It took a moment for him to register my presence. Then his eyes jumped to mine. I flinched, terrified by the certainty that we'd done this before: me looking up at him; him looking down on me – a solemn-eyed boy of ten, untouched by the wind and rain.

The child quickly recovered from the shock of seeing me. Then his sunken, sick-looking face hardened into loathing and, without taking his eyes from mine, he hissed to the person up above me – to Dom: 'He's here.'

The bunk squeaked overhead as Dom shifted suddenly and I heard my brother gasp in fear. The little white child reached his whole arm over the edge and gripped the middle rung of the ladder as though he meant to crawl down, headfirst. He glared at me and bared his little teeth, and they were black against the snowy white of his lips.

That scream bubbled up inside me and I opened my mouth to let it out.

'Hey, sweetheart.'

I leapt, my scream nothing more than a soundless rush of air, and Ma drew back in surprise. 'Did I give you a fright?' she whispered. 'Sorry, love.' She brushed my hair off my face. 'You know you were asleep with your eyes open? You looked a bit creepy, staring at the ladder like that. Were you dreaming?'

I blinked at her, frozen and disoriented, the blankets bunched at my chin. The storm still gushed and buffeted outside the house. Downstairs the telly burbled cheerfully and Dad and Dee chattered away to each other.

Ma smiled at me. 'The Eurovision's just about to start. D'you want to come on down and watch it?'

I nodded dumbly, not trusting my voice. Ma handed me my dressing-gown and stood to wake Dom. He jolted awake, the bed squealing as he jerked into a sitting position.

'Who's there?' he cried.

Ma laughed. 'You're as jumpy as cats, you two! Come on! I kept your dinner, and there's apple tart and custard for after.'

At the mention of food my stomach contracted and I was overwhelmed by a dizzying cramp of hunger. I heard Dom above me, escaping his blankets in a flurry of urgency. The bed lurched as he leapt from the ladder. 'I'm *starved*,' he said.

Ma said, 'Hey, *watch* it!' as he pushed past her out the door and onto the stairs. They entered the kitchen together, their voices under me now, coming up muffled through the floorboards.

I sat hunched on the edge of the bed, listening as my family moved about downstairs without me. I was shaky and sweating, folded over the emptiness in my belly, too dizzy to move. The hunger in me was as sharp as a pain. My hands were trembling with it, and my head ached so badly that I had to squint in the weak light. I wasn't sure that I could get my feet under me. The door looked miles away, across acres of bare wooden floor.

Then, above my head, Dom's bed creaked slyly.

I was up and moving in a flash, staggering out the door on legs so wobbly that I thought I'd fall head over heels all the way to the bottom of the dark steps. I somehow managed the stairs, clinging to the wall, my knees buckling with every step. I was making frantic sounds in the back of my throat because I could feel that little child behind me, his black eyes hating me, his little hands ready to push.

I stumbled into the kitchen in a sweat of fear, looking over my shoulder and almost crying with relief. I turned to Dom. He was sitting at the table, grinning. Ma laid our dinners down, and the sight of them blew everything else from my mind. I rushed over and grabbed a spud, cramming it into my mouth before my arse even hit the chair. I groaned at the lovely gravy, the delicious salty potatoes, the frothy, ice-cold milk. I couldn't get them into me fast enough.

Across the table Dom was shovelling food into himself, his whole attention focused on cramming down the spuds and chops and forkfuls of buttery turnip. Swallowing without chewing, he paused only to drain almost an entire glass of milk, then went on eating.

I lowered my shaking fork, staring at him.

He was delighted with himself; happily, blissfully, ignorantly stuffing his face, while I looked on, barely capable of holding it together. It hit me at once that Dom didn't remember! He had *no idea* what had just happened, no memory of the little creature that had been sitting on his bed.

Had I dreamt it all? Was that possible?

Finally, Dom seemed to have filled himself; he took one last draining swallow of milk and sat back. Then he grinned at me, patted his belly and belched, loud and long.

'Nice one!' Dad called from the sitting room 'Neuf points!'

Dom grinned even wider and stretched like a satisfied cat.

'It's starting! It's starting!' called Ma as the music for the Eurovision swelled up from the telly.

Dom rose heavily from the table and winced, doubling over.

'Je*sus!*' he laughed. 'How much did I just *eat*?'

The food in my belly heaved. The door to the stairs, a gaping hole behind me, breathed ice down my spine. This morning neither of us had been able to remember a thing about our bad dreams. Just like now, we had stumbled downstairs crazed with hunger and stuffed ourselves fit to burst, with nothing but the vaguest recollection of the night before. Even now, I had no clear idea of what last night's dream had been about – only that it had woken me, left me staring and terrified in the dark, the taste of mud on my tongue, the image of soldiers in my head. Well here we were again, demented with hunger and, as far as Dom was concerned, with no memory of what had happened upstairs. But one thing was different.

I remembered. I remembered *everything*.

Because this time I'd been awake. I'd been awake the whole time.

Dom was grinning back at me from the sitting-room doorway. 'Pat,' he said, 'you coming?' His grin faltered a little and he stepped back into the kitchen. 'Pat? You're white as a sheet. Are you alright?'

'Pat?' Ma called from the sofa, 'What's wrong?' I could hear her beginning to get up.

I shook my head at Dom, my eyes wide, and held my finger to my lips. The last thing I wanted was to try and explain this to Ma and Dad. What would I say to them?

There was a monster, Ma. A goblin-boy. He scared me.

Dom frowned, spread his hands, questioning: *What?*

I called in to Ma, 'I'm grand. There's nothing wrong with me. Just got a bit of wind is all.'

'Well, rip a fart then,' laughed Dad.

'*Dave!*' There was the sound of Ma thwacking Dad with her book, then general shuffling and giggles as she arranged herself on the sofa again and Dee climbed back on her lap.

'Come on, lads, first song's coming on soon.'

I stood up from the table. The floor did a massive ninety-degree tilt under my feet and I staggered. Dom crossed the room in a stride and caught me.

'Bloody hell, Pat,' he whispered. 'What's the matter with you?'

I took three deep, controlling breaths in and out of my nose and held onto him while I got my legs under me. Then I nodded and he let me go. I didn't fall over. That was good.

I think I faded him out for a minute, ignoring my surroundings as I tested my equilibrium, because he surprised me by taking my arm again. 'Pat!' he whispered. '*Talk to me!*'

Oh Jesus! 'Talk to me!' Typical Dom! What the hell was I meant to say? *Well, Dom, I'm a bit freaked out because a little white goblin-boy was sitting on your bed talking to you. Oh and hey, you don't remember this, but you were more than willing to listen! In fact, you sent it down to take a peep at me! Would you like me to tell you that, now? And while I'm at it, will I tell you how he looked at me while he was getting ready to climb headfirst down the ladder? Will I let you in on a secret? He looked like he wanted to eat me, Dom. He looked just like he wanted to eat me and you don't remember this because you were asleep, but I was awake. How's that? Good? Okay, now let's go on in and watch the Eurovision and we'll finish this conversation when we've gone to bed. Where, by the way, I think that little goblin-boy may be living. How's that Dom? Glad we had this chat now? Glad we talked things through?*

Dom stepped away from me, a strange expression on his face. 'What's wrong with you?' he whispered. 'Why are you looking at me like that?'

The tone of his voice and the hurt look on his face stopped me cold. I realised that I was glaring at him, my hands balled into fists, my shoulders hunched like a boxer. I straightened. I shook my head.

'I'm scared,' I said.

This totally threw him. I could see him doing a double-take and running things backwards in his head to see what he'd missed.

'I'm bloody terrified,' I said. 'I don't know how I'm standing here talking to you, actually having words come out of my mouth without crying or screaming or something. But I *can't* talk about it now – you've got to promise you won't try and make me, Dom! You've got to promise that we can just go in and watch the Eurovision and pretend that everything is alright. Because I just don't want to have to ...' Suddenly, I grabbed onto his two shoulders like a drowning man clutching a life belt. It was a gesture that surprised even me, and Dom staggered back a little bit in shock. But he managed to keep his feet under him and he kept his eyes locked on mine. 'Promise me, Dom!' I whispered. 'Promise me you'll just go in there with me and pretend everything is alright? *Promise* me. Because if I try to talk ...'

I'll lose it! I thought. *I'll lose it and I'll start to cry, and if I start to cry I won't stop!* And it wasn't just that I didn't want to look like a big Jessie. It was Nan. It was the house. It was my books. All the things I'd lost. It would all just pour out of me. It would *pour out of me* and I'd be broken. I'd cry so hard I'd be *broken*.

I began to lose it. My nose started to run and my eyes started to water. I was on the verge of breaking down. Oh God, I didn't want that to happen. *Dom*, I thought, *don't let this happen!*

Dom grabbed the top of my arms and shook me once – hard.

'*Hey!*' he said. 'Get it together.'

That settled something inside me, like a big stone dropping down and blocking something off. I took a huge, sharp breath and held it. Dom kept his eyes locked with mine – fierce, absolute, determined – and held onto me while I found the control I so badly needed. Then I nodded and pulled away.

Breathing deep, one hand resting on Dom's chest, I scrubbed my face with the sleeve of my pyjamas. Dom awkwardly patted my arm. We stood quietly for a minute while I got my breathing under control.

'How do I look?' I whispered.

Dom grimaced. Yeah. I could imagine.

I snorted back my tears and scrubbed at my face again.

'Stop that – you're making it worse.' Dom looked over his shoulder, but there was nothing suspicious from the other room. They hadn't heard us. 'Let's just go in,' he said. 'They have the lights off. You'll look fine with only the fire to see by.'

Alright then. He held onto me all the way up to the door, then let go as we entered the room. We sauntered in together as though nothing was wrong and took seats at opposite ends of the sofa.

I can't remember much about the Eurovision that year. I could tell that Ma thought it was strange I wasn't more into it. The Eurovision was *our* thing, hers and mine. Usually Dom would sit in the background, reading a book or listening to his transistor or something; that kind of music just wasn't his scene. Dad and Dee usually fell asleep after the first three songs. (No exception that year. I distinctly remember Dad snoring through most of the northern European entries.) But Ma and I, we'd have an all-night running conversation on the costumes, the crappy lyrics, whether or not we'd remember the song in a week, a month, a year.

I did my best. I remember *some* give and take. But all the time my mind kept drifting upstairs, kept seeing that pale arm snaking over the edge of the bed. Kept thinking, *I've to go back up there, tonight. I've to go back up there.*

I remember the Swedish entry, ABBA, coming on. I remember thinking, *Oh yes. They're going to win.* Ma and I even sang along, bouncing in time to the music, my arm around her shoulders; it was *that* good. Then I caught Dom looking at me from the end of the sofa, his dark eyes anxious, and the last line of the song died in my throat.

I remember when ABBA won the TV station cut to the news before the victory performance was over, and Ma leapt up and ran into the kitchen to turn on the radio. Larry Gogan was still commenting on the show and he played the song all the way to the end. Ma raced back in and grabbed me by my hands and hauled me to my feet, and we danced all around the kitchen, singing along at the tops of our voices.

In that moment, I felt feverishly happy. I was almost hysterically happy. And when the song was over I remember thinking, *No! No! Don't let it stop. Let it go on forever.* So that I could go on forever, dancing and singing in the kitchen with Ma. And not have to go upstairs.

But it did stop, and it was dead late, and Dad carried Dee to bed, and Ma started doing the dishes. I stood in the middle of the kitchen, the harsh centre light beating down on me, while Ma and Dom had a conversation with each other that was all sound and no words and seemed to come from very far away.

I stood there in my pyjamas and dressing-gown, tired and lost and bloody terrified, looking at nothing in particular, thinking of nothing but how scared I was. Then Dom came quietly up behind me, took my elbow in his hand, and led me up the stairs.

7. The Feel of Moonlight

The Feel of Moonlight

The night brings all kinds of surprises, doesn't it? Nothing is ever quite what it first appears to be. Things don't ever go quite as you anticipate.

We climbed the dark stairs, Dom's hand on my elbow. When we got to the bedroom he guided me inside, then turned and shut the door with a quiet little *snick*. We didn't turn the lamp on. The moon blared in through the two windows, fragmenting the bedroom into hard shadows and gleaming white surfaces. It was all as crisp and as clear as a black-and-white photograph.

I scanned the room, my eyes jumping from place to place. Dom stood at my side, holding my elbow, quietly supporting me, waiting for my cue. Every molecule in my body seemed ready to fight or flee. I was thrumming with anticipation. But gradually, as I looked around and as the room asserted itself on me, I began floating down into reality. I felt myself calming, reconnecting with my surroundings – and I realised that there was nothing here. Absolutely nothing.

I looked at the bunk, forced myself to really take it in. The covers were lumpy and steeped in darkness, the bottom bunk, in particular, a depthless well of darkness, but innocent of any horrors. There was no vibe here. Nothing at all. The room was empty, just a sparsely furnished bedroom, shabby and filled with dust. My whole body loosened at once with relief.

I can honestly say that if I hadn't had that reaction – that completely unexpected reaction – there would have been no earthly power that could have made me remain in the house. I had built myself up into such a frenzy in the kitchen that the relief of this – this *nothingness* – was almost a physical blow. My legs started to shake; my lips began to quiver. Absurdly I thought, *Oh great. Dom is never going to believe me now.*

I must have looked pretty pathetic, because Dom got a blanket from the bunk and wrapped it round me like a cloak. He still hadn't said a word. He led me to the window, where he left me sitting while he went and grabbed his own blanket before joining me. We sat like two Apaches, our backs to the draughty windowpanes, silently regarding the empty, threatless room.

He was no fool, my brother. I have no doubt that had he tried to get me to talk, I would have clammed up. But obviously Dom had a better handle on me than I would have ever given him credit for. That, or he was too afraid to ask. Whatever his reasons, he didn't say a word – just sat gazing pensively out into the room, his eyes roaming from place to place, his face unusually solemn.

Eventually I started talking and I didn't stop until I'd told him everything. I'm not sure what kind of a reaction I expected; certainly not the silence I received. He listened calmly to everything I had to say. When I was done, he waited a minute to be sure I was finished, then his eyes got far away and he rested his chin on his chest, his arms folded underneath his blanket. He chewed absently on the collar of his dressing-gown while he thought about what I'd said.

The utter normality of the room mocked my every word, and at that moment I felt even my own belief slipping. All sorts of rationales began to wriggle and crawl across the face of my certainty. Perhaps it actually *had* been a dream? I mean, which would have been the saner option? And in the long run, which would I have preferred? I may have spent all my days writing stories about creatures from hell and creatures from space and demons from within — but when it came down to it, what was worse? To be proven right and have this awful truth revealed, or to find that I was just an hysterical baby who'd been frightened by a bad dream?

I thought about that child's face, and about that child's arm and the way its teeth were black against its white lips, and I had no hesitation about which option I would take.

I waited for Dom to voice his opinion, and for the gentle but insistent rationalisations to begin.

Let him talk you out of this, I thought. *Let him rescue you.*

Dom shifted slightly. 'I was scared of that man,' he said.

For a moment I thought he meant one of the men at the pub. But then I remembered his reaction to the other man, the soldier, who had drawn me up the hill, who had led us to the poor auld fella in the sea, and I knew that he was who Dom meant. I felt a little flare of anger cut through my fear. What the hell did he have to do with anything? I'd just told Dom that a monster had crawled out of his bed and he was talking about some bloody sightseeing soldier?

'We saw him on the top of that hill,' continued Dom, 'and all I could think was, *That's him; that's the bad man. He's found me. He'll take me away.*' He looked at me to see if I understood.

I understood alright. The bad man. Those were the exact words the goblin-boy had just used. The bad man. Only Dom had thought them first – hours ago.

'It was a really loud thought, Pat. Do you know what I mean? It filled up my head.' Dom made a gesture at his temples, a squeezing gesture, and squinted his eyes to indicate the kind of pressure he had experienced. 'It seemed to push all my other thoughts out of the way. All I knew, all that *mattered*, was that this was the *bad man*, and he wanted to take me away … When we got to the hill, and he wasn't there, Jesus, Pat.' Dom closed his eyes. 'It's no lie, I thought I'd *die* from relief. I thought I'd bloody faint.'

His eyes filled with tears then, and I was a bit lost as to what to do. I hadn't expected this; I hadn't expected Dom to be upset. Afraid, maybe; scornful, definitely – but not emotional, not *upset*. It shocked me that I hadn't even noticed how scared he was.

'That soldier is a *terrible person*, Pat. He's *terrible*. He makes me ...' Dom pressed his fist to his mouth. I could see the skin whitening where he was pushing his lips against his teeth, but he didn't let the tears come and when he spoke again his voice was steady. 'He's done something awful, I just know it.'

'How do you know?'

He shook his head. 'It's like someone told me. I just … I just *know*.'

'Well, he's not half as scary as that boy thing. At least he isn't living in our bed.'

Dom moaned. 'Stop. That's not funny.' He pushed his fingers in under his eyes, then looked at me sideways, knowing what way I'd react when he said, 'Maybe we're going the way of Nan.'

I huffed an impatient breath. 'Don't start that rubbish again,' I said. 'This is real.'

'Oh yeah,' he whispered, pulling the blanket tight around him and looking bleakly out into the room. 'Real. I'm afraid of bad men and you're seeing demons. No way we're losing our minds.'

A knock on the door made us jump like frogs. Dad stuck his head around the corner to find us saucer-eyed and clutching each other, wrapped in our blankets on the windowsill. He was momentarily surprised, then his eyes narrowed in suspicion.

'What are you two up to? You look like Sitting Bull and Tonto perched there.'

We just kind of gaped uselessly at him, and he rolled his eyes to heaven and directed us to bed with a jerk of his thumb. 'Into the leaba, the two of you. Your mother'll have your guts if you catch a cold.'

We complied and he went downstairs singing 'Waterloo' quietly to himself. We heard him and Ma go into the sitting room. When the sounds of their voices were safely muffled by the sitting-room door, Dom crept down the ladder and stood wrapped in his blanket by the side of my bunk.

'Can I sleep in with you?'

I shifted all the way over to the wall without a word of complaint. Truth be told, I was never so grateful for the warmth of my brother crawling into bed beside me. He lay with his back to me, wrapped head-to-toe in his blanket and looking out across the room to the dressing-table mirror.

'Pat?' he said.

'Yeah.'

'I wish I believed in God. Then I could say a prayer.'

'Say one anyway.'

'Will you?'

'I always say my prayers.'

'I know. Say one now, okay?'

'Alright ... Dom?'

'Yeah?'

'Just go ahead and say one anyway. It couldn't hurt.'

'Alright.'

But I don't think he did. Dom was no hypocrite, not even when he was scared out of his wits.

☠ ☠ ☠

Jolly hands me a mug of tea. He has a knack with tea, does Jolly. Of course it tastes of petrol – that's unavoidable – but somehow Jolly always gets the tea good and hot. I seal my letter and tuck it into my breast-pocket along with my pencil. Shamie is watching me from his niche across the trench, his pale-blue eyes the only colour in the dry mud-mask of his face.

I nod at him and he understands. I've asked my darling Lacy to talk to May for him, to try and get May to stop returning Shamie's letters. I doubt it will make any difference. I don't think Shamie understands how much May meant it when she said he'd have to choose: he could have the British uniform or he could have her, but not both. I think he still believes he has a chance of getting her back. I'm less than sure of that – beneath her smile, my sister has a core of steel that not even Shamie's charm can melt.

Jolly passes between us, his back to me as he hands Shamie a cuppa.

"'Ere you go, Wee Paddy.'

Shamie smiles gratefully up at him. He doesn't climb out of his niche, just curls out an arm and brings the cup into himself. He's crouched like a little mud gargoyle in that snug cell. He closes his eyes in bliss as the petrol-scented steam rises up into his face.

The sun is blazing down for once. We've finally stopped steaming under its glare and now every one of us is pale-grey cracked mud from the knee up. From the knee down, we're still caked in heavy slime and trench slobber. Jolly flops down beside Shamie and gestures at me.

'Been writing 'ome then, Big Paddy? Reminding them to send you some burfday cake next week?'

I nod and smile. Jolly's a decent bloke. They're all decent blokes, our new trench mates. Them being the ragged ends of three Lancashire-Pals Regiments; and Shamie and I, the last men standing of the Meath Volunteers.

Jolly looks around and sucks his teeth. 'Wot a place to celebrate your burfday,' he sighs. 'Dunno why yer here, anyroad. Shouldn't you be off home in t' Em'rald Isle, burning down post offices and blowing up peelers like good Irish rebels?'

It's said with no rancour, and despite how unintentionally cutting his words are, I just smile. Jolly is a Marxist and doesn't believe any of us should be here. He skates the thin ice of insubordination every minute he's alive. If we weren't blessed with such a decent sarge, most any day would see us marching Jolly out before dawn to meet his maker.

Shamie feels the sting of Jolly's remark as deeply as I do, but we smile and roll our eyes tolerantly at each other. If you're Irish, you must be a rebel – even if you're side-by-side with a bunch of Tommies in a trench full of mud, fighting the Kaiser in the name of the English King.

My expression amuses Shamie and he grins. His mud-mask cracks into crazy lines and dust puffs up from his cheeks. This makes me laugh and I feel my skin stretch and pull under its own coating of mud. Shamie's grin widens. His eyes sparkle over the rim of his cup, and his monkey-faced delight breaks his mask into a million flaking pieces.

I sit forward, a cold feeling growing in my chest. What's wrong with Shamie's face? He looks so old.

Jolly says, 'Give us a song, Wee Paddy.'

Shamie nods, boyish shyness incongruous on his suddenly ancient face.

It's a trick of the mud, I think. It must be.

'None of your black Mick rebel songs, now,' Jolly tells him. 'Sing summat nice.'

I feel the world tilt as Shamie cocks his head back and begins to sing. He's launched into his favourite hymn, the 'Panis Angelicus'. Coming from an old man's throat, his voice is bell-clear; a swallow in May, it soars over the squalor of the trench. Soldiers, like clay statues of men all up and down the section, have paused in eating their dinners and are looking at him with wistful expressions. But the ground is heaving beneath me and the air around Shamie is filled with dancing grey spots, like ash. My tin cup slips from my fingers. It clatters to the duckboards; the precious tea splashes onto my gaiters and over my boots.

Jolly looks over as I slide from my perch and land on my knees in the clay. There's something dribbling from my nose. I can feel it, cold, running in thin rivulets from each nostril. I raise my hand to brush it away, embarrassed. But it is only water. Shamie's voice is lifting easily into the highest registers of the song, and Jolly is leaning across as if to reach for me. I open my mouth to tell him that I'm fine, but choke on the sudden gush of seawater that comes pouring from my throat and nose.

I fall forward.

There's confusion and voices for a moment, and the upside-down churning feel of being caught underwater. When I come out of it suddenly – returning to the bright sunshine and the sound of flies – I'm on my back in the clay, with the dark shapes of my companions cutting the blue sky above me.

Big-hands Charlie, shirtless from crumb-up, is anxiously shaking Jolly by the arm and insisting, 'It's the gas! It's the gas! I seen it drowned men like that before!' But Jolly is on his haunches looking at my face, and he knows it's not the gas. I roll onto my side, coughing up another mess *of salty water, and gulp in a lungful of the sun-bloated air. Shamie – all blue eyes and terror, heartbreakingly young – is gazing at me over Jolly's shoulder.*

The first time I try and say it, it's lost in a gurgle of water in my throat. I sit up, struggling to speak. Though I have no idea what it means, I need to tell Shamie this. It's very important that he knows. Finally I can breathe and I yell up into his frightened face.

'Francis found a place to hide, Shamie. He's found a place to hide!'

I woke up calling for Dom and found his side of the bed empty and cold. Dee was crying in the room across the hall. No, she wasn't just crying – she was bawling, screaming, as if she'd been stung by a wasp. I lurched to the side of the bed and scrambled for the centre of the room, looking around for my brother. Not here. Dom wasn't here.

He's in the bathroom, you dope. He's taking a piss.

Yes, yes. Plausible. But no. I knew he wasn't. He wasn't in the bathroom. I backed to the window, my eyes on the empty bunk and I knew that wherever he was, Dom wasn't in this house. Dee's screams reached a desperate pitch across the hall. I heard Dad murmuring to her, the floorboards creaking as he walked up and down.

Dad. I flung myself out the door and into my parents' bedroom. Dad swung around in surprise. Dee was in his arms, bawling hysterically. He was rubbing her back and, though she was obviously not quite awake, she had bunches of his T-shirt clutched in her little fists, clinging to him in terror. Dad's eyes were clouded with fatigue. In the adjoining room I could see Ma, a lumpy shape lying in their bed. She raised her head to look at me and then let it fall back in exhaustion and dropped her face into the crook of her arm.

'It's alright, Dom,' said Dad. 'Deirdre's just having a bad dream.'

That stung me, even then. '*Dad!* It's *me*! Patrick!'

He looked at me blankly and shook his head a little. 'Uh. Sorry. Sorry, bud. Look. Everything's alright, okay? We're looking after her. Go on back to bed now.' He returned to wearily trudging the floor. I watched him a moment, ridiculously angry at him, then closed the door. Fine. I'd find Dom myself.

I ran to the bedroom, meaning to get my jumper and runners, and paused at the window, looking down into the garden. I wasn't at all surprised to see Dom down there, strolling along in his pyjamas, but the sight of his companion made my knees unhinge.

The little white goblin-boy was prancing along beside my brother, his delighted grin a black half-moon in his chalky face. He was chatting away, obviously in the middle of a very animated and amusing conversation. Dom was smiling his lopsided smile and sauntering along, idly swinging a stick at the untidy bushes against the wall. He seemed perfectly comfortable in the company of this naked little creature. The boy said something and Dom laughed, glancing at it with the same affectionate amusement he usually reserved for me.

I threw myself at the window, fumbled the latch and shoved up the sash. Dom's voice floated up to me on the cold air. 'Really?' he said. His stick swung, *thwack thwack*, against the bushes.

'Oh, yes,' said the creature. 'Look. Put your arms out like this. Then put your head back …'

I stuck my head over the windowsill. The little creature flung his arms wide and put his head back. If he'd have looked a little to his left, he'd have seen me peering down from the bedroom window, but he only had eyes for my brother. And he was looking at Dom with a kind of tragic joy – a kind of heartbroken devotion that would have been moving had it not been on the face of such an awful creature.

'Now close your eyes,' he said. He watched my brother do as he was bid. 'Do you feel it? Do you feel the moonlight?'

The tolerant smile that had been quirking my brother's mouth got a bit more crooked, and he shook his head. 'Nope! I just feel cold.'

The little creature's face dropped. He frowned at my brother for a moment, disappointed. Then he grabbed his hand. 'Do you feel it now?'

Dom's crooked smile fell away and, though he still stood with his head back and his arms out-stretched, his whole posture sagged. A low, amazed sound escaped him. The goblin-boy smiled up at him and nodded. 'You do, don't you?'

Dom's eyes opened slowly and he looked up at the stars in wonder.

'Wow,' he said, a long, drawn-out syllable of awe. 'Wow.'

'*Dom!*' I cried. 'Let *go!*'

Dom flinched and gaped up at me, his face a naked mask of confusion. The little creature tightened his grip on my brother's hand and screeched in fear. Dom didn't seem to hear it; he continued to stare up at me with utter disbelief. 'Wh… Pat? What the hell? How did you get back up there?'

I leant far out the window. If it had been possible, I would have flown out of the window – dived out and landed on that little creature and torn my brother from its grip.

'Dom,' I cried. 'Let go of its hand! Let go!'

The words seemed to sink in, and Dom turned his puzzled face to the little creature who was tugging and hauling at him in an attempt to get him out of my sight. I saw Dom's eyes open briefly in horror, and then the goblin-boy's own eyes welled up with tears. They ran as black as tar down its white face and my brother's expression softened and I saw him bend forward to hear the words the little creature was frantically gabbling.

'He'll hurt us, Lorry! He'll take you away! You've got to come with me; you've got to be safe. You've got to be safe!'

Dom began to turn back to me, but as he was turning away the little creature snatched at him, opened its mouth, threw back its head and screamed.

'*Loooorryyy!*'

I clutched at my ears – the scream was awful, a horrible desolate cry. At its sound, Dom swayed, his knees buckled, his eyes rolled back to just the whites. He seemed to pass out on his feet and, as I watched, helplessly leaning out over the ledge, the white goblin-child led my unresisting brother up the path and further into the tangled garden. Out of my sight.

8. Take Me Away

Take Me Away

I took the stairs two at a time, my bare feet pounding the battered wood. I made no attempt to muffle my thunderous descent, but Dee was screeching at the top of her voice and I knew that Dad wouldn't hear me. I wanted him to hear me. I wanted him to follow me, and help me. But I knew he wouldn't. I was alone when I burst into the gloomy kitchen, and alone still when I slammed my way out into the back garden.

I stalled there a moment. The shadow-swallowed gate to the beach road was on my left, the tangle of overgrown garden to my right. The apple trees raised white arms over my head, and I listened.

Dom was here somewhere. He was here, and he was with that horrible little creature. Their footprints, clear and sharp on the damp sand of the garden path, led away into the furtive shadows of the undergrowth. I just stood there, my heart hammering, and was too afraid to follow them. I glanced up at Dad's window. Dee's squalling continued upstairs and now she was repeating the one phrase over and over.

'The man, Daddy! The *man*! The *man*!'

I shouted up at the window: 'Dad! *DAD*!' But there was no response.

A scraping sound to my left sent me crouching, my bowels loosening with fear. For a moment, my eyes created a phantom: a soldier in a long coat with gleaming buttons. He was young, maybe twenty, and handsome in a clean-cut kind of way. His eyes were shadowed under the peak of his military hat, his mouth a hard line in the moonlight. He glared at me from the darkness, so very real that I raised my hands to ward him off.

Then the moon shifted through the tree branches and the man broke up into harmless shapes and wedges of light. I was left staring at the innocent garden wall. A stealthy rustling in the bushes to my right drew my attention, and I saw a flutter of white disappear under the dark overhang of a tree. The creature was leading Dom away from me, taking him deeper into the confused maze of bushes.

I glanced once more at Dad's window, swallowed my beating heart back into my throat and followed Dom's footprints down the cold sand of the shadowed path.

'Dom?' I shoved aside heavy pine branches and clutching snags of bramble, shivering at the frigid drops that showered down my neck and at the horrible slimy dankness of the sand beneath my bare feet. It was awful in here, overgrown and confining. It felt as if the sun never shone and only cold things and damp things lived here.

I pushed through a particularly dense patch, the shadows released me, and I was out in the open again. I was on the very edge of the long lawn that led down to the old biddies' bungalow. Their home was a dark shape at the far end of the lawn. All around me were pools of darkness cut from the moonlight by walls and shrubs and the heavy overhang of trees.

The old outhouse sat to my right, ringed with beds of gnarly lavender, its beach-pebble walls gleaming under the moon. Dom was slumped against it, his posture a rag-doll parody of his usual grinning slouch.

He was watching me without recognition, his face pale and slack with fear, his breath a rapid pant. His legs were splayed, his arms hanging limply at his sides. His chin rested on his chest. Only his eyes were moving, and they followed me with all the terrified panic of a cornered deer.

That thing was with him, its expression twisted up in terror, hissing at me in warning. It had positioned itself between me and Dom, its white hand pressed to Dom's chest, propping him against the wall. I felt my fear give way to rage at the protective way it seemed to shield my brother from me.

I stepped forward, my hands bunching into fists. I think I may actually have growled. It was that fecking hand, that hand against my brother's chest, holding him up. And Dom's eyes, how frightened they were and how they were looking at me as though *I* were the monster here. I wanted to grab that horrible little boy-thing and pull him apart. I wanted to *shred* him and scatter the pieces. I wanted to make sure he never stood between us like that again — never made my brother look at me like that again.

'Get away from him,' I said. 'Take your hand *off* him.'

I didn't even recognise my own voice; it was so deep and low. Dom made a soft moan of fear, and the little creature opened its mouth in a childish mewl of panic. They clutched each other like frightened toddlers.

This really made me see red.

'For *God's sake!*' I bellowed. '*Get away from him!*' I began stalking towards them, my hands up. I honestly think that, had I ever reached them, I would have strangled one or the other of them, it didn't matter which, whoever I got my hands on first. I was so thoroughly blinded with rage.

The creature flung itself against Dom and spread its arms as though to hide him from me. Up 'til now, it had only been holding Dom's hand or pressing its palm to Dom's chest, but now it leant its full body against him, pressing him against the wall. The creature was tiny, barely coming to Dom's chest, but at the contact Dom moaned in distress and his legs sagged under him. He slipped down the wall a little. His eyes lost their focus, his mouth dropping open in shock. I could see his hands fluttering against the wall as if he was having a fit. And I swear, *I swear*, I heard a hissing noise where the creature's naked flesh came into contact with the warmth of my brother's body.

I was about to fling myself on them when a torrential sound surged behind me and made me turn in my tracks. The soldier was coming through the bushes – a flickering mirage of shadows and light; a mosaic of fragmented light that somehow made up a man. It was as though a spotlight was being passed over the leaves and branches of the heavy undergrowth, only everywhere it hit, it created the illusion of a tall man striding purposefully forward, stalking through the foliage to get to us. His long coat swept out behind him, the buttons gleaming. His face was a grim mask of determination, his eyes pinpoints of furious illumination beneath his army cap. I had no doubt in my mind: *this* was the bad man.

The goblin-boy screeched in fear, and I stood frozen, a witless paralytic, as the soldier left the trees and crossed the lawn in distance-eating strides. He passed me, without looking at me, and though I could have reached out a hand and grabbed him, had I the will, I still can't say that I ever actually saw him. I still can't say he was ever anything more than a scintillating trick of the light.

The soldier closed the distance between himself and the terrified creature in seconds. But as he got within reach, the little goblin-child – its cheeks wet and shining with black tears, its face contorted with terror – turned and leapt into my brother.

Both the soldier and myself screamed, though his scream was nothing more than an echo in my skull, and I ran forward, my hands up. The soldier flung his arms over his head in an expansive gesture of horror and I ran straight through him as he exploded into fragments, like leaves of light.

I skidded to a halt beside Dom and slammed to my knees, shouting his name. He was crouched against the wall, his hand to his heaving chest, his eyes wild. He didn't seem to notice me, just kept heaving in air and pulling the front of his top as if the fabric were strangling him.

I paused, my hands hovering without touching him. Where had that child gone? Had he just disappeared? Exploding into light like the man? Had he in some way leapt through Dom and into the stones behind him? Had he ... had he *entered* my brother somehow? My brother who now crouched against the wall, his eyes rolling, his breath whistling in and out of his throat like someone breathing through a straw?

Was the child *inside* him?

Suddenly Dom grabbed at his throat, a whole new panic rippling across his face. He began to gag, and I grabbed him. This wasn't asthma; this was *choking*. Dom was choking! I pulled him roughly towards me. My first thought was that he had somehow swallowed his tongue.

At the feel of my hands on him, Dom screeched and punched me. It was a cracking left hook to my jaw, and I was on the ground with my face in the dirt before I registered the blow. I rolled onto my back, clutching my face, tears of pain flooding my eyes. Dom leapt to his feet. And then he kicked me. He kicked me so hard that I actually felt my ribs creak under the impact. I've never forgotten that – the feel of my ribs bowing at the impact of my brother's kick. Thank God he was barefoot, because I have no doubt he would have done serious damage if he'd been wearing those army boots he loved.

I was so stunned, so totally out of my depth, that I didn't even try to fight back. I just curled onto my side, wrapped my arms around my head, and took it. He must have kicked me at least another three times, and punched me too, hitting the back of my head and my shoulders. All the time I was pleading with him, 'Dom! *Dom!* Stop! Dom, please! *Please!*'

I could hear him muttering to himself, a little more emphasis on whichever word happened to coincide with each blow. 'How do you like *that,* eh? How does *that* feel? Come on! See if you can take him! See if you can take him *now!*'

Finally I unwrapped my head from my arms and risked looking up. I held out my hands. 'Dom,' I croaked. 'For God's sake, it's me!'

He released a little 'gah!' of surprise, his fist already cocked back for another punch. His whole face fell, and he froze that way for a moment, his left arm poised over his head, his hair falling down into his eyes, his right fist knotted in the fabric of my top.

Then he was scrambling away from me, his eyes locked on mine even as he was shaking his head in denial. He scooted away on his arse 'til his back was against the wall of the outhouse. 'Pat,' he said.

'Oh Pat. Oh Patrick. Oh Pat.' Over and over again, 'til he silenced himself by shoving his fingers in his mouth and biting down hard on his own flesh.

I knelt on the grass with my hand to my jaw, my other arm wrapped around my ribs.

'You hit me! You *beat me up!*'

He just kept looking at me, his fingers crammed into his mouth.

'That's it,' I said. 'I've had enough. I'm getting Dad.'

I was halfway across the lawn when he tackled me from behind. He brought me to the ground with a *whomph* and pressed his whole weight down on me. 'Don't,' he whispered as he pressed his arm down on the back of my neck, pushing my face into the grass. 'Please don't.'

Oh, I don't think so, I thought, *not again*. There was no way Dom was going to work me over again. I wouldn't be lying down this time. 'Get *off!*' I elbowed him in the head, not pulling my punch by any means, and he fell back immediately.

I'd always been stronger than Dom, slightly taller, slightly broader, definitely faster. He may have been able to talk rings around me, but I'd always had the physical advantage. For once, I was willing to use that against him. I rolled, carrying him with me, and pinned him on his back, my arm across his throat. I pushed down on his Adam's apple with my forearm. 'What the *hell* are you *doing*, Dom?'

'Don't get Dad. Don't tell Dad. Please.' He seemed to fill with fresh panic at the thought, and he began to struggle again, trying to heave me off him. I pressed down harder on his neck and he clutched at my arm, trying to push me away.

We grappled with each other for a moment, our teeth bared, our hands slipping and re-positioning. Dom kept trying to kick his legs out from under me, and I kept recapturing them under my own. Finally, he just submitted, all the fight leaving him, and he lay there panting, my weight holding him down, my arm pressed across his throat. He closed his eyes and put his free hand up over his face.

I waited a good minute, increasing the pressure just a bit, to make sure he knew I still meant business. Then I slowly released him and sat back on my haunches. I began to rise, my intention to go back to the house and get Dad, but Dom grabbed my wrist. I tried to pull my arm free, but he clung on, his words coming like a torrent as he tried to prevent me from leaving.

'Dad's going to Dublin tomorrow night. He won't be back 'til Friday. What good's it going to do telling him this?'

I snatched my arm away. 'Are you *serious*? I'm not staying in that house! I'm not even going back in there! We've got to leave!'

'What are we going to *tell them*? What could we say that doesn't …' Dom swallowed. He looked absolutely miserable, and I sat slowly down onto the wet grass, knowing what he meant without him having to say it. Dom's big fear. Dom's terror.

What if we go mad, Pat? What if we go mad like Nan? Can that happen?
'Dom,' I said gently. 'They won't …'

'They'll think I've gone like Nan. They'll think I'm mad.'

Oh Jesus. I didn't know whether to hit him or hug him he was so scared.

'You beat me up, Dom! What am I supposed to do?'

He couldn't hold my gaze, and he dropped his head, closing his eyes tightly. 'I'm sorry. I don't know why I did it. It's hard to even remember that I *did* do it. I was so scared Pat. I was sure … I was sure you were the bad man, and I was so frightened that you would take me away!' He looked at me again, his eyes liquid and terrified. 'I *am* going like Nan, aren't I? I'm going to be like Nan. It's happening to *me.*'

'I'm pretty sure you're not losing your mind,' I said.

'Then what's wrong with me, Pat? *What's wrong with me?*' He was frantic now, thoroughly convinced that everything had come down to this one thing: that he was losing his mind, that he was going insane.

'You're being haunted.'

There. I'd said it. The words stopped us both cold, and we crouched there on the wet grass, staring into each other's faces with equally shocked expressions.

Then Dom laughed. So did I. It was that or do something far more hysterical.

'Oh,' gasped Dom. 'What a relief! And there I thought it was something serious.'

The night seemed to close around his words, and our laughter died. We looked around us, suddenly too aware of the watchful shadows, of the dark path back to the house, the cold sand where the sun never shone. I put my arm around my brother and pulled him up by the shoulders.

Dee would be asleep by now; I just knew that. Ma and Dad, would be asleep. Me and Dom were the only living souls awake – the only living souls. We both shivered, and I tightened my grip on Dom.

'Let's go inside,' I whispered.

9. Cheryl

The next morning I woke alone. I lay motionless, listening to Dom's quiet breathing in the bunk above me. At some stage during the night he must have crawled back up the ladder and gone to sleep in his own bed.

It was very early, the sky a Virgin Mary blue against the windows, the birds chattering the tail end of the dawn chorus. Perfect day. I rolled stiffly to the edge of the bed and got up. Every bruising moment of the night before was an ache that had me slow and wincing, careful as an auld fella.

Dom was fast asleep, his face pressed to the sidebar of the bunk, his hair a mess of tangled curls hanging over his eyes. The shark-tooth necklace was snagged up on his pillow, the heavy fang shining dully. If Dad saw it he'd give out yards – Dom wasn't meant to sleep with it on. I tucked it under his loosely curled fist. His knuckles were raw, and I covered his hand with the blanket so that I wouldn't have to see them. I didn't wake him. He looked so untroubled and the room seemed so innocent, washed in morning light and buoyed by birdsong. I left him alone and slowly made my way downstairs, trying to figure out how to deal with things that just didn't seem real anymore.

It was a surprise to find Ma already in the kitchen. She was rattling about at the sink ,and I could tell by her posture that she wasn't in good form. She sensed me by the door and rounded on me immediately.

'What in God's name did you two think you were up to last night? Your dad's had to go down the shops at all hours of the morning! Didn't even get a cup of tea or a slice of toast! And you *know* Conner's bringing Nan back today … What's wrong with youse?'

I felt a moment's confusion. Then my eyes fell on the empty bread bag and the two empty milk bottles sitting in a scatter of crumbs on the kitchen table. I groaned and clutched my head at the memory of Dom and me staggering in from the garden in the dead of night, the two of us launching a famished and barely conscious assault on the bread and butter. I remembered us glugging down a whole bottle of freezing-cold milk each, and my sinuses ached at the recollection.

'You need a new block of cheese as well,' I said, not meaning to sound smart-arsed but realising, too late, that I did.

Ma glared at me, furious, and I half expected her to stride across the kitchen and hit me with the wooden spoon she had in her hand. Then her eyes widened and her attention zeroed in on my jaw.

'*What happened your face?*' She was over in a flash, grabbing my jaw and turning my head to the light, all frowns and sharp concern.

'I fell off the bed last night,' I lied, smooth as butter. 'It woke Dom up.'

'And then you thought you'd help yourselves to the groceries?' Still clutching my jaw, she squinted up at me. When had I got taller than her?

I didn't even hesitate. 'We woke up starving,' I said, looking her in the eye. 'Couldn't get back asleep without something to eat.'

'You aren't the bleedin' famous five, Sonny Jim! There's no midnight feasts in this house!'

'Sorry, Ma.'

'We're not made of money.'

'Sorry, Ma.'

'Is it sore?' She was looking at my jaw again, really examining it.

'Yeah.'

She sighed through her nose and then let me go, dismissing me from the kitchen. 'Go,' she said. 'Get washed and dressed. You know that lot are always early when they're bringing Cheryl home.'

I headed back to the stairs, hardly believing my lucky escape. She was letting me get away with it! I paused at the door. 'Ma? Will I wake Dom?'

She glanced over at me, the sharp wintry light falling on her face. She looked tired this morning and unusually old. It had been a tough night for all of us. 'How was he last night?'

In other words: *Any asthma?* I thought of that desperate choking noise coming from my brother's throat, and looked her in the eye again. 'He's alright,' I lied, and then, little closer to the truth: 'I think he might be coming down with a cold. He could probably use a lie-in.'

She nodded, obviously worried. 'Yeah,' she said. 'Yeah, let him have a little sleep.' She pointed the wooden spoon at me. 'But you, mister! Up and get a wash. You smell like baked monkey.'

That made me laugh and I trotted upstairs to have a wash and to check on Dom, who was still sleeping like a baby.

☠ ☠ ☠

Ma was right about Dad's brother arriving early. I was hardly back downstairs and tucking into my cornflakes when we heard the heavy rumble of a big car pulling up the beach road. Ma froze, her face a mask of pure disbelief.

She claimed that they did it on purpose, hoping to catch her in curlers and a nightdress, stubbing her fags out on the dirty dishes. That way they'd finally be able to tut at their baby brother and pity him for the slag he'd married. I'm not sure they were *that* malicious, but they definitely considered Ma to be beneath them. And they definitely treated Dad as if he were retarded and couldn't wipe his own arse without their written instructions.

Whatever the reasons, this was probably the least considerate of their unscheduled drop-offs. It was barely half-eight on a Saturday morning, for God's sake!

Ma threw her dishtowel into the sink. She held her hands up on either side of her face, her fists clenched and released a grit-toothed *urrrgh!* of frustration. Then she slammed her palms down on the counter and gripped the edge tightly.

In the nine months since Nan's freefall into senility, Dad's three half-sisters and four half-brothers had minded her for the sum total of three weeks between the lot of them. And never, ever, for more than two days at a time. This last week had been the longest Ma had gone without having to take care of her mother-in-law, and it had taken our home burning to the ground for Dad's family to offer even that paltry assistance.

I watched my ma hunch over her hands. She was breathing deeply, trying to quell her sudden rush of anger. She was gathering it into herself, shoving it down somewhere unseen. I imagined it simmering away inside her, never quite extinguished, never quite exposed, and

I had one of those bright, rare moments of awareness when you see someone familiar in a new and startling light.

As the big engine sound pulled up outside the garden wall and died, I thought of Dad's family. I thought of their big cars and their stay-at-home wives and the money they all rolled in. I thought of our little house, and how Ma and Dad had moved Dee back into their room so that Nan could have Dee's room to herself. I thought how Ma and Dad didn't go to the pictures on a Friday night anymore; how Ma had given up her night class, how she brought Nan to the bathroom three or four times a day, how she bathed her, how she hadn't hesitated to take her in. I thought about how she sometimes answered the same question over and over and over again, all day long. (*What's for tea, Olive? What's for tea? What's for tea, love? What did you say was for tea?*) I thought about how gentle Ma was with Nan; and how shocking her statement in the kitchen had been (*I think I hate her, Dave.*) Because Ma had never, ever – not *once* – spoken impatiently or in haste to Cheryl in all the time she'd been in our care.

I had accepted all this. I had taken it all for granted. Because I had assumed that this was what women did; that it came naturally. Now, sitting at the breakfast table, looking at my mother and realising how much she had given up, I felt sick suddenly at how under my radar she was most days.

I searched for something to do or say.

'Will I make a pot of tea, Ma?'

'No!' she snapped. She paused a moment and then added a little more gently, 'Thanks, love.'

The latch rattled, and Ma glared through the window as the gate opened.

Oh. It wasn't Conner. It was Martin. I felt myself relax a little bit. Of all Dad's siblings Martin was the one least likely to breeze in and act the overlord. He was only eight years older than Dad; he had been only three when his father married Cheryl. The rest of Dad's family were the same generation as most of my friends' grandparents. They'd never had much time for my dad. Most of them had already moved out and started families of their own by the time he arrived on the scene. I think they considered him a bit of an embarrassment: the squalling brat their father had conceived late in life with a woman most of them considered to be a housekeeper at best, a gold-digger at worst.

Of all of his brothers and sisters, only Uncle Martin had shared any kind of childhood with Dad, and, I must admit, I sorta liked him. He was kind to Nan, when he was around, and though he still spoke in that high-falutin' manner, he was capable of holding an actual conversation rather than giving a continual series of lectures. He was an interesting man, actually, and a genuinely nice guy. He came through the gate carrying Nan's suitcase, and I saw Ma's shoulders soften slightly at the sight of him.

'Your dad's upstairs lying down with Dee,' she said. 'Go and tell him that Nan is here.'

On the way up the stairs, I heard Ma open the door and her curt greeting of, 'Martin.'

Then Uncle Martin's cultured voice, straining against the weight of the suitcase: 'How are you, Olive? She's asleep in the car.' The rest of their conversation was reduced to murmurs as I rounded the turn in the stairs and went up to the landing.

Dad was awake, Dee asleep beside him in the bed, her head in the crook of his arm. He looked up from the pillow and gave me a weary smile as I peeped around the door. 'They're here,' I whispered. He sighed and nodded, and I left him to it, closing the door as quietly as I could so as not to disturb Dee.

I entered our room just as quietly, expecting Dom to be asleep in the top bunk. It brought me up short to see him standing by the wardrobe. The heavy wardrobe door was open, revealing the long mirror within, and Dom was gazing at his reflection with a strange kind of concentration. Frowning, he traced the contours of his face in the glass as if working out a puzzle in his head.

I thought of that child leaping into my brother and my momentary fear that it had possessed him. With a dry feeling in my throat, I closed the bedroom door and stood with my back against it. Dom didn't notice me at all, raptly engrossed as he was in examining his own reflection.

As I watched him, he closed his eyes, took a long deep breath and held it. He stood there a moment, one hand resting on his expanded chest, the other on the mirror. Then he released his held breath and his whole face lit up with delighted surprise. He opened his eyes, breathed in, released it again, and gave himself one of his sunny grins.

'Well,' he said to himself. 'How about that?'

'Dom?' I asked.

Slowly, as if his thoughts were miles away, Dom turned his head. He gazed at me blankly, and then his eyes widened with sudden comprehension.

'Oh!' he said. He looked at me, then back to his own reflection, then at me again. As if registering for the first time our identical faces. Then he smiled at me — the same broken-hearted adoring smile that

I'd seen on the face of the goblin-boy – and I felt myself press harder against the wood of the door.

'Lorry!' he said. 'Look how big we are!' He spread his arms as if to demonstrate our recent spurt of height and breadth. He lifted his hands and flexed the fingers, marvelling at their length. Then he clenched a fist in front of his face and grinned at it with savage glee. 'Look at us!' He shook his fist. His face was full of love, and fierce, protective triumph. 'Look how strong we are! No one can *ever* take you away now!'

My left hand crept across the surface of the door and closed around the reassuring globe of the handle. I could feel my pulse beating in my wrist. In my throat. In my temples. The urge to scream, to simply let go and scream, was so strong that I clamped my free hand over my mouth. My tears ran between my fingers and I tasted their salt on my lips.

Whatever reaction Dom had expected from me, this obviously was not it. He took a step towards me, his face filled with anxious concern.

'It's alright now,' he assured me. 'There's no need to be afraid anymore.'

'Dominick,' I whispered, my hand curled beside my mouth like a frightened old lady's. 'Please. Stop messing.'

At my use of his name he paused, his hand still held out as if to comfort me, his head tilted. Then his expression changed, his hand withdrew and he took a small step back. I saw fear begin to rise in his eyes as he took stock of me again. As he perhaps saw me properly for the first time – as he realised I was not who he thought I was.

His mouth formed a question that never came. My grip on the doorhandle tightened.

'Dom?' I said.

Then the handle turned beneath my hand and I was shoved forward slightly as the door was pushed from the outside. I stifled a little shriek of surprise. Dom's eyes snapped to the door. There was a moment's pause and then Dad's voice, muffled came through the wood: 'Boys? Can I come in?'

I met Dom's eyes and moved aside on numb legs as Dad shoved the door open against my weight. He peered around the doorjamb at us, obviously puzzled at my blocking the way.

'You alright?' he asked.

I nodded, my eyes not leaving Dom, who was staring at our dad as though he were some frightening stranger.

'Dom!' said Dad. 'You're up! Good. You feeling better?'

Dom nodded creakily. His eyes were bigger than ever, filling his face.

Dad looked him up and down. His mouth twitched. 'Alright. Get dressed, will you? And come on downstairs. Your uncle Martin's here with Nan.'

'Yes, sir,' whispered Dom.

Dad cocked an eyebrow at him. 'Sir?' he said dryly. 'Well. That's different.' He glanced at me. 'Don't dawdle, Pat, okay?'

He shook his head as he shut the door. I heard him say 'sir' to himself, and he chuckled as he made his way down the stairs.

I put my back against the door again and stared at my brother. Though my heart was still tripp-trapping like an over-wound clock, Dad's arrival had changed something. I now realised that I wasn't alone. One shout, one heavy bang on the floor and my dad would come running. I belonged here. That thought gave me a thin thread of courage.

Dom, on the other hand, seemed suddenly filled with vulnerable confusion. He backed away from me, shaking his head, and raised his hands as if to stop me from speaking. He seemed to want to say something, but couldn't find the words. As he retreated across the room, he managed only a string of broken sounds or syllables that went nowhere.

'I …' he said. 'Wha … who …?'

Finally, he backed himself against the wall at the end of the bunk and stopped there, his hands up, his eyes glittering. In the garden, the gate creaked and we heard Dad and Martin's voices as they went to get Nan from the car. From the room across the hall, Dee's sleepy voice began a tremulous calling: 'Mam? Mam? Maammyyy?'

Dom's fear became more and more apparent as these sounds crowded in. He pressed his fist against his lips in that way Dom had, his eyes darting around the room, as if trying to figure out where he was.

'Look,' I said. My pounding heart made even that one word shaky.

His eyes snapped desperately to me.

'Look,' I repeated. 'You need to get dressed. Can … can you remember where the bathroom is?'

He nodded. The unshed tears in his eyes shivered with the movement.

I held my hand out, signalling him to stay where he was. Had he made a move towards me, I think my heart would have burst, or I would have dropped down dead of a brain haemorrhage. Dee's insistent calls were becoming panicked. I heard Ma shifting something in the kitchen and I called down to her, my voice perfectly level and strong, 'I'll get her, Ma. You're alright!'

There was a moment's silence downstairs, and then: 'Thanks, love!'

'Dee?' I called, amazing myself again at how strong my voice was. 'I'll be in to you now. If you wait a minute, like a good girl, I'll give you a jockey down the stairs.'

After a small pause came a tearful little, 'Okay, Pap.'

'Good girl. Just hang on a mo. Okay, pudding?'

'Okay.'

I hadn't once broken eye contact with the … with Dom. My hand was still held up, to keep him in place. Now, I spoke again to him, and a weird calm came over me. I was surprised to find myself rather commanding under its influence. Dom seemed to be comforted by this, and he listened willingly to each of my instructions.

'You need to go have a wash. Can you do that?'

He nodded, his fist still pressed to his lips.

'Wash your teeth and comb your hair. Alright?'

He nodded again.

'I'm going to lay your clothes out, and then I have to go downstairs. You come on down when you're ready and just … just … *sit in a corner*. Alright? Don't … don't touch anyone … don't *talk* … just *sit*. Okay?'

He nodded and I sidled further into the room, keeping as much distance as possible between us. Without taking my eyes off him, I took Dom's clean clothes out of the drawers and put them on top of the dresser. I looked at him significantly so that he understood they were his. He just stood there, his eyes jumping from me to the door, to the clothes, to the mirror.

Then I edged back to the door, afraid to turn my back on him. I eased the door open and positioned myself so that it stood between us.

CITY OF LIMERICK PUBLIC LIBRARY

'You're not to come out 'til you've heard me take Dee down the stairs. Do you understand me?'

Another big-eyed nod.

I stood peering around the edge of the door at him: my brother, trembling and terrified, his back against the wall, his hand pressed to his mouth. He looked back at me as though I were his saviour and his damnation all in one. My heart was pounding again; I could feel its frantic rhythm in each breath I took. This was Dom standing here. I didn't want to leave him alone. I *shouldn't* leave him alone. At the same time, I wanted nothing more than to slam the door on him and lock it and run as far from him as possible.

'Listen to me,' I said. 'You are *Dom*. Understand? You're Dom.'

He didn't answer me, but before I shut the door he shook his head – a firm and vehement denial that made the tears fly from his eyes.

No. he was saying. *I'm not. I'm not Dom.*

10. Cheryl and Francis

My calmness deserted me as soon as I closed the door, and I began shaking so hard that I could barely stand up. It was the thought of turning my back on him that frightened me the most. What if he decided to go for me? What if his confusion and fear turned to rage, like it had in the night? What if he waited 'til I was on the stairs, with Dee in my arms, and then came after me with his fists flying? What if I turned around and found him standing beside me, the goblin-boy's hungry look on his face?

There was a dull clunk from our room. It wasn't much of a sound – perhaps he'd bumped into something, but it shot a flare of panic through me that almost made me piss myself. I bolted from the door, stumbled over my tangled feet and slammed into Ma and Dad's room. Dee was sitting in the middle of their bed and she jumped in fright at my wild-eyed entrance.

I grabbed her and spun to go, but she immediately began to squall.

'You said me a jockey, Pap! You said me a jockey!'

Jesus! I dropped to one knee, my eyes on the shut door across the hall. She scrambled from my arms and over my shoulder and clung to my back like a little pink monkey.

'Giddyup, Pap!'

I staggered to my feet and warily carried her into the hall. She was kicking her chubby little legs, knocking her heels into my ribs and bouncing up and down in an attempt to get me to make horsey movements. But my eyes were on my bedroom door and I sidled down the hall, keeping my body between her and it.

'Giddyup! Giddyup! GiddyUP!'

We were at the head of the stairs now, me half twisted to keep my eye on the door, she bopping up and down like a lunatic on my back.

'Stay easy, Dee. Stay easy for Pap.'

But she just kept bopping up and down and telling me to giddyup, so that I had to turn and make my way properly on the stairs for fear of her pulling us both over.

At the turn in the staircase, I felt the hairs on the back of my neck rise up in a stiff ruff, and I felt sure that when I looked around he'd be there: his face white, his eyes black, his hands reaching. But he wasn't, and I managed to get Dee into the kitchen, without somehow dying of fear or breaking both our necks.

She slithered from my back just as Martin and Dad were shepherding Nan in from the garden. The kettle on the hob began its high-pitched whistle, and Ma started fussing over tea. No one noticed my rubber-legged stagger around the kitchen table and my shaky collapse into a chair facing the stairs.

Ma pucked me on the back of the head as she crossed behind me with the tea things. 'Say hello to your uncle Martin.'

I pulled my eyes from the stairs and gave what felt like a very pale-lipped greeting to the men. They were helping Nan off with her coat;

neither of them looked my way. Nan just nodded and smiled in that vague way she had when she hadn't a clue what was going on. Dad swung Dee up into his arms.

I went back to staring at the stairs.

Ma pucked me again on her way back to make the tea.

'Where's your brother?' she asked, and the horrible joke of that question had me snorting a hysterical little laugh out my nose. *I don't know, Ma. I think I might have lost him.*

'He's having a wash, Ma.'

She put the teapot on the table, giving me the fish-eye. 'What's up with you?'

Whatever way I looked up at her, Ma stopped dead. 'What's wrong, Pat?'

I wanted to tell her – I really did. I felt like it was written all over my face anyway. I felt like I was sitting in front of her, the very picture of someone screaming *help me help me help me,* at the top of my lungs. But obviously Ma couldn't read me, or I wasn't as transparent as I thought, because she just kept standing there, waiting, that questioning frown on her face, and I just kept looking at her, saying nothing.

I've never felt Dom's absence more keenly than I felt it at that moment. He should have been right there beside me, like always: explaining, involving, assuring. But there was a whistling void that should have been filled with his voice. He was silent. And so was I.

'I have a headache,' I muttered.

Ma put the back of her hand to my forehead. 'You feel hot,' she said. 'I wouldn't be surprised if you come down with pneumonia, leaping in and out of the sea like eejits. Put a spoon of sugar in your tea, it'll buoy you up.'

She moved off, and I recommenced my vigil of the stairs. A spoon of sugar in my tea. Of course. Problem solved.

I felt the family, as if far away and underwater, gradually gather around the breakfast table. They put Nan opposite me, and she sat nodding and smiling at everyone. Food was doled out, tea was poured. I kept my eyes on the stairs, moving my head if someone got into my line of vision, responding only to pass plates from left to right, hand over the milk, accept the breakfast that remained untouched on my plate.

Dom would come down and it would be a joke. He would come down and he would grin at me and he would mouth *gotcha* and I would kill him and it would all have been a joke.

'I hadn't realised you came here every year, David,' said Uncle Martin, on the moon somewhere, making polite conversation. 'It's an amusing coincidence, isn't it?'

'How do you mean?' asked Dad, his voice equally distant. 'Pass the butter, will you, Olive love?'

There was no sign of movement upstairs. No sound at all.

'Well, with Cheryl having grown up here, it's funny that Olive's family would choose Skerries for their holidays.'

I vaguely registered a charged pause in the conversation, but my attention was aimed upwards. I was looking at the painted boards of the ceiling. Listening.

'You didn't know?' asked Martin.

'That Mam grew up here? Don't be ridiculous, Martin. Sure, Mam was a Royalette. She was raised in Dublin.'

'No. Skerries. I'm sure of it. Cheryl only moved to Dublin in her late teens. I thought you knew that. It's no big secret, though she never did speak much of her life before she married Father.'

'Yeah. Well. I doubt she got much encouragement to.'

I barely had time to register the dryness in Dad's voice before I finally heard what I'd been waiting for. I looked up again. There: a subtle creak on the ceiling. And following on from that, a whole series of quiet movements: footsteps, a soft scraping, a door opening and closing.

My eyes snapped to the stairs.

'They had their own ways, those two,' said Martin.

'I suppose so,' huffed Dad. 'Mam always said she was born on the stage of the Theatre Royal. Dad seemed happy enough for her to leave it at that.'

Dom was standing at the top of the stairs now. I knew it. I could feel it. He was standing and listening, the bedroom doors all closed around him, the bathroom door shut at his back. My brother, standing in the little airless closet that was the upstairs landing, looking down the steps and wondering who lay at the foot of them, listening to the voices of his family and wondering who they were. *No, no. That's wrong. He's grinning. He's imagining me imagining him and he's grinning.*

Ma asked, 'Do you want a hot drop, Martin?'

There was a soft scuffing on the stairs and I was trying not to pant now, gripping the table.

'Thank you,' said Martin. 'I would.'

He was at the turn in the stairs now, coming down slowly. I saw his knee, then his leg as he came around the corner. Then Ma leant forward to pour Martin his tea and blocked my view. I stood up suddenly from my chair, leaping to my feet so as not to lose sight of him as he entered the kitchen.

My abrupt movement drew everyone's attention to me, so Dom and I had a moment to make eye contact when he hit the bottom step. He just stood there, one hand on the wall, looking shocky and uncertain.

My voice was dry as chalk when I said, 'Come here. Sit by me.'

Ma and Dad glanced at him and I saw identical frowns crease their foreheads.

'You look a bit ropey,' said Dad.

'Only to be expected,' said Martin. He smiled at Dom. 'You've all been through a rough time.'

'Have a cuppa, love,' said Ma, pouring Dom a cup and lacing it with the cure-all sugar.

'Come here,' I said again, 'and sit by me.'

He lurched across the room in jerky steps and dropped clumsily onto the chair beside me. We sat side by side like two broken robots, stiff and awkward, as the breakfast table slowly regained momentum around us. He laid his hands on either side of his plate. His shoulder was only inches from mine. and I could feel cold rippling off him. It was like sitting beside an open fridge. No one else seemed to notice anything. Were they blind?

Ma was cutting Dee's breakfast into little pieces, her mouth a firm line of concentration. Dad and Martin had gone back to unravelling Nan's past. Dad was fiddling with a piece of toast by his plate, crumbling it slowly and methodically with his free hand. Nan was off with the fairies, humming gently to herself and gazing at the tablecloth.

Only Dee seemed in any way perturbed by Dom. She was sitting on Dad's knee, filching toast and bits of bacon from his plate. When

Dom sat down she'd begun to smile, but had quickly stopped and stared at him as though he were a puzzle she couldn't quite work out. Slowly her puzzlement turned to concern, and as I watched, she leant closer in to Dad. Her little fist tightened in his shirt. A small frown grew between her sandy eyebrows.

'Daddy?' she said. 'Who dat?'

She was staring at Dom, and I wondered what it was she saw that the others couldn't. I looked at him from the corner of my eye. There were waves of cold rising from him that made the hairs on my left arm stand up. The left side of my body was skittering with goose flesh. Dom seemed afraid to raise his eyes and just kept staring, staring, staring at his plate of congealing food. His profile was familiar, the way a mask would be familiar: all the planes and hollows in the right place, but none of the spirit.

'Daddy, who dat?'

At the quiet repetition of her question, Dom seemed to realise what Dee was asking and he snapped his attention to her. She flinched under his startled gaze and tugged Dad's shirt in earnest.

'*Daddy!* Who dat boy?'

Dad stopped talking and looked down at Dee in exasperation. 'What *is* it, love?'

At the same time Ma reached over for her. 'Dee, come here and eat your own breakfast. Poor Daddy hasn't had a bite of his yet; it's all gone into your tummy!'

Dee was protesting and pointing. 'But who *dat* boy? Who dat *boy?*' But no one was really paying her any attention.

Dom was so tense that I swear his body was vibrating slightly. His hands had curled to fists on either side of his plate. His eyes were roaming the surface of the table as though there may be a code written there in butter smears and breadcrumbs that would give him some way out of here, an answer to the question of how to escape.

I pushed down a surge of nausea. What was I going to do? No one but Dee seemed to see anything wrong. I glanced at Mam, Dad, Martin – quick little flashes of glances. They were perfectly at ease. The cold was rolling off Dom like a fog. His little sister had just asked who he was. And yet they didn't seem to have a clue that there was anything wrong.

Then Nan spoke, her voice warm and clear and connected with life, just as it had been the day before that bloody stroke, before she had been pushed off the edge of the world into the grey nowhere she now inhabited.

'Francis, you look so cold, dear. Drink your tea. It'll heat your belly.'

We all stopped talking. Oh God. It sounded so like Nan – our proper nan. The woman who spent three weeks a year travelling with her cronies. The woman who lived for her garden, and read two books a week. The woman who would sing 'Second Hand Rose' and do the Charleston at the drop of any old hat. I hadn't realised how badly I'd missed her, until I heard her speak in that voice again.

She was smiling at Dom in *that* way: that kind, straightforward, trustworthy way. The way that let you know she'd never bullshit you and she'd never betray you. She gestured at his tea. 'Drink it up, Francis, it'll do you a power of good.'

Dom stared at her, confusion and hope vying for dominance in his face. He made a funny noise in the back of his throat and everyone looked at him in sympathy. They assumed he was upset because his nan thought he was someone else. But I knew different. I understood, suddenly and with a jolt, that Nan knew him — I mean she knew *him*, the him *inside Dom*. Nan *knew* him. But he didn't know her. I could see how he *longed* to know her, how he needed to know her, to have one little thing here that he could hang onto, that could anchor him.

But it did him no good. He searched and searched her face for some clue, and I could tell he found nothing. Nan gazed serenely back at him, her eyes filled with the same clarity of recognition she would have given me only nine months earlier.

'Who do you think he is?' I whispered.

Mam shushed me with a wince. 'Just play along with her, love,' she said to Dom. 'She thinks you're someone else.'

He turned and looked at her with Dom's brown eyes, his confusion, his sorrow almost physical. *But I* am *someone else*, that look said. He turned back to Nan, searching her face again, and in a bright flash of understanding I realised he was going to ask her who she was. He opened his mouth to speak, and I reached under the table and pinched him hard on the thigh. *Shut up.*

At the same time, Dad leant over and took Nan's hand in his. 'That's Dom, Mam,' he said gently. 'It's Dom.'

Nan smiled around at her son, a look of genuinely amused bewilderment on her face.

'David,' she said, 'what on earth are you talking about?'

Dad gasped; it was unbelievable to see her like this. It was as though the last terrible nine months had never happened and here she was Nan, back after a long trip, giving us the dry-eye and laughing along with us under her breath.

'Mam?' asked Dad, far too much hope in his voice.

Nan's clear-eyed amusement clouded over into confusion. Her face crumpled into the strained, polite smile that had been her permanent expression for so long. Dad's hope faded as his mother searched his face, trying to recall who he was, trying to catch the gist of a conversation already lost.

'I thought ...' she said. 'Wasn't ...?' She looked over at Dom and smiled uncertainly. 'Francis?' she asked. She paused, then just drifted off, her eyes slipping over the surface of things, sliding absently to the right of us; remembering or forgetting, who knew? But not with us anymore. Not like she had just been.

There was a soft knock on the door, and it broke what threatened to become a heartbreaking silence. Ma leapt gratefully to her feet and went to answer it.

It was one of the old biddies. She came in laughing and shaking her head, scattering bright raindrops from the lacquered white helmet of her hair. It was the tiny one, half a head shorter than Ma, and all decked out in sprigged cotton, wafting floral scent. She brought the glittering sunshine of a fresh spring day through the door and stood in its radiance, hands clasped, looking around the room with an expectant smile on her face.

'Well, now ...' she said.

Ma realised the old doll wanted an introduction and, with a tolerant little roll of her eyes, presented her to each of us in turn. 'Margaret, you know our son, Dominick.'

Dom surprised us all by standing and gravely extending his hand. It was a gesture so alien to my brother that Ma actually laughed. But this *wasn't* Dom, was it? It was the Dominick-*thing*. It was the goblin-boy. It was *Francis*, and he had, it would appear, impeccable manners. He offered his hand as a matter of course; as a token of politeness so ingrained in him that only unconsciousness would have prevented it. You could tell by how quickly he was out of his chair and had his hand extended, by how smoothly he said, 'Pleased to meet you, ma'am.'

The old biddy blushed like a girl and took his hand.

She'll feel how cold he is, I thought. *She'll scream.*

But the old lady just smiled. 'What lovely manners,' she said, already turning her eyes to me.

'This is our other boy,' said Ma. 'Patrick.'

I nodded, incapable of a smile, and the old lady tilted her head. I could hear her thinking to herself, *Ah, here's a sullen one.*

Dee played the shy cat and buried her head in Dad's shirt. Uncle Martin reached across the table and shook the old biddy's hand. 'How do you do?' he asked.

'Well, I'm fine, thank you,' she replied, turning her attention to Dad. 'David, how are you?'

Dad forced a smile onto his face and shrugged. 'I'm grand, Miss Conyngham. How's your sister?'

'Oh, same as ever. At war with the world.' She laughed at her own joke, then turned her speculative gaze on Nan. 'And who's this?' I knew by her voice that she could already tell Nan wasn't quite with us.

'This is my mother,' said Dad. He got up and crossed the room to hunker by Nan's chair. He spoke gently to her, snagging a thread of her attention somehow. 'Mam? This is Margaret Conyngham, from the back house.'

Nan blinked at him; her eyes wandered in fits and starts to where the old biddy stood with her hand extended, a patient smile on her face. The two women looked at each other for a moment. Then I saw a jolt of unexpected recognition hit the old biddy. Her smile fell. 'Oh my,' she said. She sank into a stiff crouch by Nan's knee, and took Nan's hand. She pressed it gently and gazed up into Nan's face.

'Hello, dear,' she said. 'How have you been?'

Nan just kept staring with wary concentration. Eventually the old biddy nodded, cleared her throat and looked down. She spent a silent moment gazing at Nan's hand which lay twined in her own. She seemed to be struck by this: the sight of two old ladies' hands, all naked joints, paper-thin skin and fine blue veins.

'How strange to suddenly notice one's hands,' she murmured. 'How fragile they look.'

She carefully placed Nan's hand back in her lap and straightened. Then she smoothed down her skirt and blinked, slowly looking around the kitchen at things only she could see.

'God bless us and save us,' she said quietly to herself. 'Isn't life a kick in the trousers?'

Dad went to ask something, but before he could speak the old biddy shook herself and laughed and filled with sunshine again. She turned a beaming smile on my mother, her teeth too perfect to be anything other than dentures. 'You have a phone call, dear! Best not keep them waiting. They're calling from Dublin!' Ma raised her eyebrows in pleased surprise and began to escort her to the door.

'Me come?' asked Dee, hopping down from her chair.

The old biddy held out her hand. Dee ran to take it, and they accompanied my mother up the garden path, disappearing together into the bright spring morning. The kitchen – filled with light now – was momentarily silent in the sparkling aftermath of the old lady.

Then Nan snorted in amused disgust. 'That wasn't May Conyngham,' she said.

'May Conyngham?' cried Dom. He ran to the door, staring up the garden path as if trying to get another look at the old biddy. 'May,' he whispered.

'Imagine, Fran!' Nan said to him. 'Imagine that old dear trying to pass as May.' She gave a sunny little laugh. 'Oh, what a hoot!'

Dad sighed in exhausted frustration. 'Come on, Mam, let's get you in by the fire.'

Martin rose to his feet, with the intention of helping get Nan settled.

Dom dithered by the door, tense and wide-eyed, his attention torn between Nan and the garden where the others had disappeared. He was looking more than a little crazy. I went to stand by him.

'Dom,' I murmured. 'Let's go upstairs.'

'Stop calling me that!' he hissed.

He watched as Dad and Martin manoeuvred Nan up and out of her chair. His eyes smouldered with rage as they took her by the arms, apparently infuriated by the sight of the two big men on either side of a fragile, confused old lady.

'Where … where are you taking me?' she asked as they hustled her into the sitting room.

Dom went to shoot after them and I grabbed his arm to stop him. It was like grabbing ice. His flesh was so cold that my fingers sizzled. I let go, crying out and clutching my hand. He came to me immediately, leaning close to comfort me. 'It's alright, Lorry,' he whispered. 'I won't leave you.'

His breath was like dry ice on my face; his fingers burned as they touched my arm. I pulled away from him. How cold *was* he? How cold could anyone *get* without …?

Dad called from the other room. 'Stop fluting around, you two, and clear the table.'

Dom turned to glare through the door at him. 'What will they do to her?' he said.

'Dom,' I whispered. 'Just go upstairs. Please? For me? Just go upstairs and wait while I clear the table.'

He shook his head, his eyes on the sitting-room door. 'I'm not leaving you with them. Not anymore.'

He was standing with his back half turned to me, his shoulders hunched, his fists raised slightly. My fingers were still tingling from where I'd grabbed him. My cheek burned from where that icy breath had come from his mouth – from Dom's mouth – and frozen my skin.

'Dom,' I said suddenly, 'eat your breakfast!'

I didn't know where that had come from; the words sounded ridiculous even as I said them. But Dom was so cold. He was cold as a corpse. And I wanted him warm. I wanted him alive. And people who are alive *eat*, right?

Dom turned to me in surprise. Then he laughed. It wasn't a Dom laugh, by any means, but it wasn't a scary-movie-creature laugh, either. It was a genuine laugh, a kind of a delighted laugh.

'Alright,' he said. 'All right, Lorry. I'll eat my breakfast.'

Jesus, that made me want to punch him. 'I am *not* Lorry,' I ground out. 'I'm *Patrick*, and you're *Dominick*. You're *Dominick Finnerty*. Got it?'

He gave me a very level look, and sat down. 'Eat your own breakfast,' he said, taking up his knife and fork.

It became a battle of wills to finish the congealed mess on our plates, and I was pretty sure we'd both be dead of heartburn by the end of the day. But I crammed it down so that he'd cram it down, maintaining eye contact all the time. When we were finished, he helped me clear the table and then stood behind me, emanating cold, while I washed the dishes. All his attention was focused on the sitting-room door. I could hear Dad and Martin in there, chatting; the TV was on.

'Why are you just standing there?' I hissed, my elbows deep in suddy water, goose flesh in scattered patches up and down my back. 'Why don't you just go upstairs?'

'I'm looking after you,' he whispered. 'I'm watching your back.' He glanced at me briefly, looking me up and down with his dark eyes. 'I'm keeping you safe, Lorry. Until you're back in your right mind again.'

Then he turned his attention back to the door, his shoulders hunched, his weight balanced evenly between his two feet, standing vigilant and ready should anyone try and to get past him to me.

11. You Can't Freeze a Tomato

As soon as I could get the dishes done and my hands dry, I shooed Dom up the stairs and out of everyone's sight. I felt like I was herding a ticking bomb round the house. I felt like any minute now, everything would blow up. I needed time. I needed space. I needed to think things through.

We were almost at the top when Dad's quiet voice called up to us: 'Lads.' He was peering at us from the turn in the stairs. 'Martin's leaving. Stay with your nan while I walk him to the car, will you?'

Damn.

'Dom's not feeling well, Dad. He was going to lie down.'

Dom's voice came flat and deliberate from the stairs above me. 'No, I wasn't,' he said. 'You're the one who needs to lie down.'

Dad looked from one to the other of us with a confused frown. 'What's up with you two? You're like the hormone sisters this morning.'

Normally that would have made me laugh, but I was stretched a little thin for chuckles today. Instead, I blinked down at the old man, trying to give nothing away, hoping he'd relent and let us escape upstairs. Exactly how creepy we looked, standing one above the other in the gloom, staring down at him with our identical faces, I can only guess. Pretty bloody creepy, I'd say.

Dad's eyes lifted to Dom, and my heart sped up a bit as something crossed his face – some fraction of understanding. 'Whu …?' he said uncertainly. His eyes widened, his pupils spread, and he stared past me to where Dom stood, cold and silent, on the stairs above us.

I took a step downwards. *Can you see it, Dad?* I thought. *Jesus, Dad! Try and see it!*

But he only frowned and shook himself, scrubbing his hands through his hair, and let his eyes slip away from us. 'Whew,' he said. 'Weirdness.'

My heart fell. *Oh Dad.*

He turned his back on us. 'Come on down to your nan,' he said. 'Just for a minute while I walk Martin to the car.'

'Dad!' I called, and he looked back. 'Are you leaving today?'

'Yeah. After dinner.'

'Stay 'til tomorrow, Dad. Please.'

If I'd said that in front of Ma, she'd have lost the rag with me, entirely; told me to get a grip and stop acting like a baby. Dad just grimaced in helpless sympathy and spread his hands. 'Can't, bud. Sorry. Justin needs me.'

We need you! Dom and me! We need you!

'Just 'til tomorrow, Dad? Just one more day?' *Just one more night?*

He locked eyes with me, and for a moment I thought he'd stay. Then he gave a shrug of those expressive shoulders and tilted his head in apology. 'Sorry, bud. I'll stay a bit late and watch *Dr Who* with you, if you like?'

I nodded. Dom, standing behind me like a black hole, said nothing.

Dad half laughed. 'Jesus!' he said 'What are you like? All you need is a river of dry ice and a full moon and we'll have the total *Hammer House* effect. Cheer up! You'd swear I was heading off to war or something.' He clapped his hands as if to cleanse the air. 'Come on down now! Sit with Nan for me.'

Then he was gone.

Dom stayed silent, and when I started back down the steps he made no move to follow me. 'Come on,' I said, without looking at him.

'Wouldn't you rather I went upstairs?'

The bitterness in his voice made me glance around, and I caught a diluted glimpse of what had creeped Dad out. Dom was almost lost in shadows, his face and his hands ghostly highlights, his eyes black-light pinpoints in the gloom. I wondered if I'd looked the same when I was standing there. Of course I had – we were twins, weren't we? I shuddered. Imagine staring up at two of *that*; it was amazing the old fella hadn't run a mile.

'Just keep your mouth shut and don't touch anyone,' I said and made my way to the sitting room without waiting to see if he'd follow.

He didn't, not right away, and I had time to do two prowling circuits of the cramped room, my hands in my hair, before I found enough composure to sit. Nan was sitting on the sofa, drowsing already. The TV was on, the sound turned down. The fire was low and hot in the grate.

I chose the threadbare armchair facing the door and sat waiting. My arse had hardly hit the cushions before I was fighting the urge to leap to my feet again. It felt like I was trapped in an airless room without windows or doors, and I wanted to *pace*. I grabbed the arms of my chair and dug in hard, forcing myself to sit still, because I could walk myself to the moon and back and still not escape this.

He came in quietly. Dom and not at all Dom. My brother's lazy, C-shouldered slouch, squared off somehow and tilted forward now, so that he led the way with shoulder rather than hip; Dom's under-the-eyes, affectionately mocking smirk replaced with dark-eyed speculation – like someone sizing you up from behind partially opened shutters.

His attention was almost immediately snagged by the TV. At first he just blinked at it, trying to figure it out. Then he was over and touching it – the flickering screen, the sides, the back – tentatively at first, then with genuine, almost scientific interest.

'Gracious,' he murmured. Bill and Ben were on, those crazy twins. Dom tapped the glass of the screen and peered at the figures moving across it. 'A laterna magicka of some sort?' he whispered. 'A picture show in miniature?'

He turned shining eyes to me, his enthusiasm for TV overwhelming everything else.

'Sit down,' I snapped. 'Just sit down, and shut up, and let me think.'

He glowered again and turned back to the telly. He peered into it one more time, pressing his face to the glass the way people do at aquariums. Then he reluctantly went to sit at the opposite end of the sofa from Nan. He regarded me with tight-lipped concentration, his hands folded in his lap, far too grim and upright to be Dom.

Dom. Where was he? Had I lost him?

It happened all the time, didn't it? All the time. People were snatched away, and they didn't come back. Gary Halpin's brother, for example – snatched away at the age of seventeen. Smeared along the side of the Tonlegee Road, his bike a scattering of parts. Grandda Joe – he just fell down dead. Alive one minute, dead the next. Nan – still here, but snatched away nonetheless. It happened all the time, and holy water and Latin and all that *Hammer House of Horror* bullshit didn't bring them back.

I had to get that thought out of my head somehow, so I slammed my palms down onto the arms of the chair, raising twin puffs of dust and making Dom jump.

Nan muttered but didn't wake up.

'Where's Dom?' I said. 'What have you done to him? How do I fix this?'

His face darkened. 'There is no *Dom*, Lorry. There never was a Dom. Why can't you remember? The old lady remembers.' He gestured at Nan. 'The little girl knows. Why don't you?'

I gripped the arms of my chair very, very tight.

'I want. To talk. To Dom,' I said.

He looked me up and down, pity not quite winning out over anger. 'What have they done to us, Lorry?' he asked quietly.

'There's no *they*. There's just *us*. There's just Ma and Dad, Nan and Dee and *us*!' I leant forward, appealing to whatever I could find of my brother in there. 'Dom,' I hissed. 'Wake up. Please! Fight him, Dom. *Please*.'

He tutted in frustration and looked away. This made me want to hit something, so I clamped my teeth shut and sat very still for a moment, throwing bolts and turning locks all down through my body, not looking at him. Eventually I was tied down enough to speak to him again. He was watching me with frowning impatience.

'Dom,' I said.

He grimaced.

'Dom! Why is this happening? Why?'

'*Why?*' He spread his hands in exasperation. 'Are you only asking that *now*? All that time in The Grey, were you not constantly asking why? I was! *Why* did they hurt me? *Why* did they take you away? *Why* did they send me to that place?' He searched my face. finding only incomprehension. 'You didn't want to go, Lorry. They took you from me – but you didn't want to go. Don't you remember? Say you remember!'

I shook my head. His face fell, his desolation and sense of loss so obvious that I actually felt sorry for him. He lowered his hands. He looked so betrayed.

'How could you have forgotten?' he whispered. 'You were screaming. You tried to hold on to me, but they pulled you away. They had to do it again and again, because each time they dragged you off, you'd get free and come running back to me. They were big, though. Big men, so much bigger than us. And there were more of them than you could fight, and eventually they took you away. I was hurting so much that I couldn't help you.'

He put a shaking hand to his throat and his eyes focused inwards, remembering. 'Then the pain stopped, and the choking, but I couldn't move my arms and legs anymore. I kept thinking, *Please let him hold my hand*. I wanted so desperately ...' His voice hitched and he had to take a second. 'I wanted so desperately for you to hold my hand, to give me a hug. I couldn't understand why they took you away. And then they sent me into The Grey, and the world was *gone*. And after a while the soldier came, another big man, just like the others, with his anger and his noise, and he was in The Grey with me and I was running and running. For years, it seems. But

I never *forgot!*' He glared up at me then, his eyes black as night, and this time he was accusing me, all the pity gone from his face. 'I *never forgot*, Lorry. I spent all that time *remembering* and *waiting* and *where – were – you?*'

'I was *here.* I've never been anywhere but here! Listen to me. Maybe … maybe you *were* alive once …' His eyes widened at that and he glared at me. 'Maybe there was a Lorry too, once. But I'm not him! And you're not my brother!'

'Take that back,' he whispered.

He was gripping the sofa with tremendous pressure, his face and body rigid with anger – or perhaps with terror; it was hard to tell. I was stunned to see mist beginning to rise from his shoulders and hair.

'*Take it back,*' he cried.

'Dom!' I whispered, pointing to his hands. Blossoms of frost were beginning to radiate from his clutching fingers, spreading in glittering patterns across the fabric of the sofa.

He didn't seem to notice. All his attention was focused on my rejection of him. He had begun to shake with rage. There was a rim of hoarfrost developing around his lips, where his angry breath was condensing. It was his anger; his anger seemed to be dragging the heat from the air. I could feel it now, emanating from his corner of the room like a door opening onto a black void. The angrier he got, the colder it became.

You can't freeze a tomato. My dad's voice came to me sharp and clear, as if he were in the room. He'd told me that at Christmas. *You can't freeze a tomato.* Somehow the freezing process bursts all the cells in a tomato's flesh and, though it looks alright while frozen, it damages the way the tomato is held together. And when it's defrosted, the tomato falls apart.

'Stop it!' I said, beginning to panic for the damage this might be doing to my brother's body. 'Stop!'

'She knows me!' he screamed, pointing at Nan. 'Explain how she knows me!'

When he lifted his hand, it left a perfect five-fingered frostprint on the sofa cover.

'Calm down!' I shouted.

He made a dive for Nan. I think his intent was to shake her awake.

'Lady!' he shrieked. 'Tell him! Tell him you know me!'

'Don't touch her!' I dived for him and wrestled him away from her, yelling in pain as my hands made contact with his frigid flesh. I dragged him backwards and we landed on the floor, my arms wrapped around his chest. His attention switched instantly to me and we were suddenly grappling with each other again, scuffling on the dirty floor like street thugs. 'Calm down!' I yelled. 'You're hurting yourself! You're hurting *Dom*!'

It was like wrestling frozen stone; there was no yield or give to his flesh at all. I just hung on, my arms around his chest, as he struggled to get away from me. I don't think he intended to hurt me or even to fight me. But I had grabbed at him, and our blood was high, and he just wanted to get away. He elbowed me hard in the ribs and it was like being hit with a sledgehammer made of ice.

'Lemmego!' he screeched.

'Just calm *down*! You're hurting yourself!' My head smacked the floor as we rolled again, and I saw stars.

Then I was hauled up by my collar, my father's voice an unaccustomed bellow in the already overcrowded space. 'What the *hell* are you doing?'

I'd never before experienced my father's physical strength, and it stunned me to be jerked bodily to my feet and hurled into one corner while my brother was similarly manhandled to the other side of the room. I rebounded off the wall and stood, breathless and dishevelled, my burnt hands tucked into my armpits, my hair hanging into my eyes.

Our father stood in the middle of the small room, a hand held out to each of us like the referee at a boxing match. He didn't know which of us to be looking at, so he swivelled his head between the two of us.

'What. The *hell*. Are you *doing?*' he repeated.

Dom glared at him from the opposite wall, eyes black, skin pale and marbled blue, and I was raging suddenly, at my dad, for being able to stand there and ask what the *hell* we were *doing* when Dom was dying in front of his eyes. I glowered at him, all kinds of words knifing through my head, none of them making it past the blockade of my throat. Dom just loosely clenched his fists and said nothing. Dad's fury morphed very quickly to exhaustion and disappointment. He flung up his hands in despair, then covered his eyes.

'Jesus,' he sighed.

Nan's voice surprised us all. 'You always were a hot-headed little man, Francis.'

She was still huddled up on the sofa, in the exact same position she'd been when asleep. But she was smiling up at Dom in clear-eyed amusement. Dad looked at her, and he seemed to reach the end of his tether. He shook his head, his face crumbling, and waved at us in shaky dismissal.

'Get out of my sight,' he croaked.

'Dad,' I said.

'OUT!' He didn't even look at me, just pointed at the door.

As Dom and I left the room, I heard Nan say, 'Ah, they're just lads, David. Let them blow off their steam.'

Dad said nothing that I could hear, and I didn't look behind me as I led the way to the room that I now shared with this thing called Francis.

12. Little Green Pills to Combat the Cold

Little Green Pills to Combat the Cold

I slammed my way into the bedroom and just kept moving. If I stopped, I'd die. I'd scream. I'd explode. Why couldn't Dad see? What was wrong with them that they couldn't bloody *see*! Dom was the colour of chalk, his eyes were pitch-black, frost was bloody well coming out of his *mouth*! Why couldn't they see?

I prowled from one side of the room to the other, my fingers dug into my scalp, my eyes so wide they hurt. If it wasn't for Nan and Dee, I'd have thought I was imagining it. Hah. Yeah. That was great: a senile auld wan and a wee girl who thought fairies lived under the stairs. *Super grounding in reality there, Pat. Oh God.*

I spun on my heels in the centre of the room, pulling my hands down my face. Then suddenly I was launching myself at the furniture. I flung myself at the wardrobe first: a two-fisted thump against its dark wood that had me recoiling instantly, my burnt hands held high over my head, my face contorted in pain. *Shit.* I turned and kicked the dressing table. This hurt my foot, and I hopped backwards across the room until I clattered into the bunk. The bunk. The damned *BUNK*.

I grabbed the side-rail and shook the whole bed, repeatedly jerking it towards me and banging it violently against the wall. I think I got about three or four really good bangs in before Dad bellowed up the stairs. I'm not sure what he said, but *this is the last straw* was loud and clear in his voice.

I stopped, clinging to the side-rail of the bunk, my cheek resting on my forearm. Panting, I waited for the old man to hurtle up the stairs and maybe give me the first thrashing of my life. But I heard no more from him, except his footsteps retreating down the stairs and the clattering of the pipes as he filled the kettle.

I bowed my head in defeat, resting my forehead against the cool metal of the battered rail. The sweat of anger still burned on my face, but the rest of me was freezing, and I began to shiver with cold. There was an arctic draft sweeping over my back and shoulders, and I knew exactly where it was coming from.

Dom was behind me. While I had been raging about the room, he had come quietly in and shut the door. Now he sat on the windowsill, his knees drawn up, his head leaning on the glass. He was looking down into the garden, his eyes narrowed against the light. He was heavy and still, and the cold rolled off him like an incoming tide. I may as well not have been in the room for all the attention he was giving me.

What was I going to do?

For lack of any other ideas, I crossed to the dressing table and got myself a jumper. And a cardigan. And a scarf. I pulled them all on, keeping an eye on Dom as I did so.

'What age are we?' he asked, still looking into the garden.

'Sixteen in August.'

He blinked at that. 'Five years,' he said in disbelief.

'What?'

'We've been in The Grey for five years.'

'Dom, what's The fecking Grey?'

'The Grey, Lorry. You know…' He moved his hand about. 'Just … The Grey. When everything …' He looked about him, gesturing at the walls, the ceiling, me. 'When everything … faded out.'

I squeezed my temples, but didn't bother reminding him that I'd never been anywhere but here, full technicolour all the way. 'I think you've been gone a lot longer than five years,' I murmured, thinking of his reaction to the TV. 'Can you remember anything specific? What year was it when they took Lorry?'

He just shook his head, little shakes, a nervous movement, over and over, his mouth working, his eyes roving the landscape below. Eventually he squeezed his eyes shut against the light and rested his forehead against the glass. 'I remember them taking you. That's all – and then The Grey … being in The Grey – and then the bad man chasing me, on and on. That's all. Before that we were happy. You and me, May and Jenny.' He thought of something and his eyes shot open. 'That old lady, the one who knows me. What's her name?'

'Nan? Her name is Cheryl. Cheryl Finnerty … er … yeah, Finnerty is her married name. Dunno her maiden one. She's our nan.'

He sighed in tired exasperation. 'I don't know any Cheryl.'

'She's senile. She doesn't know anyone …'

'She knows *me*!' he cried. 'She said my name! She said *Francis*! You heard her!' He groaned and laid his head back again, as if shouting had given him a headache. 'This world is so full of noise and colours,' he moaned. 'It hurts.'

'I'm going to get you out of him,' I told him evenly. 'You can't stay.'

'Urgh!' He whacked his head back against the glass in frustration and glared at me without lifting his head from the window. 'Why can't you remember? You knew me before! When I found you in the bed; when we were talking in the garden! When the soldier came and you were frightened! Why can't you remember now?'

'That was Dom!' I yelled. 'You were talking to Dom! And he *didn't* know you! He thought you were me! Don't you remember? When you had him by the hand and you were rabbiting on about moonlight and you looked up and you both saw me? Don't you remember how scared he was?'

'He … he was scared of the bad man … The bad man was leaning out the window.'

'It was *me leaning out the window!*'

'Lorry was frightened …'

'Dom! *Dom* was frightened! Because he realised I was upstairs! He realised he was holding hands with a frickin' *ghost* in the frickin' *garden* in the middle of the *night*! Of course he was scared!'

He grabbed his head. He was getting upset again; I could tell by the way the temperature was plummeting. My breath began to fog in the air and, even through my three jumpers, I felt needles of cold chill my arms.

You can't freeze a tomato, I thought. *Jesus.*

I hunkered down cautiously by his side. I tried to make my voice low and unthreatening.

'Listen,' I said, 'Isn't it obvious that you don't belong here? Just think about it for five seconds and it'll be obvious. This isn't your life. This can't be anything *like* your life! This is *Dom's* life.'

He groaned, the heels of his hands pressed to his temples. 'I thought that when I finally found you, we'd get everything back; that we'd be alright again … I thought …' He gasped, leaning back. Frost bloomed with an audible *hiss* across the glass behind him. I watched in horror as its jagged icy pattern fanned out around his head. He looked like a religious icon, with his tormented face and his frozen halo, outlined against the vivid blue sky.

'You have to calm down,' I whispered.

He flashed me a look that was all goblin-boy and nothing of Dom, and when he bared his teeth at me I was surprised that they weren't yet black against his white lips. 'Calm down?' he snarled. 'I finally get out of The Grey. I finally find my brother, and when I do it's just *lies* and *noise* and damnable *colours*. And *you* … you don't even *know* me.'

'All I'm saying is … don't get so upset.'

He chuffed out a bitter little laugh. 'You're one to talk.' He looked over my shoulder. and when I followed suit I saw that my assault on the bed had loosened the plaster on the wall. Several big chunks of it had fallen onto the blankets.

'Shit,' I said.

'Your language is terrible,' he whispered.

It was my turn to half laugh. 'You've met me on a bad day.'

My laugh seemed to surprise him, and I felt him relax a little. His eyes lost some of their midnight-blackness, warming a shade closer to Dom's usual chocolate brown. I lowered myself to my knees beside him. It felt like I was edging my way around a tiger. The two of us were so volatile.

'Are you cold?' I asked him. He shook his head in surprise. 'Look at the window behind you.' He did and pulled back, shocked at the ragged silhouette etched in frost on the glass. 'Look at my hands.' I held them out to him, palms out. The flesh was pinched, pink and raw.

'I burnt them when I grabbed you downstairs.' He was appalled, and I leant forward to press my advantage. 'You're hurting my brother. Just by being in his body. You're going to kill my brother. Please. Please, please, please just leave Dom alone.'

'But …' He looked down at himself, then back at me. 'What are you asking me to do?'

'You know.' I made a shooing gesture with my hands. 'Get out of Dom's body. Let him take control again. Just …' I made that ineffectual motion again.

'Lorry,' he said, seemingly torn between being amused and bewildered. 'What are you talking about?'

'Let Dom go!' I shouted. 'Get out! Just leave him!' I shoved at his shoulder, knocking him into the glass and his lip curled in warning.

'Don't hit me again,' he said His eyes began to darken. That fog began to curl up from his shoulders.

Calm down, I told myself. *Softly. Softly.* 'I tell you what,' I said. 'Just let me *talk* to Dom. You don't have to leave. Just … please just let me talk to Dom.'

Bright angry splinters of frost glittered on his mouth as he answered me.

'There is no Dom. I'm Francis.'

I shot to my feet, my hands clenched. I had to gather every stitch of patience I'd ever had and wind it around myself just to keep from flying to the four corners of the room. 'I know you're confused,' I ground out. 'But listen to me now. My brother, Dominick Finnerty, lives in this body. You, Francis … something-or-another … have taken it over. You are *inside my brother's body*. He's in there with you. You have to …'

He stood suddenly and came very close, looking up at me from

Dom's ever so slightly shorter height. He was glaring into my eyes, reading my face. Looking for what? Deceit? Malice? Something hidden behind my words? I held his eyes, and it wasn't long before his expression softened and I saw him start to consider the impossible.

He looked down at his hands, the too-smooth hardness of his flesh, the blue marbling of veins beneath his milky skin. He turned and watched the last of his frosted silhouette dispersing from the window.

'Let me talk to Dom,' I whispered.

He didn't seem to hear me. He began turning from left to right slightly, as if looking for an exit. His movements became jerky and stiff, and he began to crackle with cold – literally. It was as if I could hear the cold off him, the brittle sound of hundreds of needles hitting a tiled floor. Tendrils of fog began to curl from his hair.

I wrapped my hands in the ends of my scarf and grabbed the tops of his arms. I yelled into his face, 'Calm down before you kill Dom!'

He desperately met my eyes, his legs starting to buckle. 'Can't. Too scared ... Can't ...'

'Jesus. Jesus *Christ*.' I was angry all over again. I dragged him, stumbling, to the bunk and flung him onto the bottom bed. I reefed all the blankets off the top mattress and piled them on top of him. I rifled through all the drawers and just piled everything on him: jumpers, kaks, pajamas, everything I could lay hands on. I bent down to him, snarling into his frightened face, 'Calm down. Calm the hell down.'

'Y-you ... calm down,' he whispered, his lips barely moving. He sounded so like Dom that I nearly shouted for joy. But the terror in his eyes brought me to my knees.

'Dom?' I asked.

My heart fell when he managed a tiny shake of his head, his eyes desolate. Still Francis. His lips were blue now, and though there was ice starting to form on the top layer of blankets, he wasn't even shaking – he was too cold. 'Help me,' he managed, and then all that came from his lips was the hollow whistle of his breath on immobile lips.

I pushed myself away from the bed and staggered to the hall. I had no idea what to do. Downstairs, Ma had come back from the old biddies' place. I could hear herself and Dad in the kitchen. She must have just come through the door because Dad was telling her about us.

'… on the floor like gurriers. I nearly killed them. I swear, if they'd've said a word to me, I don't think I could have contained myself.'

I put one foot on the stairs, then another, an indecisive downward movement.

Ma's shadow passed across the wall at the turn of the stairs as she crossed from one side of the kitchen to the other. 'The girls aren't coming for Easter,' she said. 'They're afraid they'll get caught by the bloody bus strike.'

'Ah babe, I'm sorry.'

'S'alright,' she said, not quite managing to hide her disappointment. 'Sure, they'd only be underfoot anyway.'

I have to calm Dom down, I thought. *I have to calm him down.*

I thought of Ma and Dad, of calling them up to witness what had become of Dom. I thought of the yelling, the panic, the chaos that would follow. I imagined them dragging Dom's body out of the bed, stumbling with him to the car. The frantic lunatic search for a hospital or doctor. And all the time Francis, trapped, rigid and frozen, more and more afraid in a world less and less familiar, with people who had no clue – it would kill him. It would kill Dom. I couldn't do that.

I backed quietly up the steps and stood perfectly still and silent on the top landing. Then I turned and went through Ma and Dad's room to the adjoining room at the far end of the house. Nan's room.

I never actually made a conscious decision, if you can believe it. There was no moment of *Hey. What if I do this?* I just went straight to the little wooden box on Nan's dresser and emptied Nan's medicines out onto her bed. There were a lot of them: packets and boxes and vials of stuff. But there were two in particular that I was looking for. There, Nan's sedatives, a bottle of little yellow tablets and a bottle of green — both full. No one would miss any.

I weighed them in my hands, trying to decide which ones to give him. I decided on the green ones. Nan took three half-tablets a day. They kept her calm. I wondered how much I should give him to keep him calm. A whole tablet? He was pretty bad. How fast would it work? If I gave him a whole tablet, would it work faster than a half one?

Shit. I was wasting time. I pocketed four of the little green pills and shoved all the boxes and bottles and vials back into Nan's wee box. I didn't even pause to make sure everything was in order. I just crept back across the top floor, hoping to God that no one downstairs heard me creaking about overhead. My hands were shaking as I filled Dee's night-time bottle with water in the bathroom. I sloshed half of it on the floor while crossing the landing.

His lips were solid curves of blue marble by the time I got back to him, and I thought I was too late. But then his eyes moved under his half-closed lids, seeking me out and fixing on me as I dropped to my knees by the bed. I balanced the bottle of water and rooted in my pocket for the drugs.

I cradled a little green pill in my palm for a moment, wondering if I should cut it in half. Then I just slid the whole thing between his lips, lifted his head a little and dribbled some water in after it.

'It's called librium,' I said. 'Swallow it.' His eyes found mine, and I knew he was scared to. 'Swallow it, for Christ's sake, or I'll kick your arse.' I dribbled more water down his throat for good measure, laid his head back on the pillow, and then sat on the floor, watching his face and waiting.

13. The Monster of Peladon

The Monster of Peladon

he Grey. Yes. That's such a good description of it. You always had a way with words, didn't you, Fran?

☠ ☠ ☠

I snorted awake, my face mashed into the blankets, drool drying in sticky strings under my cheek. My mouth was gluey, and I had that foul-breath feeling of having been in a deep sleep. My eyes found his before I was with it enough to remember where we were, and I got the feeling he'd been watching me for a while. I was still sitting on the floor, my head lying on the bottom bunk. I blinked rapidly and sat back, working my tongue about to get rid of the glue. Dee's bottle was still a quarter full, and I drained it in a couple of swallows before clearing my throat and coming to full consciousness. 'Jesus,' I mumbled.

'You were asleep,' he whispered. He was pale, pale, milky pale, but his flesh had lost all the icy hardness of before and his eyes were just brown – Dom's clear, brown eyes. He was lying on his side, a mountain of assorted covers over him, his hair a messy tangle on the pillow. He quirked his mouth, knowing what I was thinking. 'It's still me,' he croaked. 'Still Francis.'

I couldn't hide my disappointment, and he couldn't hide a bitter twist of his lips at my reaction.

'How do you feel?' I asked.

He made a face and turned his head a little. 'Wash your teeth,' he said mildly.

'Sorry.' I put my hand over my mouth. 'How do you feel?'

He thought for a minute, as if scanning some interior landscape. 'Slow,' he said. His eyes wandered to mine and he gave a blurry little smile. 'But calm.' He giggled.

You're stoned, I thought. *You're waaavey, man. You're up a tree.*

'Let's get these covers off you,' I said and I began to disinter him from his blanket cocoon.

With each layer that I removed I felt the cold rise up from him, but it was bearable, a chilly draught rather than the glacial blast of before. I was still glad of the extra jumpers, but I was no longer in danger of frostbite. While I was putting most of the clothes away, he pushed the final blankets off and blearily pulled himself up to sit on the edge of the bed.

'Was I asleep long?' I asked, eyeing the window and trying to figure out the time by the sun.

He shrugged one shoulder, *dunno*. 'It felt an age.' He looked at me tiredly. 'I tried, you know … what you asked.' Seeing my lack of comprehension, he sighed and made a vague motion with his hand. All his movements were treacle-slow, and lazy. 'Jumping,' he said. 'Leaping …' He dropped his hand and grimaced at me. *Come on*, that grimace said, *get with it!*

Oh. 'You tried to leave Dom? My God! Did it work?'

'For goodness sake!' He spread his arms, as if to show himself to me.

'Quite obviously it didn't.'

I blushed deep and ducked my head. What a dope I was. What a bloody idiot.

'Where are you going?' He tried to follow me as I headed for the door, but his legs weren't too reliable and he ended up clinging to the bunk. I paused at the threshold but didn't look back.

'I'm going to wash my teeth,' I said. 'Don't leave.'

I was grey and ancient-looking in the spotty bathroom mirror, my eyes those of someone who has forgotten how to sleep. I splashed cold water on my face and brushed my teeth with vicious force, the suds pink with blood as they chuckled down the drain. I closed my eyes and sank onto the toilet seat. I rested my head in my arms and just sat there for a minute or two, inhaling the cat-pee smell of the ancient lavatory and thinking of remarkably little. It was as though something inside me had shut down for a moment, leaving me functioning on a physical level but asleep where it counted most. I felt distant and tingly, as though my entire soul had a case of pins and needles.

Then a floorboard creaked on the landing and I leapt to my feet, dashing into the hall without really thinking about it, ready to defend Dom from anything.

Dad leapt about a foot into the air. Hot tea slopped from the two mugs he was carrying, and he hissed in pain. 'Jaysus! Pat! What're you up to?'

I lowered my fists, my heart skittering around my chest. We shuffled around each other for a minute on the small landing, then I opened the bedroom door and let him in.

Inside the room, we stood about uncertainly: Dad with the dripping mugs in hand, me hovering, Dom on the edge of the bottom bunk, eyeing us warily. Eventually Dad just kind of shoved a mug at each of us, and it was a case of catch it or wear it.

Once I had that mug in my hand, it was all I ever wanted to just sit down and drink that tea. I could feel each mouthful going down my gullet, the heat of it, the glorious heat of it hitting my stomach. And it made me realise that I was starving again. Not as incapacitated with hunger as before, but still, emptied out and hollow in the way that I'd now come to associate with waking from dreams I didn't quite recall.

I drained the cup to the very last drop, then cradled it against my forehead, trying to remember all the things I knew I'd dreamt. The ghost of the steam warmed my closed eyelids and my cheeks. My face felt swollen and bruised with exhaustion. Memories danced just behind my eyes, thin and intangible and vital − the ghost of the echoes of other people's dreams.

Damn it, I thought. *Damn it. Why can't I remember?*

'I'm sorry I have to go,' said Dad. He was sitting on the windowsill, his eyes hopping from me to Dom, from Dom to me. His arms were folded, his long legs stretched untidily in front of him: he was all hair and legs and eyes, a bigger, older version of me and Dom. The kindness and understanding in his face made me love him, and made me sad because there was nothing I could think of to do with it. Like the dreams, he was miles away, just out of my reach.

'You know I have to go, right? We need the money, and Justin needs me to run the factory.'

I think I nodded; I don't know what Dom did. Whatever our reaction, Dad creased his mouth up and dropped his eyes to the floor. He looked tired. We all looked tired. It was like the whole family needed to go to bed and sleep for a year. Wake up with everything better. Our house back, our nan back. Dominick back.

Dad scrubbed his hand over his face and tried a smile on for size. 'Lookit,' he said. 'You're lads. You have to blow off steam. I understand. You have been through a hard time, and … bloody hell, lads … you've been great. I'm not surprised you finally went off the deep end; it had to have been coming for a while. I'm just a bit shocked that you did it in front of your nan.'

He gave us a look that said, *Come on! What were you thinking? Your nan for God's sake!*

'I'm not going to give you the you-have-to-look-after-your-mam-and-sister speech. You know that already. I trust you to pull your weight. But I won't be here, lads. I need to know you can keep a lid on it. It's too easy to lose the rag at your age. I do *not* want your mam pulling you off one another, the way I did today. Are we understanding each other?'

His level stare said, *You have your orders now. Don't let me down.*

Who's going to look after us? I thought. *We're falling, Dad. We're falling. Why aren't you able to catch us?* I said nothing. Dom mumbled a mechanical little, 'Yes, sir.'

Dad looked hard at us for a minute. 'Alright,' he said, just about ready to put the subject back in its box. 'Oh, and lads …' He raised his eyes to the bundled covers of the top bunk, the long line of bare brick where I'd smashed the plaster from the wall. 'Tidy up that mess before your mother sees it. And if the old biddies make us pay, you're working every weekend at the factory 'til you've made it up to me. Got it?' I nodded. Dom stared at his feet. Dad sighed. 'Give us your cups,' he said. '*Dr Who* is on in half an hour. You gonna watch it with me?'

We handed him our mugs, Dom's still half full.

'Jesus!' Dad peered into Dom's mug. 'This tea is stone-cold! Sorry, about that, bud! Maybe I picked up my old one by mistake.'

He turned to leave. I leapt to my feet.

'Dad!' I cried. He turned back. 'Do you think we look different?'

Cold surged over my hand as soon as I said it, blasting out from Dom with anxiety and fear and I stared at my dad, willing him to notice. *Look at Dom, Dad. Don't you think he looks different? Don't you think he looks cold? Don't you think Dom looks dead?*

Dad scanned my face, completely at a loss to know what I wanted from him.

'Dad, look at Dom! Don't you think Dom looks sick?'

Dad's face pinched in momentary alarm and he stooped down to look at my brother who remained perfectly still, watching him from the bunk. Dom's face was polished white and immobile as a mask; his wary eyes were black as pitch. Dad took one look at him, sighed and dropped his eyes, his shoulders stooping in relief and exasperation.

'Your brother's fine, Pat,' he said, straightening up and giving me a quick, disappointed frown. 'And I can't bloody *stay*, alright? Stop acting the maggot.'

Dad fumbled his way out of the room and I was left with an empty, angry, broken feeling in my chest.

Dom glared at me. After a moment, he struggled to his feet and clung to the bunk while he got his bearings. 'Tell you what,' he slurred. 'This is no bloody fun.' Then he walked, careful as a drunk, out after my dad.

I was thoroughly incapable of speed, and despite Dom's loose rein on his coordination, he had already disappeared into the sitting room when I got to the bottom of the stairs. Ma was clearing up carrot and potato peelings, the smell of chicken casserole flavouring the air. Dad was washing the cups. They both gave me tight-lipped glances as I crossed the room, Dad's softened with a last-minute wink.

Dee was sitting in the armchair facing the door, her little legs sticking straight out ahead of her, Bobo, her toy dalmatian, clutched in her lap. Dom was standing by the sofa and she was staring over at him with deep uncertainty. As I crossed the threshold she flicked her eyes to me.

'Where Bom?' she whispered.

'C'mere,' I said and hefted her up into my arms. She wrapped her legs around my waist, hugging Bobo between us, and rested her head against my neck, her attention on Dom.

'Who dat boy?' she whispered.

'That's Dom, Dee. It's just Dom.'

She looked up at me, her eyes searching. 'Where Bom?' she asked, thoroughly confused.

'Dee. That's Dom, there. He … he's playing a game. He's pretending to be someone else. Will you play Dom's game with him?' I felt horrible saying that to her. I felt squalid and wrong.

She frowned at me. She shook her head. 'Me not like dat game.'

'Alright,' I said. 'Don't worry.'

'Me not want to play,' she said. 'Me want *Bom*!'

'Shh, now … don't be so noisy. It's alright.'

Her voice was getting a dangerous pitch to it, and I began to jig her up and down, all the time casting nervous glances at the kitchen door. She laid her head back down onto my shoulder and hid her face in my neck. 'Me not like dat game,' she mumbled.

Dom knelt at Nan's feet. He took her hand between his two hands, and looked up into her face.

Ma came in carrying the tea things and put them on the little sitting-room table. She was talking over her shoulder to Dad. '... turns out the old biddies know your mam. They were being pretty coy about it, as if they thought Cheryl mightn't want us to know. But it turns out they were really close friends.'

She went back out. Dad murmured some surprised things in the kitchen.

Dom and Nan gave them no heed at all.

Nan was watching the TV, apparently oblivious to the young man kneeling at her feet. Dom turned and followed her eyes to the screen. There was a cartoon on. Dom seemed to lose himself in it for a moment, his eyes following the hectic colours of *The Pink Panther* (that rinky-dink panther) as they swarmed across the screen. He still had Nan's hand in his own, still kneeling at her feet. They looked so normal, these two people – these stolen people – watching bright colours that neither of them comprehended.

Dr Who was going to be on in a minute. It was episode three of 'The Monster of Peladon' and we were dying to see what happened with the beast of Aggedor. We loved *Dr Who*. If this were my Dom, he'd be hopping up and down on the sofa, willing the fecking *Pink Panther* to finish.

Last time, just before the episode had started, he'd come dancing into our sitting room, shuffling in backwards, wagging his arse and grooving his arms, singing about where'd your mama and papa gone from that stupid 'Chirpy Chirpy Cheep Cheep' song; he'd been singing the same two bloody lines all day, and I'd thrown a cushion at him.

After the episode was over, we'd been strung out with expectation and excitement. We could hardly wait another seven days to find out what was going to happen. The cliffhanger had seemed cruel and unusual punishment. Now, I couldn't have given a crap. Sarah Jane and the Doctor could have fallen off the edge of the world for all it meant to me. Dom was gone. He was gone. I wanted him back. I'd have given anything. I'd have let him sing the same two lines of any bloody song he wanted. He could sing it until my ears bled. Until I went deaf. Just as long as it was him, really him.

My life had become one long cliffhanger.

Dad skirted around me with a jug of milk and a teapot. He put them on the table. Ma raised her voice and continued their conversation through the door.

'… want to bring her for a walk tomorrow. I tried to explain how … you know … out of it she is. They didn't seem to mind.' She dropped her voice to normal as he went back into the kitchen.

Dad's intrusion seemed to break the hypnotic power of the TV. Dom blinked and turned back to Nan. 'Cheryl,' he said, tugging her hands and drawing her wavery attention to him. 'Who do you think I am?'

Nan gave him a playful little smile. 'Stop your messing, Fran! You're always teasing!'

He stared into her face, pressing her hands between his. I could see him trying hard to remember her. Dee turned her head, her curls tickling my neck, and we watched the two of them in silence. I tightened my arms around my sister, pulling her up a little, holding her closer.

'Why can't I remember you?' whispered Dom. 'Did you perhaps work for my mother?'

Nan tutted and rolled her eyes.

He squinted up at her, trying, trying. 'It's so hard to recall. Everything just bled away inside The Grey. Now I find it so difficult …' He shook his head. 'I am so sorry, ma'am. I just don't remember you. Can't you tell me who you are?'

Nan was irritated with him now. 'Ah stop, Fran. I'll tell May on you.'

Dom's eyes opened very wide suddenly and he sat back, dropping Nan's hands as if they'd burnt him. Nan rubbed her fingers, a little moment of pain showing in her face. 'Goodness,' she said, 'how cold you are! You really ought to put your gloves on. The snow is piled high.'

Dom knelt very straight and stiff, his face an open wound of revelation. I could see that he knew. He knew who Nan was, and he wished he didn't.

'You're Lacy,' he whispered at last. 'You're Lacy-Doll.'

Nan's eyebrows shot up, and she gave a delighted little laugh. 'Oh, no one's called me Lacy-Doll since I was a girl! How lovely!'

'What wrong with dat boy?' whispered Dee.

'He's upset,' I answered. 'And he's Dom, Dee. Call him Dom.'

'I'm's cold.' She was shivering quite badly all of a sudden. I pulled my cardie open and wrapped it around her, cocooning her against my chest so that only her little head stuck out, and her little legs.

Dom rose shakily to his feet, looking down on our fragile old nan with a kind of blank sorrow. 'You're Lacy-Doll,' he whispered. 'You're Lacy. And that old lady. That old lady before. She really is May Conyngham, isn't she?' He looked up and around at the room, as if seeing it for the first time. I could practically hear things clarifying for him, little cubes of understanding falling, *clunk, clunk, clunk* into place.

'What is it?' I asked, though I had kind of guessed.

He looked at me and maybe it was the librium, or maybe it was just that he had nothing left to feel, but I thought he was terribly calm when he said, 'May and Lacy are three years younger than me. They're seven years old. That … that means I must be nearly eighty years old! How did that happen? How? A few days ago … maybe a week, at the most, I was ten. We were ten years old, Lorry! All of a sudden we're fifteen and now …'

'Time flies,' said Nan, nodding sagely. 'It surely does.'

The temperature in the room began a steep downward slide. 'Dom,' I warned.

'Yes.' He held a hand out, flapping it at me without looking in my direction. 'I know, I know. Calm down.' He breathed in deep. 'Calm down,' he whispered.

Dad came in, peered at the telly and jumped. 'Ah lads! It's started! Why didn't you call? Sit down!'

He shooed Dee and myself into the armchair. I watched Dom do a slow spin in the middle of the room, his hand to his mouth, his big eyes blank. Dad grabbed him and pushed him down onto the fireside stool. 'There we go!' he said and plopped himself down beside Nan.

'Olive!' he shouted. 'Doctor's on!'

Ma scurried in, drying her hands. She paused in the middle of the room. 'Dave, it's freezing! Put some wood on the fire.'

Dad looked around her to see the telly and dragged her down into the corner of the sofa with him. 'C'mere to me and I'll heat you up,' he murmured. Ma blushed and smacked his knee. He pulled her in under his arm and she rested her head on his shoulder, the two of them already involved in the show.

Dom sat by the fire, staring into middle distance. His mind must have been crawling, churning, boiling under his skull. I pulled Dee closer, like a teddy-bear, like a blanket.

On the telly, Sarah Jane Smith screamed, and I didn't even turn my head from Dom. Dom. My real-life cliffhanger. My own personal tune-in-next-week. What were we going to do?

14. James Hueston

James Hueston

We sat through the telly. We ate our dinner. Our father left us. All those things happened in neat little packages of time: one, then another, then another.

On his way out the door, Dad gave me a fierce hug. 'Love you, bud,' he said, and I hung on to him for a fraction of a second after he tried to let go. He patted my back and clunked my forehead with his own. 'Got to go, sonny boy.'

He turned to give Dom a hug and laughed in disbelief when Dom stuck his hand out instead. Dad shook hands with him, the corners of his mouth twitching. Then he pulled Dom into a hug anyway. Dom's arms remained at his sides. Dad released him and grabbed Dom's face between his hands, shaking it gently to and fro, looking into Dom's eyes.

'Listen to me, bud,' he said. 'You're never too big to hug your old man.'

Later, in a phone call to Ma, Dad would mention the mysterious burns on the palms of his hands. He thought maybe one of the bleach barrels at work had sprung a leak; it was the only explanation he could come up with. No, he couldn't remember exactly when he got them, but they hurt like blazes.

I helped carry his bag to the car, Dom trailing behind. It was beautiful outside, the air tinted a clear pink, scented with the outgoing tide. The sandy garden was cold under the bruised shadow of the house, but the car was still in sunshine. It threw the mellow gold of the late-evening sun back at us from a dozen gleaming points, and radiated a day's worth of heat up from its metal body. I leant against it, soaking it up.

Dom stayed in the shadows, his face glimmering in the oncoming dusk. We watched as Dad put his things in the boot of the car.

'I'll be back Friday, bud, okay?'

I nodded.

He waved at Dom. 'See you, son.' Dom lifted his chin in goodbye. Dad's hand lingered in the air, hurt finally showing through his amusement. 'Well, okay then,' he said.

He tousled my hair and got into the car. I stood back as the engine coughed to life. He pulled out into the lane, his indicator tick-tocking. Then he was gone, and I was alone.

It felt like a hundred years since Dom and I had pimp-walked down the strand, singing and swatting at each other with sticks. A million years. A lifetime. But it had been yesterday. Yesterday morning, I'd had a brother. I'd had a best friend. He'd been fun. He'd been interesting: my slow-burn, articulate, counterweight. Now I was lopsided, a boat with one paddle, rowing frantically and spinning in a slow, maddening circle around the space that should have been him.

'This was a beautiful garden once.'

I turned, glaring at him over the warm stones of the low wall. I couldn't care less about his bloody garden. He gave me his speculative look and stepped uncertainly from the shadows. The light obviously bothered him, because he immediately shaded his eyes. He tried to stand, as I had done, facing into the evening sun. But instead of comfort it seemed to cause him only pain, and he gasped and stepped back into the shade, his hand clamped over his eyes.

'Are you alright?' I asked, grudgingly.

He nodded, his hand still over his face, his teeth gritted. Eventually the pain seemed to subside and he opened his eyes, cupping his cheek in his hand and looking blankly into middle distance.

'We've lost our brothers, haven't we?' he murmured.

My heart constricted as I realised we'd been thinking the exact same thing. 'No,' I said. 'We'll get them back.'

He raised his eyes to mine, and the smile he gave me was so sad and so kind that I almost liked him. That was such a betrayal of Dom that I scowled. 'What made you think I was Lorry?' I asked.

He shook his head, looking me up and down, as if trying to figure it out himself. 'We're twins too. Lorry and I. Maybe that's why?'

He gestured down at himself, then at me, as if to remind me that Dom and I were twins. As if I could somehow have forgotten. He looked straight at me with Dom's clear brown eyes. 'I feel so lost without him,' he said.

Twins? Lorry and Francis were twins!

I was trying to process this wacked-out information while he kept talking, quietly working things out in his head. 'In The Grey, it all made sense. I was alone, searching for so long. And then – then there was suddenly a *feeling*, a feeling of loneliness and pain and confusion – it was like a *sound* in The Grey. I was able to follow it, and when I did, I found this *boy*. He *knew* me. He talked to me. I thought I'd found Lorry. Do you understand? Do you know how that felt? I'd *found*

Lorry – at last.' His face brightened for a moment, remembering this joy. Then his hands fell to his sides, the happiness gone. 'Then the man came. And he was so angry. He's always angry, but now he was *furious*. He shouted at us. In the garden.'

'I *told* you, that was *me*.'

'No … well yes … I don't know. I think you were there … but *he* was there too. And he was angry. He frightened Lorry.'

'Dom,' I corrected automatically, 'he frightened Dom.' But my thoughts were miles away. I was remembering the phantom soldier and wondering – was he still here? Did he still want Francis? If so, would he hurt Dom to get to him? I looked over Dom's shoulder, past the apples trees, into the deep shade of the undergrowth. Despite the heat of the sun, the hair on my arms prickled up. I laid my hands on the warm stones of the wall just to feel something real.

'Dom?' I said, my eyes on the shadows behind him. 'Why don't you come over here, come and stand by me?'

But he was still trying to explain that night, his eyes distant. The shadow of the house was like a purple stain at his feet, and he seemed to float against it, a thing detached. 'I woke up,' he whispered, 'perfect and whole again. Part of the world again. But nothing was simple anymore.' He looked back at the house. 'Nothing made sense.'

He seemed to tune me out for a while, as he examined the house. His eyes roamed the sky-reflective windows, the rust-coloured bricks, the ivy-covered apple trees. I did the same, and tried to imagine the changes seven decades would wreak upon a home.

'Do you know who May Conyngham is?' he murmured.

I shook my head, my throat dry.

'She's my little sister.' He looked back at me suddenly. 'Imagine that.

Imagine waking up tomorrow, and that wee girl you're so fond of is suddenly an old woman, and the frilly wee sprat that was her best friend is assumed to be your grandmother.'

I couldn't. I couldn't imagine Dee aged ten, let alone in her late seventies. It was beyond me.

'I have my own grandmother, you know.' He gave a wry smile. 'She's a rotten-tempered old harridan, actually, gives my eldest sister Jenny an appalling time. In The Grey, I'd forgotten all this – my sisters, my mother.' His smile died as quickly as it had flickered into life. 'Oh! My poor mother! How must she feel? She dotes on us.' He raised his eyes to me, horrified. 'How can I have forgotten all this? It was so simple in The Grey. Everything else faded out, and there was just me, and I was looking for Lorry; then that damned man was chasing me and that's all there was! That's *all*!'

'Did he murder you?' I asked. 'That man – the soldier? Did he kill you and Lorry? Is that why he haunts you?'

Dom shook his head, his expression helpless. 'I don't remember,' he whispered. The house at his back was eating up the light. His face had become a shimmering blob, his eyes dark, tragic smudges under the hanging fringe of his hair. He looked as though he were being eaten by shadows as if the evening were sucking the last of his energy from him. I was suddenly overwhelmed with the sense that we really should *do* something. Just do *something*. Anything. I just wanted to be free of this endless claustrophobic mess.

'Let's go for a walk,' I said.

His eyes snapped up in surprise, and I could see my own desire reflected in his face.

'Let's walk to the headland,' I said, leaning towards him over the wall.

Yes. The sea — the pounding immensity of it; the wild air of the strand. We'd walk the legs off ourselves, run the entire length of the strand and climb the weed-encrusted boulders at the far end of the beach. We'd keep going 'til we were as far from here as possible. We'd drop unseen into a hidden cove and yell ourselves hoarse against the roar of the surf. Just for the sheer release of it. Just because we could.

'Come on!' I said. 'We can walk the strand. Go to Red Island.'

He wanted to. He wanted to so badly. But he remained on the shadowy side of the garden, his hands opening and closing, his face desperate. He hadn't the strength or the courage to cross back into the sun.

I couldn't stand the thought that we wouldn't go — that we'd just go back into that house. That we'd just sit there. 'We can climb the rocks!' I cried. 'We can skip stones!' Dom loved to skip stones, but he wasn't good at it, not like me. The thought of Dom pushed me into anger. 'Come *on!*' I yelled. 'Come on!' I slammed my fists down on the wall, hurting them against the stones. 'Let's go! Let's get moving!'

He began an apologetic gesture but then froze, startled. His eyes slid left of me, and I knew immediately that someone was behind me.

I spun to find a very old man standing there. It wasn't hard to recognise him — though he looked quite different to our first encounter. His extremely pale eyes would always give him away.

It was the auld fella we'd pulled from the sea.

He wasn't drunk this time, though he was faintly scented with whiskey. His bright cloud of hair was Brylcreemed down behind his ears and parted neatly on the left. Carefully washed, his face and hands were pink, his cheeks clean-shaven. He had a farmer's flat cap clenched in his two hands and he was regarding Dom with a stunned expression on his face.

'How long have you been standing there?' I said.

The old man didn't take his eyes from Dom. 'What the divil?' he said and made to move around me, heading in through the garden gate, his eyes never leaving my brother.

'Hey!' I put my hand up – had to actually place it on his chest before he finally noticed that I was trying to stop him getting in. I pushed him gently but firmly back a step. 'Where d'you think you're going?'

He finally seemed to register my presence, and the expression in his pale-blue eyes had my heart skipping a beat. 'Do you know what's wrong with your brother?' he said.

Dom and I traded a surprised look. 'What do *you* think is wrong with him?' I whispered.

The old man seemed to check himself at that, and he cleared his throat, frowning. His eyes slid to the right. I think he'd spoken without thinking and was regretting his question. 'Well ...' He stood a little straighter, retreating behind himself. 'Well,' he repeated. 'He looks a bit pale, doesn't he?'

'Mister?' I asked quietly. 'Do you know what's wrong with Dom?'

The old man's eyes widened. He seemed to be considering taking a risk. His fingers worked the brim of his hat.

'Can you help him?' I whispered. I could feel Dom in the background straining to hear, longing to just cross the last band of sunlight and stand with us. '*Mister*,' I insisted, 'can you help him?'

Then Ma's voice intruded, snapping us from our whispered communion.

'*Excuse* me?' she said. 'Can I *help* you?'

It was her special 'back-away-from-my-children' voice. Extremely polite. Extremely cold. A sharp blade of warning cutting across the evening shadows. I groaned inwardly at her tone. We were fifteen years old, and she still thought we were stupid enough to take sweets from a stranger. She was standing at the arch of the back garden wall, Dee peeping out from behind her legs.

The old man's eyes met mine for a moment, and I tried with all my might to pour a message into that brief communication. *She hasn't a clue. For God's sake, don't give us away.* He frowned thoughtfully at me for a fraction of a second, then he turned and gave Ma a smile. It was a radiant smile, a genuine kind of smile that, when aimed at you, said that you were the best thing that had happened all day, that you'd made him happy just by being there.

It gave me a jolt, this wonderful smile. It belted me across the chest like a bang from an electric fence. I knew this man. I knew him very well. I knew his smile, and his dancing eyes. I knew his cheeky delighted spark of life; the way he embraced friendship and cherished it; the way he never stopped caring.

Who the hell was he?

'I'm James Hueston,' he said. 'You're Missus Finnerty?' His voice raised to a question as he extended his hand across the garden wall. 'I told your husband I might call around to thank your boys for fishing me from the sea.'

She melted instantly, her whole posture softening, her face opening like a flower. God help us, but my ma was an unpredictable woman.

'Mister *Hueston*! Oh, come on in, please! I've just made tea.' She advanced on us. Dee trailed behind, her fingers jammed into her mouth, firmly attached by one clutching fist to Ma's loose slacks.

Instead of shaking James Hueston by the hand, Ma grasped his wrist and, in one of her impulsive gestures of affection, pulled him forward to kiss his old cheek across the garden wall.

'Oh goodness,' he chuckled, pleased, and touched his cheek where she'd left a tiny ice-pink SWALK. But when she began to usher him into the garden, he hesitated at the gate and glanced nervously up the side passage, which led to the old biddies' house. 'Uh,' he said. 'Well, I'm not sure I should come in, missus. I really just came to ... '

'Mister Hueston. I went out and bought an Oxford Lunch in case you called. You're not escaping without a slice.' She shooed and herded and clucked 'til he was crossing the garden and passing into the shade of the house.

Dom had been staring at him this whole time, and when they came level with each other, James Hueston paused and stuck his hand out again. 'So this is the other one,' he said. 'Hero number two.'

'This is Dominick,' Ma said. 'I assume Patrick already introduced himself?' She looked back over the old man's shoulder and jerked her chin at me. *Get over here!*

Dom grabbed the old man's hand and James Hueston gasped and clenched his teeth against the pain of contact. An unexpected clot of raincloud suddenly covered the sunset. The garden was plunged into chilly gloom. The old man let out a low whine of discomfort, but Dom didn't seem to notice and just kept holding on, his face a twist of emotion.

Ma looked at James Hueston in concern. 'Are you alright?' she asked.

'Just ... hah.' He gently extricated himself from Dom's icy grip. 'Just a touch of rheumatism,' he lied.

He patted Dom's arm, nodding reassuringly and holding eye contact for a moment. Then he allowed Ma to lead him through the arch and under the apple trees.

I came up behind my brother and put my hand between his shoulderblades. Cold snapped up through the fabric of his jumper. My already damaged fingertips sang out; I felt the blood in my wrist slow to a crawl. Still, I kept my hand there, hoping that Dom, wherever he was, would feel my presence.

The wind picked up, sending little ghost-devils of sand skittering past us. All the gold had drained from the air now, and it was cold. rapidly falling into twilight. Dom's back was a mass of trembling tension. 'I know that man,' he said.

'We saved him yesterday. You and I – *Dom* – Dom and I. He was trying to drown himself.'

He jerked under my hand, and his shoulders hunched. His head half turned, almost to look at me, then snapped back again to where the old man had followed Ma out of sight.

'He tried to …? Oh but Lorry, that's a terrible sin.'

Those words coming from Dom's mouth made me snatch my hand from his back, as I was once again slapped with the fact that this was no longer my brother. Dom would never have spoken of sin, except to disparage the idea of it. I hated these moments of clarity. They swallowed me. They stole my breath and my heartbeat from me.

'You've made a mistake,' he ground out. 'James Hueston would never do that. He'd never …' His voice was a harsh rasp again and he was getting a broke-backed hunch to him that alarmed me. I leant around to look into his face.

'Dom?'

'I feel so strange, Lorry,' he whispered. 'My mind feels strange. Like the parts of a magnet that don't want to touch … being pushed … together …'

He groaned, doubling over, and I tried to catch him before he fell down. Small whiffs of vapour rose from my fingers like smoke from a soldering iron. My hands screamed. There was no way I could hold onto him. I let go, and he staggered away from me, heading for the little stone bench that sat under the first apple tree. I bounced about on the balls of my feet, hissing with the pain, my burnt hands shoved under my armpits, my teeth gouging my bottom lip.

Dom managed to sit on the bench and slump back against the trunk of the tree. He released a gasping little sigh and went completely still. Except for the hectic glitter of his eyes, he looked just like a corpse.

'Hold on,' I cried, stumbling towards him. 'Hold on.'

I fell to my knees on bitterly cold sand. Ignoring the pain in my hands, I fished another green pill from my pocket and held it to his lips. His eyes met mine. His lips stayed shut, and I realised he was afraid of me. Of course he was; we were complete strangers, thrown together against our will in the worst of conditions. 'I have no idea if this is okay,' I whispered. 'I don't know what I'm doing with these. They're not sweets. They might … I don't know what they might do.'

We looked at each other for a moment; then he parted his lips slightly and let me slip the pill into his mouth.

'Can you swallow?'

He shut his eyes and I saw his throat working in jerky, convulsive movements.

I knelt beside him, my knees soaking up the damp. *Where are you, Ma?* I thought. *Why isn't Dad here? Why are we alone?* I watched Dom, his face blank, his eyes closed as he waited for the pill to work. *Ma, I thought. What if this were me? Would you see it then? Would you? If something came tomorrow and pushed me aside and stole my face … would you notice? Or would you fail me as miserably as you've failed …* I bit back on that thought. I bit viciously back and shut it down.

'I'm sorry.' His voice startled me, the dry whisper of it in the coalescing shadows. 'I'm sorry that I stole your brother.'

I tried not to let my throat close over at that. I just ground my teeth together and nodded.

'I didn't mean it. If I could … '

'How do you feel now?' I said harshly.

Before he could answer me, a long shadow cut the warm rectangle of light thrown through the kitchen door, and Dee stepped around the hydrangea bushes. She was ridiculously tiny and solemn, standing there looking at us. She didn't take her eyes from Dom. 'Mammy said come in.'

I stood, putting myself between them. 'Alright, Dee. We're coming.'

She maintained her solemn examination of our brother for a moment, lifted her eyes to me, then stepped back behind the bushes. Her shadow shrank and bobbed as she ran inside.

'Come on,' I said, 'we need to go back in.'

'Buy me a minute,' he whispered – an odd expression, but I knew what he meant.

I nodded to him. 'Don't be long,' I said and went ahead of him.

The kitchen was warm with the smell of tea, the lingering scent of dinner and turf-smoke from the sitting-room fire. Ma had sat James Hueston at the kitchen table and was busy setting out the tea stuff, biscuits, the Oxford Lunch and an ashtray should the old man want a smoke. He sat taking in the shabby surroundings, a strange, rueful look on his face.

As I came through the door, Ma was putting the cosy onto the teapot. 'You've spent a long time in England, haven't you, Mr Hueston?'

James looked down at his hands, smiling a bit. 'Oh aye,' he said. 'Quite a bit of time.' His accent registered with me then. He spoke just like my ma's brother, Gary, who'd left home at seventeen to join the RAF and only ever returned for weddings and for funerals. James had the same warm, rounded burr to his voice.

The radio was playing low in the corner, waiting for the news to come on. Ma was listening for updates on the bus strike, I guess, hoping it would be called off. At that moment, Cat Stevens' gentle voice was telling us that if he ever lost his eyes he'd not have to cry no more. I couldn't bear to sit down, so I went and leant against the Aga, its latent heat a drowsy comfort against the small of my back.

'Where's your brother?' Ma asked me.

'We left the gate open. He's gone to shut it.'

It seemed an eternity, but no one else seemed to notice, and finally there he was: Dom-and-not-Dom, staggering up to the door. I tried not to stare as he stood there swaying slightly on the threshold, but I sussed him out from the corner of my eye. He didn't look normal, not by any stretch of the imagination, but at this stage I figured Dom's head would have to be off and tucked under his arm for my ma to notice anything out of the ordinary.

He lingered a moment, the stormy twilight a turbulent grey behind him. I thought perhaps he was considering going back outside. Then, out of nowhere, a violent wind ripped through the garden behind him. It raised a flurry of sand, flinging it through the open door, and Dom lurched the rest of the way into the room with it, jerking forward as if he'd been given a shove in the back. We all jumped as the door was ripped from his hand, and slammed shut against the wind.

There was a moment of stunned silence. Then Ma laughed.

'Wow,' she said, pushing her windblown hair back off her face. 'That was some entrance, Dom!'

She twinkled a smile at James Hueston, and he grinned uncertainly at her, his attention drifting to my brother. Dom staggered back a little, his eyes on the firmly closed door. He inadvertently brushed Dee's shoulder, and she squealed and scuttled away as if afraid that he'd touch her again. James Hueston's eyes followed her as she ran around the table, and narrowed when she flung her arms around my waist and buried herself in the folds of my jumper. She turned her head a little so that she could watch Dom out of the corner of her eye.

'Bad man,' she whined.

'Don't be such a weed, Dee,' I murmured, but I pushed her behind me slightly so that I was between her and Dom. Neither of us could take our eyes from him. He was staring fixedly at the door.

Ma crouched by Dee. 'Oh, puddy!' she said. 'Don't start that again.' She ruffled Dee's hair. 'It's just the wind, okay? There's no bad man.'

Dee attached herself like a little suckered creature to Ma's neck. Ma hoisted her into her arms. She raised her head to find James Hueston watching her and gave a tired little roll of her eyes. 'Dee's been having bad dreams since we got here. It would appear that there's a bad man out to get us all.'

'Bom,' said Dee, her voice muffled in Ma's shoulder. 'Bad man gots Bom.'

Dom looked round sharply and we traded a wide-eyed glance.

Ma shook her head and tutted. 'You're a silly sausage,' she cooed, rubbing Dee's back as she carried her across the room. Dee twined her little hands in the heavy locks of Ma's hair and when Ma finally got herself seated, curled up on her lap. 'Me not sausage,' she said, but her heart wasn't in it and her thumb soon crept into her mouth. She wasn't going to be awake for much longer.

Ma kissed the top of her head. 'You'd better sleep tonight,' she murmured fondly, 'or I'll throw you in the bin.'

James Hueston leant forward, putting a hand onto the teapot. 'Will I pour you a cuppa, missus?'

Ma smiled gratefully at him.

Meanwhile Dom was staggering clumsily forward, apparently aiming for a chair. I couldn't take my eyes off him. As James Hueston poured Ma's tea, he too was surreptitiously following my brother's progress, and we both sighed with relief when Dom managed to sit himself in the chair right across the table from the old man.

'Have a cuppa,' said James Hueston, pouring tea into my brother's cup. Dom said nothing. His hands, resting on the kitchen table, were curled slightly and immobile; his face was like a waxwork dummy's.

Then James Hueston smiled, at him that tremendous warm smile, and I saw Dom's expression open, in surprise and relief. He leant forwards, like a flower towards the sun, his eyes drowsing shut slightly, his lips parted, and for the first time since we'd fought each other in the garden, Dom relaxed. When James Hueston turned to me and asked would I like a cup of tea, I didn't answer. But he went ahead and poured anyway, and I unthinkingly wrapped my hand around my mug, staring at him all the time.

James Hueston's smile had *warmed* my brother. I don't mean in any sappy hearts-and-flowers way either. His smile had actually physically *warmed* my brother's hands and cheeks. I saw Dom's fingers relax; I saw the tight flesh bloom and lose its mottled blue. His cheeks flushed gently and, despite retaining their polished stone-like appearance, they softened. For the first time in hours, some of the pain seemed to leave Dom's body, and he began to look alive.

I could have leapt from my chair and hugged James Hueston 'til his brittle old ribs snapped with the pressure, but I didn't. I raised my cup to my lips instead and quietly sipped my tea.

15. The Truth

The Truth

Ma was laughing gently as she finished her tenth cup of tea that day. She shifted Dee's loose-limbed weight in her lap and told James Hueston how we drank far too much of the stuff in the Finnerty household; how my dad always said that by the time we hit the grave none of us would ever rot, we'd be too pickled from tea. Ma said that if they dug her up in a hundred years, they'd think she was a saint because, like Bernadette, death would not corrupt her. She laid her head back in solemn beatitude, closed her eyes and laid her free hand on her breast, looking angelic.

'Saint Olive of the Barry's Green Label,' she intoned. 'Bless my teapot.'

James Hueston chortled in genuine delight, and his amusement pleased Dom who gave a rusty little chuckle.

Something banged the back of my chair. I spun to look, but nothing was there. Yesterday's storm was back, gusting against the house with force, shushing through the eaves and down the chimney so that the rooms were filled with tiny stirrings and insistent little *thud, thud, thuds* of not-quite-snug doors and windows batting in their frames. I looked around the subtly shifting room and pulled my chair a little closer to the table.

James Hueston laid his cup down, looking questioningly at my ma as he took a pack of Woodbines from his pocket. She nodded and smiled at him and asked Dom would he get the fags from her handbag in the sitting room. Dom didn't even look in her direction, just continued gazing at James Hueston like a sleepy cat. Ma seemed completely oblivious to how stoned he was, how blissed out.

I jumped to my feet. 'I'll get them for you, Ma.'

'Thanks, love. Bag's hanging on the back of the armchair.'

Dee was unconscious in Ma's lap, her curly head lolling into the crook of Ma's arm, a thin line of drool shining on her chin. Ma was going to get a crick in her neck holding her like that. I was just about to offer to take Dee in and lie her on the sofa, when I hesitated. I realised I didn't want her out of my sight. I wanted her here, with Ma and me and … and Dom. All of us together, under the hard spot of the kitchen light, within the benign radius of James Hueston's presence.

I ran my fingers through Dee's curls and went into the sitting room. Nan was snoozing on the sofa, her feet up on a little poof. I pulled the tartan car-blanket up around her shoulders and tucked her in a bit. She was deeply asleep, not a stir out of her. In the kitchen I heard James Hueston strike a match and the sweet smell of his cigarette smoke wafted in to me.

'Your husband told me about your home, missus. I'm sorry for your troubles.'

Ma made a noncommittal sound.

'Anything I can do to help while your man is away … just ask.'

I was a bit surprised at how dark it had become already. The garden was barely visible through the window. The almost blank glass made me feel watched. I hastily shut the curtains, then went and threw another few bits of turf onto the fire. The room brightened instantly.

'The two sisters have already offered their help, Mr Hueston. Thank you so much.'

There was a rueful chuckle from the old man. 'Oh, you'll have as much help as you can handle then … that Jenny's a fierce woman.' There was an awkward pause. 'May is looking well, is she? Seems happy?'

My mother must have nodded or shrugged, some wordless communication, as there was silence in the next room. I stood at the fire, brushing turf-dust from my hands, and looked around me. Nothing felt right.

Nan sighed, and I jumped as if she'd let out a yell.

James Hueston murmured in the kitchen. 'I feel I need to apologise to your boys for the state they found me in yesterday. I was … well… I was very much the worse for wear, missus, and I'd hate for them to think that I was *that* kind of a man.'

The window was rattling a low, continuous samba behind the curtain – like someone trying to get my attention. I took a deep swallow and struggled with the irrational feeling that I was somehow standing my ground. The back of my neck crawled with the sensation of being watched.

Ma's big shoulder-bag was just in front of me, but instead of getting her fags and leaving, I stood quietly listening to the shifting, living silence of the room.

The floorboards creaked, the unmistakable feel of someone moving their weight on the floor beside me. Despite the cosy heat and the kindly light, my heart began creeping slowly up my throat. A cold breeze passed over the back of my neck. It felt as though something were circling me, and I had to stop myself from backing up against the wall, to ease the vulnerable feeling between my shoulderblades.

Low and almost inaudible, a voice whispered into my ear, 'Pat.'

I jumped, and my hands flew out as if to ward something off. 'Who's that?' I whispered, scanning the room with bulging eyes.

Ma's voice drifted from the kitchen, gently encouraging James Hueston to continue. 'You'd been drinking?' she said.

'Truth is, missus ... a bit like your little girl there, I've been having some terrible dreams myself lately, and I finally tried to drown them in a bottle. It's not an excuse but ...' His voice trailed off, and the kitchen was very quiet for a moment.

The voice spoke in my ear again.

'Pat.'

I felt a little puff of breath on my cheek and jerked back at the physical intrusion into my space. A welcome spark of anger cut through my fear.

'Go away,' I said. 'Leave us alone.'

There was a pause, as though something had been shocked into stillness. That surprised me, and I felt a little rush of confidence, a real sense of my own power. Behind me, on the mantelpiece, a small china dog began to vibrate, rattling gently against the stone of the mantle. I glared at it.

'Cut that out,' I said.

The dog stopped its rapid jittering as suddenly as it had begun. Very, very quietly, but with a strength that amazed me even while I was doing it, I spoke out into the room: 'I want you to leave him alone. Do you hear me? Leave my brother alone. And leave Francis alone, too. I mean it.'

I heard a desperate rushing noise within the room, and a fierce, cold draught gusted from the fireplace against the back of my legs. There was a low, agonised moaning. To anyone else, it would have been the sound of the wind scouring the house, but I knew it was here, in the room, rising up from the walls. It was the very essence of desolation.

'You're not welcome here,' I said. 'I want you to leave.'

The wind wailed in the chimney. At that moment, I felt an awful wave of nausea stagger me backwards, and I slumped against the wall. There was a tearing sensation in my chest – a terrible kind of *rending* – and I grabbed the front of my jumper in sudden agony.

And then there was nothing. No more sound. No more sensation. Just a quiet, empty room, and an unexpected feeling of abandonment and remorse.

'Oh Patrick!' said Nan. She was looking up at me with wide-eyed dismay. 'Oh Patrick,' she said again. 'What have you done?'

'Pat?' Ma called, worry in her voice. 'Is your nan alright?'

'She's grand, Ma. She's just talking in her sleep. Hang on and I'll get her settled.' Nan and I stared at each other: me splayed against the wall, clutching my chest, she shaking her head slowly, her eyes full of tears. I wobbled across to tuck the blanket a little better around her, and stroked her cheek with the back of my finger. 'It's all right, Nan. Everything's fine. No need to be afraid now.'

'But Patrick,' she quavered. 'Your poor brother …'

I stroked her cheek and forced myself to smile at her. Her eyes began to drift shut. 'He'll be okay, Nan,' I murmured. 'We'll fix everything, don't worry.'

'Your poor brother.' She was floating off, her eyes closing, her breath deepening. I stayed by her for a few moments, the way I would with Dee, just to make sure she was fully under. Then I straightened up and brought Ma's her fags.

Everyone but Dom was looking at me expectantly when I entered the room. I handed Ma her cigarettes and made what felt like a rueful little shape with my mouth. 'I think the wind startled her a little bit. She's gone back asleep now.'

There were *ahs* and nods of understanding from Ma and James Hueston. Dom was not on the same bus at all. He was gazing at James Hueston with a kind of floaty curiosity.

'What are your bad dreams about?' he asked.

James Hueston gave him a long, searching look.

Ma shifted Dee and flicked her eyes to the old man. 'Ah, Dom,' she said. 'Mr Hueston mightn't want to talk about things like that.'

'It's alright,' murmured James Hueston. 'I don't mind.' But then he just sat there, silently looking down at the table, as though gathering the right words. He delicately picked a little flake of stray tobacco from his lip and rubbed it between his thumb and forefinger as he thought.

I couldn't sit down. I just couldn't. I went to the sink with the pretence of getting myself a drink of water and let the tap run. I could see into the sitting room from here. Nan's feet were visible, resting on the poof. She seemed fine. The room seemed perfectly peaceful. I felt powerful and dislocated all at once. I had sent that thing packing! With just a command, it had run away. Was that all it had taken? In the end was that all we'd had to do? Tell the soldier – the bad man – to leave? Command, and he would have to obey?

The window over the sink shook gently in its frame, and I glanced at it. It knocked twice. *Bang. Bang.* Very angry. Only my own face glared back at me from the glass. The feeling of dislocation grew. My eyes were dark. I looked furious with myself.

I swallowed the water convulsively. It was cold enough to splinter my teeth. I tore my eyes from my own reflection and forced myself to sit back down at the table.

'I've been dreaming the same things since the war.' James glanced at my ma. 'The First World War,' he said, and she nodded. 'I were in the service in the second war, too, but I were a mechanic in the RAF then, didn't see no action.'

Ma smiled. Her brother Gary had been an RAF mechanic at the end of World War II. She didn't mention this to James Hueston, but that didn't surprise me; Ma didn't talk much about Gary's being in the British armed forces. There were some people on our road who were pissy about it, and Ma had learnt to carry her pride in her big brother quietly, inside herself.

James was looking down at the glowing tip of his fag as though there were a picture show running there that only he could see. His Woodbine was held between his two middle fingers, the glowing end sheltered in the cup of his palm, the smoke rising up between his fingers. A lot of old men smoked like that. Dad had told me it was from hiding the bright end of their fags at work or at war.

The old man raised the cup of his hand to his mouth, the fag completely invisible to the casual observer, and took a deep pull. The smoke trickled slowly out his nose and from the corners of his mouth as he contemplated my mother.

'You believe in ghosts, missus?'

Dom jumped, and I sat straighter in my chair. I flicked a wary glance at my mother. Olive Finnerty was the most practical, down-to-earth, no-nonsense female you'd ever get to meet. She had no truck with bedtime scares or night terrors. You came complaining to Ma that you were scared of the dark, the most sympathy you'd get would be a clatter to the back of the head and an abrupt command to get a grip on yourself. My stomach tightened in anticipation of her response. I didn't want her scoffing at this old man, and maybe cutting this important topic off at the knees.

Ma regarded James Hueston thoughtfully. The house moved around us with the storm, shifting and sighing. Dee's breathing was a gentle, steady undercurrent, and the Aga ticked quietly in the background as the fire in its belly began to die down. Ma nodded. She looked down at Dee and nodded again. 'I think any person who believes in the afterlife must automatically have a belief in ghosts, Mr Hueston.' She gave the old man a very direct look. 'But I think it's more likely that a person'd find themselves distressed by their memories than by any supernatural spirit.'

James Hueston chuffed a little breath out his nose. 'Well,' he said, 'I been *distressed by my memories* for most of my life then, missus. And for most of my life they've been just that: memories, bad dreams of things that already happened. I can deal with that, so I can. But recently ...' He paused and took another compulsive drag on his cigarette, as if to stop himself talking stubbed it out, and ran a hand over his eyes.

I leant forward. 'Recently, Mister Hueston?'

He didn't look at me, just reached for another fag and lit it. He blew a long, grey blast of smoke out of his nose and came to a decision. 'Recently,' he said, 'they've been more like hauntings.'

'Yes!' I cried.

Ma and James looked sharply at me.

'Shamie,' murmured Dom, and they turned to look at him.

He was slouched lazily against the table now, watching the old man from under drowsy lids. He stretched his arm towards James Hueston a little, his palm up as though he wanted the old man to take his hand. The name Shamie bumped something in my memory, tugging at my chest. James Hueston smiled at Dom, sadly – fondly almost – and there was a moment of intimate connection between the two of them that made my stomach tighten. Ma frowned at them with wary uncertainty, and I willed her to back away, to remain an observer for just a moment longer.

'Aye,' breathed the old man. 'I were called Shamie once upon a time.'

Dom's eyes sparkled with amusement, and he began to hum softly under his breath. I didn't recognise the tune, but it was pure vaudeville, a real Nan special. James Hueston smiled in recognition of it.

'Oh aye!' he said happily. 'I remember that!' He began singing in a quiet baritone: 'I'll be your little *honey*, I will promise that, said Nellie as she rolled her dreamy *eyes*.' He grinned and began nodding his head in time with the song. Dom joined in the words, their two voices blending sweetly as if they were used to singing together. *It's a sin to say so Mommy*, said the *bird* on Nellie's hat. Last night you said the same to Johnny *Wise*.'

The two of them laughed and Dom sat back in his chair, the picture of relaxed delight. My attention was firmly on my ma, who had a confused, suspicious look on her face.

'Where did you learn that song, Dom?' she asked sharply.

I leapt in, drawing her eyes instantly to me. 'Nan taught it to us, Ma.

Mister Hueston was singing it when we first met him on the harbour.'

She regarded me with narrowed eyes. I could practically hear her running Nan's back-catalogue of songs through her mind. There were hundreds of them from vaudeville to jazz to musical; I imagined them like cards flipping on a roller-index in her mind: 'If You Knew Susie', 'Don't Sit Under the Apple Tree', 'Sally', 'My Old Man'. James Hueston's voice intruded on her thoughts, and she turned her attention to him, still frowning.

'I spent a lot of time in this kitchen when I were a lad.'

Dom nodded in happy recollection, a loopy smile on his face. He was starting to worry me. No, if I was honest with myself, he was starting to infuriate me. If there hadn't been such a tangle of feet under the table I'd have kicked the legs off him.

Wake up, you bloody lunatic, I thought fiercely. *Stop drawing Ma's attention to yourself!*

James Hueston went on talking, looking around the kitchen as he spoke. 'I were great pals with the two boys who lived here. They were … I suppose they were like brothers to me. And their mother …' He paused a minute, then flicked a glance at my ma. 'My own mother died when I were three, missus. Nancy Conyngham were like a replacement, you know? Until I were nine years old, I spent more time in this kitchen than I did in my own house.' He grinned at her; it was a sunny memory for him. She smiled back, softening. 'Fran and Lorry and I went to school together, ate together. Very often shared the same bed. You know, I can quite honestly say, they were the best years of my life.'

'Fran and Lorry,' I whispered.

'Fran and Lorry Conyngham,' echoed James Hueston.

Dom had become very still, leaning back in his chair, his arms sprawled on the table. His eyes were focused on nothing, his breathing slow and deep. Still smiling faintly, he looked as though he were peacefully asleep with his eyes open, and I knew that Francis was remembering. He was far away, reliving the memories of the short, happy life the old man was describing.

Ma's eyes were on James Hueston; she was concerned for him. Like Dom, the old man was far away, walking the private halls of his childhood. But he had already come to the end of his happy memories, it seemed, and my stomach did a slow flip as the sunshine drained from his face.

Still smiling contentedly, Dom glanced at James. The old man's wretched expression stole the smile from my brother's eyes. Dom swallowed and pulled himself up, sitting straight in his chair, as if to fully face what came next — as if to brace himself for the truth. He waited, the light glinting off the polished surfaces of his snow-white cheekbones. His eyes became so dark that no light reflected from them at all. He couldn't seem to bring himself to ask the question I knew was expanding in his chest, so I did it for him.

'The boys who lived here,' I said. 'They were murdered, weren't they? They were murdered by a soldier.'

The shock on the old man's face was almost amused. 'My God, lad! What a thing to say. Murdered! What on earth made you think that?'

Dom and I traded a confused look. We were both lost. I turned beseechingly back to James Hueston.

'*What* then?' I asked. 'What happened to Francis?'

'He died,' said James.

His eyes searched mine, trying to fathom my weird questions. Then he turned to look searchingly at Dom, and it hit me like a truck. James didn't understand! All this time I thought he'd known that *this* was Francis, right here in front of him, but he hadn't. What, then, had he seen in the garden when he'd asked, *Do you know what's wrong with your brother?* What was it he had been going to tell me?

'When I were eight,' said James, 'poor Fran died of diphtheria. He were ten years old. It were awful. An awful, awful death.' He shuddered. 'You know that disease, missus?' He looked at Ma and she nodded sadly. James Hueston closed his eyes. 'Poor Fran,' he said. 'He were a lovely lad. Kind, full of divilment. What a death.'

'Oh,' said Dom, 'oh.'

'What … what does it do to you?'

'Ah, Pat!' Ma shook her head in distress. 'Don't.'

But James Hueston tried to explain, holding his throat as an illustration. 'It chokes you, lad. Your throat swells up inside, and you choke to death.'

Choking. So it hadn't been asthma at all. Dom had been *choking*.

Dom was absolutely distraught now, his whole face working for control, his lightless eyes glittering with tears. 'Shamie,' he whispered. 'Oh, Shamie, don't say that.'

James Hueston frowned. I saw something starting to dawn in his face. Then he suddenly sat bolt upright, straight as a rod, and I knew he'd got it. Whatever it was James Hueston had started off thinking about Dom, *now* he'd got it. His eyes grew rounder and rounder as my brother nodded slowly, staring at him.

Ma cleared her throat, all her attention on James Hueston – all her concern focused on him and the distress he was showing. 'So,' she ventured, 'if you were around when the Conynghams were children, you must have known my mother-in-law.' It was clear from the tone of Ma's voice and her too-bright expression that she was trying to change the sadness of the conversation and bring James back to happier times. He dragged his attention to her, only half his mind on her question, his eyes owlish.

'Beg ... beg your pardon, missus?'

'My mother-in-law; she would have been Cheryl Byrne back then. May Conyngham said ...'

'Cheryl Byrne? Jesus, missus! Do you mean *Lacy*? Lacy is your ...?' James snapped his eyes to Dom, then to me, examining us. Dom was nodding again, empathising with his confusion. 'Oh God, I see it now!' he exclaimed. 'Their hair! Their eyes! And sure, your husband was the image of Cheryl! How could I not have noticed that?' He became utterly speechless for a moment, his hands making little disbelieving movements. 'Cheryl ... but sure, she left after the war. She went ... she disappeared into Dublin. They said she married late ... some old man with a big family. Had herself a child with him ... that must be ... her boy is your husband?' He looked at Ma as if she needed to reconfirm the facts for him.

Ma smiled and nodded. 'That's David,' she said.

There was a breathy whisper of sound from him, and he sank back in his chair. He looked very fragile to me just then, with the light blaring down on his thin old face. The flesh under his eyes and around his jaw seemed too loose and too pale. He looked as though he'd just been punched in the stomach. For a moment, I wondered at how all this might affect someone of his age. Then I felt guilty, because despite the impact this was obviously having on him, I still wanted to grab the front of his shirt and shake him 'til all the answers fell out.

'Who's the *man*?' I demanded. 'Who's the *soldier*? What happened to Lorry?'

Ma looked at me as if I had two heads, but James's attention had slid past us, to the doorway of the sitting room, and I don't think he'd heard me at all. His mouth fell open and he rose slowly to his feet.

'Lacy,' he breathed.

'I'm so glad you're here, Shamie. Laurence told me you had come home, but I wasn't sure I'd get to see you.'

Nan was standing on the threshold, the tartan car-blanket held around her shoulders like a shawl. Her long white hair had come loose in shining waves around her face, and she looked utterly changed. There was something girlish about her; she was barely recognisable.

Ma made a move to go to her, but she was pinned down under Dee's sprawling weight. I half rose from my seat, alarmed. Nan was so thistledown-looking, so fey! It felt like she might just float off if I didn't catch her quick. Dom beat me to it. With one of those alien gestures of courtliness, he stood and pulled his chair out, gesturing for Nan to take his seat. Nan didn't acknowledge him. She had eyes only for James Hueston.

The two old people stood for a moment gazing at each other, and for that moment the house was completely still – no sounds of the storm, no noise from the Aga, nothing. It was as though everything had paused just for them; as if their years of history had earnt them one perfect bubble of calm.

Then James Hueston pushed his chair abruptly backwards and strode around to Nan. All the time he was rounding the table, Nan held his eyes with this – this *gentle* look on her face. He stopped very close to her; then he hugged her, inhaling as he did so, her hair, her soft, powdery scent. Nan laid her forehead on his shoulder, and for a moment James held her close, her hands trapped against his chest, her hair falling forward across his arms.

'Shamie,' she whispered. She pulled back so that James had to hold her at arm's length. 'You shouldn't wear your uniform,' she said. 'It's not safe. They've been spitting on the poor boys getting off the boats.'

James looked down at his ordinary brown jacket and cord trousers and laughed bitterly. 'It's a bit late to be finding that out now, Lacy darlin'.'

She put a hand to his cheek, deeply sympathetic, so very tender. The rest of us may as well have been spectres for all the two of them noticed us. Our eyes hopped between them, from one to the other and back, but we'd faded like wallpaper into the background of their existence.

'Did you have trouble when you got here, Shamie? Were people cruel? There's been such awful things said …' Her lips trembled for a moment, and she bit them and ducked her head, her hand still on his cheek. She patted his face, without looking at him, and he pulled her back in, his chin on the top of her head. He stroked her hair and stared blankly at the wall behind her.

'I can't say I expected it, Lacy,' he said. 'I can't say I did. There were … It were all very different when I got home. I were still the same lad – still an Irish lad – but all some folk seemed to see was the uniform.'

'They've been so cruel,' she said. 'The whole family. The whole damnable lot. I wasn't certain I could bear it. At times I felt that I was going mad. If it hadn't been for Jenny … She stayed such a good friend …'

'May wouldn't see me,' he interrupted. The words came out under pressure, bluntly, as if he was telling a dark secret for the first time. 'I waited for her on Church Street. She spat in my face.'

Dom gasped at that and whispered, 'No'. The thought of his sister spitting in Shamie's face was obviously too terrible for Francis to contemplate.

'I think I'm going to go to Dublin,' whispered Nan, her eyes open, her forehead resting on James's chest. 'I think I'll disappear.'

James Hueston pushed her back and held her away from him so that he could look at her. He was angry with her, frustrated. 'I *looked* for you!' he cried. 'When I came back from the war. I couldn't believe you'd left. Lacy, I had a *picture*. A photograph. For you. I had his things. Why didn't you wait? Why didn't you leave word for me to find you?'

Nan ran her fingers down his jacket, counting buttons that weren't there, straightening a lapel that didn't exist. 'Ah, Shamie. He's gone. And soon you'll be gone. What use are photographs to me?'

'What do you mean, I'll be gone?'

She looked into his eyes, and there was my nan. That straightforward, no-nonsense look. 'You won't stay to take this abuse. Not after all you've been through. Not James Plunkett Hueston. To hell with them and their narrow world. I give you a month, and you'll be off, to make a life for yourself!' She gave his nose a cheeky tweak, and he ghosted a smile at her.

'You're not wrong on that,' he said. 'I went back to England within the year, joined the merchant navy, and then the RAF. I saw the *world*, Lacy.'

She tilted her head at him and brushed his hair back. 'Tell me you'll have a great life,' she whispered. It was as though he'd never spoken;

she was far away, in another world, another time, gazing up into a young man's face, their whole life ahead of them. 'Tell me you'll have the wonderful life he never got.'

James swallowed and said nothing, just kissed her forehead – a lingering kiss to seal his lips – and then pulled her in to rest his chin on her head again.

They stood that way for a long while. Eventually, my ma, spoke, quietly so as not to break the connection between the two old people. 'Mr Hueston?' she said. 'Were you sweethearts? Cheryl and yourself? Were you in love?'

James Hueston didn't stop stroking my nan's hair, but his eyes shifted to my brother. *Stop looking at Dom!* I almost shouted it at him. *Ma'll get suspicious!* Sure enough Ma followed the old man's eyes with a puzzled frown.

Dom was still standing with his hands resting on the back of his chair like the world's most patient maître d' waiting to seat a customer. He and James Hueston gazed at each other across the top of Nan's head. Dom's expression was tragic, a bleeding wound, every conflicted twist and turn of Francis's thoughts and emotions running across his polished-marble face like cloud-shadows on a hill. He was staring across the yawning gap of almost a century to the friend Francis had once loved; the friend who'd lived. A friend who knew the secrets that Francis perhaps no longer wanted to hear.

'Are you alright, Dom?' said Ma.

I got to my feet. 'I think Nan needs to sit down, Mister Hueston. She can have Dom's chair.'

James guided Nan to the chair and got her seated, tucking the car-blanket around her shoulders. She participated only on the most surface level, already miles away again. Dom stood behind them, looking as though he might fade away any minute; like he might just let go of the chair and slide to the floor. I shot a glance at Ma. She was frowning at him – squinting as if trying to see him through a fog. She had gathered Dee into a tight little hedgehog shape on her lap and was holding her very tightly. Her expression said: *What's going on?*

James Hueston turned his honest face to her, and she latched onto his words as if they were a life raft – gratefully allowing herself be distracted from the shambling wreck of her son.

'Lacy and I weren't sweethearts, missus. She were always the little pal of my heart, but we weren't never *that* way with each other. No, when we were teenagers, Lacy were engaged to my best friend. That is, she were engaged to Francis's brother, Lorry.'

Lost again, after
so long Running

At first I thought he meant – what? Some kind of child bride? Some weird Victorian arranged-marriage type deal? And then, God help me, way too slow, it hit me. Lorry hadn't died. Lorry hadn't died at all. He had grown up. God damn it, Lorry might even still be alive!

'Cheryl was *engaged*?' Ma was utterly astounded. 'Cheryl?' she repeated.

'*My* Lorry?' whispered Dom.

James Hueston's eyes began to drift to Dom again.

'Mr Hueston,' I said loudly, 'maybe you should sit down? You look shattered.' There was more of a command than a request to my voice, and I pulled back my own chair and offered it to him. He gave me a long, level look, and I tried to drill holes through him with my eyes. *Stop looking at Dom!* I don't think I blinked for about fifty seconds. Then James Hueston rounded the table, purposely keeping his eyes off my brother. He only flicked a brief glance at Dom as he sat in his chair.

'It's very cold, isn't it?' said Nan. 'That's because of Francis. Laurence says he's killing poor Dom.'

Dom leapt like a fish. He jerked his hands away from Nan. We all looked at her, a brief suspended moment of shock. Then Ma swallowed and blinked rapidly.

'Cheryl,' she said. 'You're upsetting Dominick. Please stop talking about him like that.'

Nan raised an eyebrow, looking Ma up and down. 'I'm not *complaining*, Olive. It's not anyone's *fault*. Francis is just a child. Sure, how was he to know? But if he had only listened to Laurence none of this would have happened, and Dom would be alright.'

Ma pressed her teeth together. I could see her counting slowly backwards from ten in her head. She turned apologetically to James Hueston, and I think she was talking to herself as much as the old man when she ground out, 'Cheryl can't help it, Mr Hueston. She says funny stuff sometimes, but it's not her fault. Try not to let it upset you, because … because she doesn't mean it. Before her stroke, she really was the most wonderful – the most *vibrant* woman. It would have done your heart good to see her.'

James Hueston's jaw worked slowly, as if he was chewing something unpleasant. I think he suspected the truth. I think that, unlike my ma, he could see the effect that Francis was having on Dom. I wondered if he longed to tell Ma. I wondered if, like me, he wanted to grab Ma's face and turn it to Dom and scream at her, 'Take a good look. Take a good long look at your son!'

Instead he said, 'Cheryl were always the loveliest person.'

I allowed myself check on Dom. He looked as though he were sinking – alone, desperate, confused – drifting out of reach. Nan was shivering, now, clutching the tartan car-blanket around her and frowning. Behind her, thin spidery threads of fog drifted around her shoulders. They were emanating from Dom, rising up from him in a slowly gathering mist as he stared at my nan.

'Dom!' I said sharply. He looked up at me and I was at a loss for what to say to him. I held his eyes with my eyes. I tried to tell him. *It's alright, I'm here. Look at me. Just keep looking at me. I'm here.* 'Do you want some toast?' I croaked lamely.

His shadow-eyes just glittered at me; his expression didn't change. But the fog dissipated without a trace into the air.

Ma answered me before Dom's silence became obvious. 'Toast would be lovely,' she said. 'Put the kettle on if you like.' She glanced at Dom, but of course she saw nothing, not a flicker of anything wrong. She dropped her eyes to look at Nan, who was hunched against the cold, and rocking. 'Maybe we should bring Nan back in to the fire,' she said.

'No, no,' drawled Nan, waving a hand dismissively. 'It's just Francis. If he'd stop breathing down my blooming neck, I'd be fine.'

Dom skittered back, distancing himself from Nan as much as possible in the small room.

Ma gave him a sympathetic little grimace. 'It's alright, pet. Don't pay her any notice. Sure, she'll be off on a different track altogether tomorrow. You remember the three days she thought I was Oliver Cromwell? She kept snarling at me, *Hell before Connaught, you blood-soaked tyrant*, and refusing to budge from the sofa.' She twisted a smile at him and wrinkled her nose in understanding.

Dom just kept backing off, his mouth open slightly, his arms hanging. I resisted the urge to go to him and just stood there with my heart lodged painfully beneath my Adam's apple, watching him shuffle backwards until he was smack up against the sink. James Hueston began talking, and I knew it was to distract our mother from the sight of her eldest son slouched against the counter like some cheap zombie extra.

'When Fran died, his poor mam just disintegrated,' said James, catching and holding my mother's attention. 'There was nothing left for her to give. She just sat down and never really got up; that's how it felt to us at the time. The girls took over running the house, looking after each other and their dad. But Lorry … poor Lorry.' James shook his head. 'Nancy couldn't stand the sight of him after that. Just couldn't bear to look at him. They had been so alike, you see, him and Fran. Twins.' He flicked a glance at Dom. 'Lorry came to live with me and Dad. Can't say it was … well … it weren't like it had been here. It weren't *comfy*, shall we say. My dad weren't ever home; he worked all the livelong day, and there just weren't no … there weren't no tenderness.' He watched Ma cradling Dee and nodded to himself. 'Aye. I missed Nancy Conyngham an awful lot – can't even begin to imagine how poor Lorry felt. It were just him and me from then on, all alone, the two of us. And we were so … it were … for a long time …' He struggled for words. 'Fran's death …' He glanced at Dom again. 'Fran's death just cut us to ribbons.'

'Oh yes, it did certainly,' agreed Nan softly. 'Poor Nancy was never the same, and Laurence lost all his sunshine. Remember, Shamie? He wouldn't let us call him Lorry anymore? I think it reminded him of Fran,' she murmured. 'That's what I think.'

Dom's eyes were brimming with tears. 'Poor Lorry,' he said softly. Ma shot him a look and creased her mouth and nodded, the two of them moved by the story, but each for an entirely different reason.

The old man fiddled with his cigarettes, lifted them, threw them down with a grimace, lifted them again. Finally, he opened the pack with a disgruntled 'gah!' and lit himself another fag. The sweet smoke hazed the air, and I inhaled it gratefully. It smelt like Grandda Joe and summer and normal times.

It shocked me when Nan reached across the table and helped herself to a Woodbine from James's pack, and even more so when James leant forward, natural as you please, and lit it for her. Ma gaped as Nan pulled in a lungful of smoke and held it like a pro. Evidently she was just as surprised as I was to see Nan with a fag in hand.

Nan knocked her head back, relishing the flavour, and eventually released the smoke in a fragrant blue stream that tumbled slowly through the pool of light from the ceiling lamp. 'Oh yes,' she said softly, her eyes following the curls and torrents in the light, 'your ma missed you an awful lot, Francis. She cut poor Laurence out of her life as surely as if you'd both died.'

Dom opened his mouth, his face questioning, but shut it again when James Hueston spoke.

'Been a long time since we sat and shared a fag in this kitchen, Lacy dear.' He tapped his finger on the table as he spoke, his eyes shifting from Dom to Nan. 'Do you remember? The last time we all sat round this table – Lorry, Jenny, May, yourself and myself – we played cards all night long.'

'That would have been poor Nancy's funeral,' said Nan.

'Mam?' whispered Dom.

Ma looked at him. 'Yes, love?' But Dom was looking at James, his thoughts on his long-dead but only now mourned mother, I suppose. Ma seemed to decide she'd imagined his hoarse whisper and turned her attention back to our miraculously lucid nan.

'What age were you, then?' I asked Nan. 'When Fran's mam died.'

Nan frowned. 'I was … oh, let me see … Laurence must have been …' She thought a moment, her lips moving as she calculated.

James shot a sideways glance at my brother. An acute column of cold was building around him. I could feel it advancing across the room to where I was standing. I dug my fingers into the back of my chair. James and I made eye contact for a moment.

'It were 1915,' said James, flipping ash into his saucer and turning his attention back to Nan. 'You and Lorry had been engaged for seven months. It were the year before me and Lorry joined the army. The year May found politics.'

'Oh May,' tutted Nan, shaking her head, her jaw popping.

'She were a brave woman,' countered James. 'They were all brave. All those men and women. Fighting to free Ireland.'

'You were brave too!' Nan pointed her fag at him. 'And no one should have ever implied otherwise! May Conyngham was a bloody fool to let politics come between you. She lost herself a great man when she broke your engagement. I could have strangled her.' Nan angrily stubbed her fag out. It was only half smoked, and she instantly regretted it. She gave James a sheepish look. He grimaced playfully at her and lit her another. They were as easy with each other as an old married couple, as comfy as worn slippers.

I hadn't seen my nan this alive, this *now*, in over nine months. James Hueston, this warm, generous-spirited man, had invoked her for us. He had called forth my nan and he had warmed my brother, just by being himself. What cruelties could possibly have brought a man like this to the water's edge on a winter beach? What could have driven him to surrender himself to those icy waves?

'What became of Lorry?' asked Dom. 'Please tell me, Shamie. What happened him?'

James Hueston vacillated for a moment. Then he stubbed out his cigarette. There was something final about that gesture, as if, unwilling to inflict this detail on Francis, James had decided not to continue. For a moment, I thought he might actually excuse himself and leave us all hanging. I nearly interceded, but Dom spoke again. 'Shamie,' he pleaded. *Please. I can't go on.* 'Just tell me.'

'I joined the army because he joined the army,' said James. 'I were a tough little gurrier, you know, and Lorry, he has this tender side to him. There was no way I were letting him go to war on his own. I promised Lacy that I'd keep him safe.' He smiled over at Nan, and she shook her head in grim self-recrimination.

'I should never have made you make that promise.'

'We were young, Lacy. We had no idea.' His face fell like a plummeting stone. 'We really had *no* idea.' He ran his hand over his eyes. 'So,' he said. 'Yes. Lorry joined up because … heh … because he was Lorry. And I tagged along behind because I loved him, and because it sounded like an adventure. And …' He shrugged. 'We got by. We made it through; we outlived every single one of our original platoon. Isn't that funny? Every man-jack of them dead by 1917. So,' he whispered, 'we end up in a mud-hole called Passchendaele, fighting forward and back for a few yards of muck and a shell of a town. And there we were, on Lorry's twentieth …' His eyes flicked to Dom. He seemed to stop, reconsider what he wanted to say, and start again somewhere else. 'On a … on a rainy night, near the end of 1917, we were running from one trench to another while the sky fell down around us. A really good friend of ours … Jolly … a real decent bloke … a good man … he … he slipped on the duckboards, he slammed into Lorry. Sent him flying. Sent him … sent him flying to the edge of the duckboards. And …'

'He went into the mud.'

They all looked up at me. My ma frowned with confusion.

But James wasn't surprised. 'Aye, lad,' he said quietly.

'Jolly pushed him into the mud.'

Dom mouthed the words after me. 'Jolly pushed him into the mud.' As if the repetition would force the sentence to make sense.

'Aye,' said James, eyeing me warily. 'God love him. Jolly knocked poor Lorry over. Couldn't do a thing about it.'

'And Laurence drowned. In the mud.'

James nodded, his eyes swimming. Dom repeated the word 'drowned', but without any emotion.

'It was very quick, Shamie,' I said. I flicked my eyes to Mam. 'It would have been very quick,' I said.

James Hueston tilted his head, as if begging me not to lie; as if the pain of a lie now would be worse than all the horrible 'maybe's he'd carried with him all his life. 'Are you sure?' he whispered. Not, *How do you know?* or *What are you talking about?* Just plain, honest belief that I was telling him the truth. 'Are you *sure?*'

I nodded. There was a long moment of stillness. The five of us – those who were awake, those of us freshly conscious of how utterly cruel life was – just suspended there for a moment of silence, each in our own cocoon of thought. I was thinking *So. That's how it happens. All the time. All over the world. People just fall away. There's no warning, and you can't do anything about it. No matter how old you get. You just lose people and lose people and lose them again, and you never get them back.*

I glanced over at Dom. *I'll get you back*, I promised, *I'll fix this.* But the Dom looking back at me was anything but Dom. He was Francis, all Francis, nothing but Francis, devastated and alone, looking out from a stolen face at the world he'd lost, at the friends he'd never get back. My stomach iced over at the sight of him. *When* would I fix this? How? *How?* Where was Dom? He seemed so *gone.* So utterly, irrevocably gone. Dom.

'You know the strangest part of it?' said James Hueston. He glanced up at Dom, then spoke directly to me. 'You think it will kill you,' he said. 'I thought all those things, each one as they happened, would be the last thing I'd be able to bear. But I'm *telling* you, you just go on. Life just goes on, and you travel on with it, through all the different things. And they all happen to you and you just sail through them and carry on. I thought ... ' He snapped his mouth shut. He glanced at my ma. And suddenly he was standing. He was pulling his coat on. He was pushing his fags into his pocket and looking around him in a glazed kind of confusion. 'I should go,' he said.

Ma reached for him, panicky with concern. 'Oh no, Mr Hueston! Don't go.'

James didn't seem to hear her. He turned to me again, as if he'd forgotten to pass on a message and wanted to deliver it before he went. 'See, yesterday morning, I'd had enough. I woke up, and the dreams had been so bad. I got up, and I couldn't shake them. I thought about things I hadn't thought about in years. About Francis and May, about Lorry and poor Jolly. I had ...' His hands were in his pockets; he was thinking very hard. He looked directly at me again, searingly, willing me to get the point. 'Son,' James said, 'I've had a good life. I want you to understand that. I left here when I realised this country would never acknowledge men like Lorry and me, and I washed my hands of the place. Had me a grand adventure of a life. You just *go on*. Understand? No matter what it throws at you, life carries you on, and you make the very best of it.'

I stood there frowning at him. What was he telling me this for? I didn't need to know this. I hadn't lost anything. *My* brother was coming back! But, despite my growing scowl, James Hueston just kept talking, and staring me in the eye.

'In 1947, after the second war, I married me a lovely Creole woman, a big grinning, roundy woman. We lived in Paris, where she were from. It were too late for childer, and her two boys never took to me, but we had a jolly old time together. We spent our whole lives laughing, 'til God took her. And even after *that*, I just went on. I had me a lovely life, son. I done *so much*! That's what I wanted to make clear. And after Tania died, bless her, I came back here and settled down and it's all been ... despite everything, it's all been *so good*! Life's been ...' He looked for a word, smiled when he found it. 'Life's been *tasty*,' he said. 'But the dreams got very strange these last few days and when I woke up yesterday morning it were as though none of that good stuff had ever happened. It were as though I'd only ever had the bad times.' He ran his hand over his face. 'All my hurts were distilled for me into something bitter, and that was all I could feel ... I think that it's because of Lorry, son. And Francis. I think they're more than a dream. I think, maybe they've always been more than a dream, because they never got the chance. Life never carried them on. You understand? Life never got tasty, and so all they have is their last moments and the bitterness of being *stuck*.'

He looked from Dom to myself and back again. Dom was completely blank. My ma was very quiet, her eyes roaming over James Hueston. She thought he was like Nan. She thought that this poor old man was wandering in his head, drifting in and out of lucidity, the hazy companions of his past side-by-side with the flesh and blood of his present.

James Hueston looked at me hard one more time. 'You're *not stuck*, boy. No matter what's happened, or what will happen. No matter what you lose. Life will carry you on – every tomorrow brings the hope of change. You got to know that. I wish I'd known it earlier; you got to let yourself be carried along.'

I could feel my fingernails splitting the brittle fabric of the chair-back. *What's he telling me this for? I've not lost anything. Dom's coming back! I'm going to fix it, and Dom's coming back. I don't need this old-man advice. I don't want this old-man advice.*

James saw this in my eyes, and he sighed and shook his head. Then he reached across the table and patted my mother on her arm. 'Thank you for your hospitality, missus. I mean what I said – if you need help, please send the boys for me. I'll do whatever I can for you.'

Ma nodded uncertainly.

'And thanks so much for what you're doing for Lacy. I don't have the words to thank you. I just don't have the words.'

Ma's face softened, and she nodded. James pushed his chair in and went and kissed Nan on the forehead.

'What about poor Dominick?' Nan asked, reaching up to clutch James's hand. 'I thought you'd be able to help, but it sounds like you don't have anything to give.'

Ma sighed wearily, assembled Dee into a manageable shape and got slowly to her feet. 'Oh Cheryl,' she groaned. 'Please stop.'

Dom, James, Nan and I glared at her, and her face flushed under our collective disapproval. She swallowed and dropped her eyes. She hoisted Dee's drooling weight onto her shoulder and mumbled without looking up at us. 'I'm sorry. I get so impatient … I'm so tired …'

James reached for Ma. I think he was going to try and explain, but Nan stood instead, squeezing his hand quickly before letting go and speaking gently to Ma. 'Take me up to bed, Olive love. Sure, we all need a rest.'

Ma met Nan's eyes. There was a moment of silent communication. Nan smiled and nodded. Ma swallowed hard and nodded back. 'Alright, Cheryl love.'

'I'll see Mr Hueston out, Ma. I'll lock up.'

Ma nodded gratefully at me, said goodnight to James and began to usher Nan from the room. At the foot of the stairs Nan turned and raised a hand to James who was standing watching them with his hat in his hand.

'Come visit me, Shamie,' Nan said. 'I might not be here, I go away sometimes. But, if you come visit … I think I might know you.' She squinted at him, uncertain of the sense of what she was saying.

'I'll visit, Lacy. Wild horses couldn't stop me, and that's the truth.'

Nan nodded without smiling, and the women disappeared around the bend in the stairs. James Hueston turned to me, about to speak, and I held up my hand. I felt my anger with him written all over my face. 'Not here,' I hissed, and I gestured at the door as much as to say, *Outside*.

Out we went. As the lights came on upstairs and all across the top of the house, we headed into the garden with Dom trailing behind us, silent and blank as a wall.

17. Cold Comfort

I led the way under the apple trees and out into the front garden. The breathless quiet that had descended when James and Nan first saw each other still had its hold on the night. The sky was a brilliant bowl of stars high above the purple silhouettes of the hurdy-gurdies. I was like a cold cyclone at the centre of all this peace, my anger so violent that I felt like I was spinning. I turned sharply in the middle of the garden and found myself face to startled face with James Hueston, who had expected me to bring him to the gate, I suppose, and was brought to a jarring halt by my sudden turn. Dom slouched at the back wall, looking up at us from under his hair.

'What in God's name was that all about?' I got right up in the old man's face, so he had to draw himself back a bit. I could see him force himself not to blink. I was reminded instantly of the brutish men of the day before and how they had pushed this poor old man around. But, my God, I was angry and, despite the uncomfortable echoes, I found myself poking him in the shoulder with a less than gentle finger. I just couldn't seem to hang on to my temper anymore. James Hueston had pushed my last button.

'You listen to me, *Mister* Hueston.' A jab to the shoulder and the old man fell back a step. 'I don't *need* you to tell me that life goes on. Alright? Because I haven't lost *anything*.' Another jab and another step back. Dom straightened and came forward from the wall. I kept my face close to James's. 'Dom's just *stuck*.' Jab. 'He's just *stuck*.' Jab. 'And all we have to do is get Francis *out of him* and everything will be *okay!*' Another vicious jab, and James was three more steps closer the wall. 'Don't be looking at me with big eyes and giving me sympathy speeches, because they're *bullshit*. I haven't lost *anyone*. Dom's coming *back*.'

My hand was grabbed suddenly, and the searing pain of Dom's icy touch cut through my anger. He bent my jabbing finger so far back that I thought he'd tear it from the root.

'You touch him again and I'll snap it right off, you hear me?' His white face was right up against mine, and I could see blue marbling threaded under his skin, feel the frost on his breath. I forced myself to nod as I stared into his ocean-black eyes. 'It's not Shamie's fault,' he grated. He gave my finger one final twist before releasing me, and I staggered back a step or two, cradling my screaming hand.

My heart was hammering away in my chest and my whole body was howling *fight fight fight*. I wanted to hold someone down. I wanted to pump my fist into their face. I wanted to grab them by their throat and squeeze 'til my hands were tired. I wanted to make someone pay and pay until they gave me everything back.

'Dom's not dead,' I snarled. 'He's *not*.'

Dom held my eye for a moment, making sure I didn't fly at his throat or something, and then he turned to James, his voice softening in brotherly concern. 'You alright, Shamie?' He reached to touch

James's arm, and the old man flinched back in fear. Dom paused in mid-gesture, his face crumbling. James stared at his hovering hand, back to Dom's face and at his hand again. Dom finally dropped his hand to his side, looking lost.

James Hueston scanned him up and down, taking in every detail of Dom's terrible condition in a way he hadn't been capable of 'til now. He shook his head, his eyes filled with that awful bloody sympathy. 'Fran,' he said finally, 'it *is* you in there, isn't it? What have you done to that poor boy?'

'His name is Dominick,' I growled. 'It's Dominick. Don't be calling him Fran. His name's not Fran.'

James Hueston turned that bloody sympathetic look on me, and I wanted to slap it from his face. 'Son,' he said gently, flying in the face of my rage, 'your brother isn't here anymore. He's gone.'

I flew at him, my hands clawed, but Dom flung an arm out, without looking, and stopped me. It was like running into an iron bar set in concrete. I just bounced off him.

'What did you see?' Dom asked James. 'When you met me in the garden, you saw something. You were going to say something to Pat … you wanted to *tell* us something, and then their mother came out and we all had to pretend.'

I shuffled up beside Dom and the two of us looked at the old man with equal intensity. I didn't envy him, out here alone with us, the hunched and staring freak-twins: one of us on the edge of violence, one of us a black-eyed monstrosity. To his credit, James didn't step back. He held his ground and met our eyes. I think he was searching for the words least likely to set me off.

'Last night I woke up from another dream,' he said. 'We were in

Passchendaele again, me and Lorry. Its always Passchendaele these days. Only things weren't the same. Things were weird ...'

I ground my teeth in frustration. 'Jesus *Christ*! What the hell has that got to do ... ?'

James snapped his eyes up to me and I stopped. I clenched my hands and my teeth and forced myself to shut up. 'It started off as just a memory,' said James. 'One of those moments that stays with you all your life. I often think of that day. It were a rare moment of peace in that terrible battle. We were drinking tea, Jolly brought me tea ... I started to sing ...'

'The *Panis Angelicus*.' I murmured, my fists loosening, my mind filled once more with the buzzing of flies, the pull and crack of sun-dried mud on my face, the stench of rotting bodies and the petrol-scented tea.

James nodded, apparently unsurprised that we'd been sharing dreams. 'But as soon as I started singing, it all changed and suddenly it was all very strange. Lorry fell down. Water came out of his mouth ... He tried to tell me something.' James glanced at Dom. 'Something about Francis.'

'He told you, *He's found somewhere to hide*,' I said. All the belligerence drained from me. My stomach did its now familiar lazy flip. We both turned to stare at Dom and he backed slowly away, his eyes moving from one to the other of us. His hands came up slightly, as if to ward us off.

'I didn't mean it,' he whispered. 'I didn't ...'

'When I woke up,' continued James, 'Lorry was there as usual, glaring at me from the corner of the room. I'm used to him being angry – he's always angry – but this time he was bloody furious, and for the first time in years, he scared me.'

'What do you mean?' cried Dom. 'What do you *mean*, Lorry was there?' He stepped forward, and now he was the one with the dangerous edge to his voice and I was the one stepping protectively in front of the old man.

'Son,' said James, 'Laurence has been with me every step of the way since the day he died. I don't know why – maybe because we were such good friends; maybe because I was there when he died. Who knows? But he's followed me ever since. There's not been a night I haven't woken up to see him standing at the window or glaring at me from the corner of the room, anger radiating off him like a curse. I thought for years that he was angry with me. But he's not. He's just *angry*. He's just bloody furious. All the time. It's like that's all he has left, maybe all that's actually left of him: his rage.'

Dom's face fell. He was beginning to understand – and so was I. I turned to him. He shook his head; he stepped back.

'The man on the cliff,' I said, 'the soldier. That was *him*. And in the garden. The phantom ...' Dom continued to move away from me, backing slowly towards the deep shadows of the arch. 'The phantom who was chasing you ... the *bad man* ... that was Lorry. That was *Lorry*, you bloody idiot. It was Lorry all along!' Dom continued to shake his head and retreat. I yelled after him, blindly lashing out in my fury. 'You've been running away from your own bloody brother, you git! You stole Dom for nothing! You bloody coward! You coward! Why didn't you just bloody *look*, why didn't you bloody *listen*! It was your *brother*! How could you not know?'

Dom turned clumsily at the arch. He staggered briefly and then ran back under the apple trees. The shadows swallowed him and I made to follow. James Hueston grabbed me by the arm, his fingers surprisingly strong. He twisted me around to look at him, thrusting his angry face into mine this time, making *me* fall back with the weight of *his* anger.

'Shut up,' he said viciously. 'Let the poor bugger go.' We glared at each other for a moment, then James released me with a little shove so that I stumbled back. His expression softened instantly. 'Of course he didn't know. How could he? All these years he's been looking for a gentle, laughing ten-year-old boy − not a furious man, not an English soldier.' He hesitated, reluctant. 'Maybe you wouldn't recognise *your* twin, either.'

Something about the way he said this made my knees turn to water. I remembered the whisper of 'Pat' in the sitting room, and I pressed my fingers to my cheek at the memory. 'What did you see?' I whispered. 'Before Ma came out. What were you going to tell me?'

'I weren't sure at first. I thought … well, I thought your poor brother was just being haunted, like me. It takes its toll, and I guess I thought he were sick from it … but as we got talking, and he called me Shamie and he sang Fran's song and … just so many little things. That *cold*.' He shivered, and looked at me, the outrageousness of what we were discussing clear in his eyes. 'God help us, it really is Francis, isn't it? He's inside that poor boy.'

I nodded. He swallowed.

'Last night, I woke up from the dream and Lorry was there, standing in the corner of the room, as usual, glaring at me. But he had a boy with him. A boy I never seen before, until I got here and I realised it were your brother. It were Dom.'

'You had a dream about Dom?'

'Lorry had him by the scruff of the neck. Poor lad was kicking and screaming. All I could hear was the sea … Normally when Lorry tries to talk, all I can hear are those bloody Jack Johnsons exploding, but this time all I could hear was the sea pounding, a heavy surf filling up the room.'

'You were remembering,' I whispered. 'You were just *remembering*. We saved you from the sea, and you dreamt about us.'

'I weren't dreaming, son. I've seen enough of Lorry these last decades to know when I'm dreaming. He were there. And so were your brother. It were like Lorry wanted to show me him; like he had dragged him from somewhere just to show me. Lorry had a good grip on him, but your brother were fighting like a dog; eventually he got loose and ran away. Lorry ran after him … and that was that.'

I stared at him, my fingers still pressed to the memory of my own name whispered in ghost-breath against my cheek. Dom was a ghost. Francis had pushed him from his body, and now he was a ghost. Who had I sent away? Who had it been that called me? My mind turned from this thought. It just rolled over and went numb.

'I don't know what to tell you, son, except what I told you before. Life will …'

I held my hand up to stop James talking and began to turn away from him, my head full of buzzing.

'I don't know what to tell you …' he called after me.

I left him alone in the sandy garden and as I passed through the arch and into the cold shadows of the apple trees, I heard the gate click behind him and a bottle roll away from under his feet as he shuffled home through the debris of the amusement park.

18. Hate the Boy

Hate the Boy

All the upstairs lights were off now, but the kitchen light still spilt out from behind the hydrangeas, cutting a luminous path through the gloom. I stood in the dark under the apple trees and listened to the sound of Francis crying. It was the hoarse, choking, hopeless sound of someone who knows there's nothing that can be done.

I had only heard someone cry like that once before, and that had been Dom – the real Dom. It had scared me then, and I had never heard crying like it since. Even when Grandda Joe died, even when Dad lost Grandad Peadar, the crying had been different. It had been done in the comfort of another person's arms, with the knowledge that you were safe and protected and had nothing to be ashamed of. This? This was the lonely bitterness of guilt, and the understanding that you stood alone in a pitch-black world.

We were twelve, when I'd first heard that kind of crying; we'd been fishing with Dad and Grandda Joe. The two men had walked ahead, carrying most of the tackle and the picnic stuff back to the car. Dom and I were trudging silently along behind, our own rods bouncing on our shoulders. We were pleasantly shattered, content to put one foot in front of the other and nothing else. The tar sucked at our feet and heat-devils made the road shimmy and waver against the air. It was baking hot. The tall brambles on either side of the winding country lane hung breathless and still.

We didn't hear the car. The encroaching hedges and dead summer air conspired to flatten the sound and it was on us before we knew it: a little pale-blue Ford Anglia with a lumpish shape at the wheel; here then gone in an explosion of sound and exhaust. The driver probably never even saw us; he was bombing along so fast. I shoved Dom one way and threw myself the other, and we ended up hung on the brambles like tinker's washing, our rods slung across the branches of the hawthorn. We looked at each other across the haze of exhaust smoke, our mouths hanging open. Then I laughed, and Dom's slow grin spread across his face, and we wordlessly peeled ourselves from the thorns.

The bird was in the middle of the road when we rounded the bend. It must have been hit by the car, or caught in its downdraft and slammed against the road. It was fluttering in an erratic circle on the hot tarmac, its movements too uncoordinated even to be an attempt at flight. My stomach turned over at the sight of its pained convulsions. Its gaping beak and emotionless, suffering eyes made my skin crawl in sympathy and revulsion.

I lay my rod down on the verge and went and hunched over the bird, my hands out, my intentions uncertain. It flopped and spasmed and gasped. My hands hovered over it. I couldn't bear the thought of touching it – feeling its broken bones, perhaps, grating under my hands; its guts coming out, maybe; or something awful with its eyes. I could have picked it up easily, but I ended up just shuffling around after it, my hands poised but useless.

I was pushed gently to one side, and Dom hunkered down in my place. Unhesitatingly he put his hand down on top of the fluttering creature, holding her between the cup of his hand and the road. Her glossy head stuck out between the arch of his thumb and forefinger, the neck straining. Her bright-yellow beak was open unnaturally wide, the tongue poking far out. Her gold-rimmed eyes glittered. Dom took her head in his other hand, gently closing her beak within the grip of his fingers, then twisted his hands quickly in opposite directions, breaking her neck in one swift movement.

I straightened too quickly at the sight. The heat wrapped around me, and I twisted away, staggering off to dry-retch into the long grass beneath the brambles. It was cooler there, in the shade of the tall hedge, and I stayed crouched with my hands on my knees, waiting for my heart to slow down.

When I turned around, Dom was standing with the bird at his feet. He was looking at it, his arms hanging loosely at his side, his face blank. Then his chest jerked as if he was going to puke or hiccup, and he made a strange noise, and suddenly he was crying. His knees buckled just a little, and his head dropped back so that his mouth was opened wide, and he *cried*. It didn't last long – a frightening thunderstorm, passing quickly in summer – but for its duration I remained scared and frozen, watching him as I'd watched that poor bird, too cowardly to do anything.

Here in this frostbitten garden, in the dark, the crying sounded just the same. The same desolation. The same loss. Francis leant to one side of the kitchen door, his back to the wall. I stepped from the cold shelter of the apple trees and stood opposite him. The rectangle of light from the kitchen was a golden border between us, and I could barely see him in the shadows. I watched, my jaw tightening, as he laid his head back against the bricks and let his grief consume him.

He had stolen my brother. He had pushed my brother out into the howling world of ghosts, and now he stood there bawling with the same sorrow that Dom had shown when he had taken that poor bird's life. *But you did this out of cowardice*, I thought. *Without mercy. You are not Dom.* I felt my thoughts grey over. My hands balled into fists.

That day, when Dom had finally stopped crying, I had gone to him in a sudden rush of protectiveness and gratitude, and grabbed him. He'd been so surprised that he'd yelled. Then he had subsided into the hug, his arm twining around my waist. After a brief moment, he'd wiped his nose on the shoulder of my jumper and I'd pushed him off, swatting him in relieved disgust. We'd ignored the dead bird, retrieved our rods and continued on.

There would be no continuing on today, no hugs, and I didn't wait 'til Francis had finished crying. Instead, I strode across the bright splash of light, my fists raised above my head, and slammed them down on the tops of his shoulders with a cry.

He grunted and fell to his knees, and I raised my arms again, bringing them down on his arched back in a double-fisted *thump* that vibrated up my arms to my teeth. He let himself fall to his side, wrapped his arms around his head and just went on crying. I brought my foot back in silent rage, fully intent on kicking him in the head. I've no doubt that kick could have killed him – I was mindless and blind – but, at the last minute, I stopped myself and punched him instead, hard on his back. The blow echoed hollowly in his chest and reverberated in my head. He did nothing, and some of the deafness of my rage faded as I realised he was still crying, huddled against the wall, heedless of my blows, weeping in long, groaning breaths as if nothing else existed but his grief.

I flung myself onto my knees and hauled him around to face me. I shook him furiously.

He didn't even seem to register my violence. 'I didn't mean it,' he whispered. 'Oh, help me. Help me, God. I didn't mean it.'

'Yes, you *did*. You stole Dom's body. You *killed* him. *You killed him!*'

His eyes opened with renewed horror. 'NO!' he said. 'Don't think that. I *didn't* mean it. I didn't! I would *never* ...'

He was desperate for me to believe, but I was desperate for someone to blame, and my rage had finally crested beyond thought. I don't know how far I would have gone — what depths of violence I would have sunk to — had I not punched him in the mouth then, hard enough to split his lip.

The edges of the wound opened white against the blue of his skin, but no blood came out. *Of course not*, I thought, *corpses don't bleed.* This sucked all the power from me, and I released him, staring at the bloodless wound on his mouth.

He curled against the wall and rested his head on his knees. Dom's heavy curls fell in limp rat's tails onto the soiled denim of his beloved new jeans. He sobbed again and laced his fingers over his head, Dom's raggedly bitten fingernails digging into the backs of his hands. 'I'm sorry,' he whispered.

'If I could kill you, without hurting Dom's body, I would. You've broken everything. You've *ruined* everything.'

'I only jumped to get away from the man,' he said, his voice thick and muffled.

'Shut up.'

'Oh God, it was Lorry. Lorry was here all this time.'

His breath broke up again into ragged little sobs, and he lost control for another moment. I let myself topple over backwards into the sand and dug the heels of my hands into my eyes, listening to him cry.

'I mean it, Francis. Shut up, or so help me God.'

'I wuh … wanted to protect … I … I can't remember … I can't remember if it was you or your brother.'

'It was DOM!' I yelled, rolling onto my elbows to face him. 'It was DOM, you stupid bastard! Can't you at least remember which of us you *killed*!'

'I wanted to *protect* him. I jumped in front of him, I tried to cover him with muh … with my body.' His teeth were bared, and his hands fisted up by the sides of his face in a physical effort not to break down. He stared at me with eyes that showed white all around the iris. He was raw, as raw as I felt. We were bleeding all over the place from invisible wounds.

'Something *happened*,' he said. 'Something *slipped* and suddenly I wuh … suddenly I was in a tiny dark space. It was too hot. There was no air. And we were pressed up against one another, struggling against one another. This other person. I thought …' He scrambled to his knees and put his face close to mine in an effort to get me to understand. Dom's face, his black hair plastered down over white skin, purple bruises under his eyes, the white split in his lip gaping, his eyes as black as pitch. 'I thought it was *the bad man*,' he cried. 'I thought he'd got me at last. And I *fought* … I *pushed*. Do you understand?'

He tilted his head, his miserable pleading expression an awful parody of Dom, and I had to shut my eyes tight and bury my face in my hands just so I didn't have to see it.

I dropped back onto the sand and rolled over onto my side with a groan. *Jesus, you bastard*, I thought, *can't you at least let me hate you? Can't you give me that much? That I can hate the boy who killed my brother?*

I don't know how long I lay there, but I think it was a long, long time. I remember thinking how nice it would be if I just fell asleep there and never woke up. But there was never any danger of that happening. Eventually the cold began to really eat into me, and I began to shiver uncontrollably. My face was aching from tears I didn't know I'd been crying. When I took my hands away from my eyes, I felt the hot tingle of blood rushing back into the compressed skin.

James Hueston had been right – life pushes you on. And right then my body had had enough of lying in the frost and was demanding that I get up and do something about it – no matter how much my heart wanted to lie there and die.

I rolled onto my knees and stiffly pushed myself to my feet. Dom was gone, but his footprints in the sand led into the kitchen. I staggered after him, following him inside and heading upstairs to the room where it had all begun.

19. Maybe Now, in Dreams

Maybe Now, in Dreams

I stood outside our bedroom door for what felt like the hundredth time that day. There was no light, only a thin wash of moon filtering though the bathroom window and dying out on the landing. It was nothing more than a milky suggestion of light, enough to trick the eye and fool the brain, and just enough to prevent me missing a step and falling down the stairs. I didn't think I'd ever be afraid of the dark again. It had thrown all it had at me, and in the end it had done its worst. There was nothing left for me to fear.

I put both hands flat against the wood of the door and listened. Nothing. The whole house slept, Francis with them it seemed. I laid my forehead on the blistered paintwork. I'd really worked him over. I'd beaten the crap out of him – out of what was left of Dom. My knuckles were singing high and clear at how much damage I'd done to them. I couldn't imagine how much hurt I'd inflicted on him. I ran my fingers down the door, feeling the pits and cracks that I couldn't see.

If it were me – if Francis had stolen my body and pushed me out into the cold – Dom would have worked something out. He wouldn't have stood around watching as I disintegrated. He wouldn't have beaten the shite out of my body and terrified Francis 'til he couldn't stand up anymore. He wouldn't have sent my ghost away when I came to him for help. He would have *talked*. He would have *worked something out*.

Dom.

I slapped the wood gently with the palm of my hand. I could do this. I could figure it out. If Francis could leap in and push Dom out, then why couldn't Dom do the same? My eyes opened wide in the dark, seeing nothing. I was suddenly filled with hope, and it was better than despair. It stopped the trembling in my legs and arms, and let me breathe. But there wasn't much time. I had no doubt that Dom's body was dying; it might already be ... I breathed deep and pushed myself off the door, throwing that thought behind me. Dom was out there somewhere, with Lorry. We'd find him. Francis was terrified and probably a bit crazy, but he was no coward, despite what I'd said to him. I knew he would never have killed Dom on purpose. He'd help, if he was able. He'd help. All I had to do was ask.

I shook myself, literally, my eyes open wide in the ghost-light. I took another deep breath through my nose and quietly opened the door.

I didn't see him for a moment, because my attention went automatically to the windowsill, and then to the bed. It was only when I stepped forward and closed the door behind me that I looked down and saw him sprawled on the floor.

I'd seen three dead bodies in my life: Grandda Joe, Grandad Peadar and, long ago, almost too long to recall, Granny Fee. They'd been combed and powdered and dressed in their best, tucked into their silk-lined coffins, their hands laced in rosary-beads, their eyes properly closed.

Dom didn't look like that at all. He looked like something thrown from a car, like a doll dropped from the sky. His legs and arms were loosely flung out, his head twisted so his face was out of sight. He had obviously just fallen to the floor and lain there. God knew how long. I shuffled around so I could see him properly and knelt down beside him. I sat back on my heels, looking into his face. I could see the dull gleam of his eyes under his heavy eyelids. His lips were half open, dry and cracked. His hair fanned out around his head on the floorboards. His hand was curled in front of his face, impossibly still.

People say that the dead look as though they're sleeping. Well, Dom didn't. Dom looked dead. He looked absolutely, irrevocably, unmistakably dead. I reached for him, without thinking about it, and snagged him by his shoulder and the front of his jumper, and rolled him onto his back. I pulled him onto my knees, my arm around his chest, his head resting on my thigh. His arm tumbled out of my grip and unfolded loosely, his elbow and then his hand knocking against the floorboards in quick succession.

Knock-knock, who's there?

I gazed down into his inanimate white face, and I meant to just say, 'Dom?' But something unannounced burst in my head and in my chest. Suddenly I was four years old, kneeling on the floor, clutching my brother to me and yelling through my panic the only word that seemed to be left to me, 'Maaaam! Maaammyy! Maaaam!' over and over in hysterical, breathy screams.

The door opened, and I presented him to her as though he were a broken toy I wanted her to fix. But it wasn't Ma. It was Nan. She was all white – her long hair, her skin, the long cotton nightie that brushed her toes and tied at her neck. She stuck her head around the jamb first; looked at us, looked behind her; came in and carefully shut the door.

'Nan!' I screamed in that high breathy, almost soundless voice. 'Get Mammy. Get Ma. Nan, get Ma!'

Nan looked at me a moment with sad eyes and then came over and knelt down beside me. She took my face in her hands, wiping my tears, shaking my head slightly from side to side as she spoke.

'Patrick,' she said quietly. 'Shhh.'

'Nan,' I croaked, my voice nearly gone. 'He's dead! Look! He's dead.' And I offered her Dom again, his head lolling back into the crook of my arm as I lifted him up to show her. She glanced at him, then turned her whole attention to me.

'Patrick,' she said again, 'Laurence says you have to go to sleep.'

I blinked at her, shocked into stillness.

'You have to go asleep, darling. Do you understand?'

I shook my head. My tears brimmed over, and she caught them with her thumbs, sweeping them to one side without taking her hands from my face or breaking eye contact.

'Laurence is going to lend you his eyes, but you have to go asleep.'

I felt my face crumple up, and I shook my head again. My tears ran down her fingers before she could catch them. I wanted to ask her to get Ma, I wanted to tell her that Dom was dead, but when I opened my mouth nothing came out but a big choking sob.

'Patrick,' she said, lifting one hand from my face and laying it on Dom's motionless chest. 'Laurence says that Francis is still trapped in here. Do you understand?' She patted Dom's chest, and I looked down at him in horror. 'He can still see us and hear us and feel us. Do you know what that means?'

I looked back at her. My eyes felt like they were going to bulge right out of their burning sockets; my mouth was open in gasping sobs that I couldn't contain. She put her hand back onto my cheek, cradling my face as if to hold me together.

'If we get your ma, it's all over. Understand? Dom will still be dead and Francis, poor Francis, will be buried inside this body. Francis will be put in a coffin and buried. Do you understand, darling? Tell me you understand.'

I stared into Nan's face and nodded. I understood.

'Alright, love,' she said. 'Now you have to go asleep. Can you do that?'

I shook my head, my eyes brimming over.

'But you have to. Laurence says that you have to go asleep and he'll lend you his eyes. He says you know what to do. He says Shamie will help you.' She searched my face. 'Do you know what to do, darling? Because I'm just the messenger. I don't have anything for you but the message.'

'Yes, Nan.' I whispered. 'I know what to do.'

She wiped my tears one more time and kissed me on the forehead. Then she bent and looked into Dom's dead face. 'Fran,' she whispered. 'Hold on, darling. Lorry is coming.' And she kissed him too, and swept the matted curls back off his cold forehead.

She ruffled my hair as she got up and left without looking back at us, closing the door carefully behind her.

I didn't think anymore. I had no thoughts left. I just pulled Dom up into my arms and pushed backwards with my legs 'til I was sitting with my back to the wall. Dom's limp body lay against my chest, my legs sprawled out on either side of him. I settled him so that his head rested in the crook of my neck, and with my free hand, I rooted numbly in my trouser pocket 'til I snagged the last of Nan's little green sedatives. I dry-swallowed them, lint and all.

Then I lay my cheek against the top of Dom's head. His cold curls pressed against my mouth and snagged in my damp eyelashes as I hugged him tightly and waited for the drug to take hold.

20. Fall to Fog

Fall to Fog

When I wake up, I don't remember where I've been. Then I recall the trenches, the slide off the duckboards, the cold swallow of the mud. I scream and open my eyes. There is a gentle light illuminating me, and I realise that I am clean and dry. My scream turns to a relieved laugh, and I look around for Jolly and Shamie. I'm sure they must have saved me from my muddy grave – but they are not here.

I am swaddled in warm dry fog, and the air is kind with the scent of hay and fresh-baked bread. All around me move the dim shapes of men. Some sit up suddenly, as though shocked awake, and then get slowly to their feet. Others run frantically and then slow to a walk and look around them in wonder. One fellow, off to my left, calls for his mother – that long, desperate battlefield wail – but he stops almost at once, and I hear him laugh and, then he sighs in relief.

I get to my feet and notice that I am dressed in my best uniform. I haven't been this clean and warm and dry in months; I'd forgotten what it was like. I look at my hands and there are no fleabites. I run my hand over my chin and there is no stubble. I inhale the gentle air again and I am suddenly, absolutely happy. There are things I should be worried about; there are things I should remember, but all I need now is to smile and keep walking happily forward.

I stroll at a leisurely pace, swinging my arms. I think, I would like to have a stick to swat, the way I used to when I was a boy.

And then, just like that, I have one! Hah! It must have been in my hand all along. I begin to swish it to and fro ahead of me as I walk. It makes a satisfying sound in the air. I begin to whistle, and soon I find myself knocking out a pretty good version of 'The Saucy Little Bird on Nellie's Hat'.

Fran would like this, I think with a smile. Maybe I can find him a stick too. We can run down to the harbour and see if the boats are in. We could maybe get some crabs for tea ...

At the thought of Fran, I am halted by an uncomfortable twinge in my stomach. I stop and bend forward at the waist until the discomfort eases. Men stroll past me. There are yet more of them coming up through the mist, an endless parade of men, it seems, all heading in the same direction. A gentle tugging at my heart urges me forward, but I resist it and turn to look back.

It is all grey behind me – a smooth, featureless wall of

mist. I think I hear someone back there, calling my name.
I think ... maybe ... Is it?

'Fran?' I call.

At the sound of my voice, the passing men turn their
indistinct faces towards me. I gasp as their eyes find me.
Their attention is a physical blow. It shocks me. My arms
rise up; my legs splay. I can feel my feet leave the ground
as I am lifted into the trembling air. What is happening?

I am turned to face forward, and I am gently set back
down on the ground. There is the sensation that this is
the right way to face – the only way. As one, the men turn
from me and continue on. The feeling of discomfort leaves
me, and I sense once again the sweet insistence of that
pull around my heart. It is calling me onwards. I begin to
walk. My mind fills with happiness, and my moment of
fear melts away. My thoughts drift to Fran and the trip
we might take to the harbour. The mackerel may be in
and we could take our rods ...

Someone calls my name. The voice is far away and
frightened, and I am almost certain that it is Francis. I
stop, and, in stopping, I fill with anxiety; I should keep
going. Men continue to pass me by, and even the ones
coming up from behind me seem further away than
before.

I am being left behind.

The tug on my heart grows ever more insistent, and I
fight to resist it. I only want a moment to listen for that
voice. But the need to move forward is relentless, and I

feel as though my insides are being pulled slowly through a painless hole in my throat. I groan with the effort of just standing still and listening.

The voice comes again: clear and certain and far away. Francis shouting, 'LORRY!' I am positive now that it is him. My lost brother. My twin. I spin without a second thought and begin to run back for him. I yell for him at the top of my lungs.

'FRANCIS!'

And I am torn asunder. I feel it, quite distinctly. I am torn in two, from top to bottom. That tug against my heart, the painless, invisible cord trying to pull me forward, rips something from me like the shirt being torn from my back, and I scream as part of me is left behind. A great flat wall of weight falls onto me and I am slapped down into the earth.

I've been hit, *I think in panic.* A shell just hit me.

The ground splits open, and I am plummeting through the solid earth. I'm slapped up and shoved down and cast from side to side in darkness. A nauseating pain consumes me. I want to breathe and I want to vomit, but I can do neither in this endless rush through the churning earth.

It ends in an abrupt bang of silence, and I am spewed up into the fog. All around me, men are running and silently screaming under the constant flash of lightning and a heavy storm of shells Their running figures smear their way through the air, horrified mouths and eyes nothing but blurred smudges on their indistinct faces. All is grey, dirty, and soundless. I am violently pushed one way then carelessly swatted back, the very air itself buffeting me. I stagger about without respite, my arms wrapped around the pain in my heart. There is no noise – only the sensation of noise, and it makes my ears ring. I am torturously close to the edge of hearing, but actual sound eludes me.

A young man runs right through me, pulling a portion of me with him like a trail of filthy smoke. My mouth opens to scream noiselessly at the horror of it; then I snap back together with a sickening twang. I wrap my arms tighter around my chest and grit my teeth at the disgusting sensation.

I glare after the man who has done this to me, and I realise that he is the only distinct person in this shifting fog. I stumble after him, latching onto his sharp figure in the mist. He has fallen to his knees beside the wavering outline of another man and seems to be trying to pull him to his feet. I squint hard, trying to get a better focus. Pain sears my head, but details spring temporarily to life. I see the duckboards beneath the two men, the rain that pelts them, the vast rushing pandemonium of war that streams by.

It is Shamie. The man who ran me through is Shamie, and he is trying to pull poor Jolly to his feet. Jolly is screaming and crying. He is lying half on, half off the slippery duckboards, his arms sunk to the shoulder in *the liquid mud. He flails against Shamie's touch and continues to try and grope about in the treacherous slurry.*

The pain becomes intolerable, and I have to press my knuckles to my temples and squeeze my eyes shut for a moment. When I am finally able to look again, everything is back to shadows and the dirty half-suggestions of shadows, except for Shamie, who stands out clear and true as a photograph in the murk.

Shamie gets his shadow-companion to stand and turns towards me, his friend's arm slung across his shoulder. He looks straight at me, and the sight of his determined face is a punch to the belly. Shamie is looking right through me, as if I no longer exist. Then he bolts, dragging his companion with him, and I stumble after, following him blindly through the shifting grey.

'Shamie!' I scream. 'Shamie!'

I stagger only steps behind, but Shamie doesn't see me. So I stumble on, as I will continue to do forever, for an eternity, keeping Shamie in my sight, hoping for a glimpse of Fran, and I realise with despair that this is hell. This is hell and I have purposely thrown myself from the very arms of heaven.

I woke with a bump, as though I'd fallen from a great height, and my first thought was, *Oh no. I'm awake and I have no pills left!* Then I realised that my arms were empty, and Dom's cold weight was gone from me. I began to grope around for him in panic, thinking he'd slipped to the floor.

I called for him, but instead of shouting, 'DOM!' as I had intended, I found myself yelling, 'SHAMIE!' My voice was hoarse, a hoarse man's voice, and I realised that I was groping about not on the floorboards of our bedroom but in a bed of dry, yellow clay. It crumbled beneath my fingers as I scrabbled about, and I called again, 'SHAMIE! SHAMIE!' as if I'd been calling that name forever and couldn't find a way to stop.

A cautious voice said, 'I'm here,' and someone put their hand on my shoulder.

I leapt away, pressing my back to the wall of the trench, and gaped up into Shamie's young face. I knew him, and I didn't know him, all at once. My head spun with the contradiction.

He stared at me, this young version of James Hueston, looking me up and down. He seemed as disconcerted as I was. 'Laurence?' he asked uncertainly.

I swallowed, afraid to look down at myself for fear of what I might see. Shamie was dressed in a grubby soldier's uniform. His nails were filthy and his hair stuck up like a dirty blond hedgehog. He had a scruffy boy's beard on his cheeks, and his pale-blue eyes were round and frightened.

'Laurence,' he whispered, 'why am I here? What did you bring me back here for?'

His tone of voice told me that *here* was not a place he had ever wanted to be again. He seemed to feel betrayed that I would bring him back.

I shook my head. 'I'm not Laurence, Mr Hueston. Don't you know me?'

The words sounded odd, coming as they did in that raspy man's voice, but I knew who I was – and I knew what was going on, too.

This was another dream. Somewhere in Skerries old James Hueston was fast asleep and dreaming in his bed. Just like I was fast asleep and dreaming on the floor of our room, my brother's body cradled in my arms. 'We're sharing a dream, Mr Hueston.'

Shamie's expression changed; all his wounded disappointment left him and his mouth dropped open a little in wonder. 'Are you …?' he stammered. 'Patrick? Is that you, boy?'

I nodded dumbly, and we blinked at each other for a minute. Then James Hueston laughed and scratched his scrubby beard, perplexed. 'Now what in God's name is this all about?' he muttered. He got to his feet and looked around, his face hardening. 'And why, of all places, are we here?'

'Mr Hueston …' I began, and he glanced down at me, a spark of amusement showing through his confusion.

'Now that's just too peculiar,' he said. 'You calling me *mister* in that voice … with that face. I can't cope with that, at all. Call me James.'

'Dom is dead, Mr Hueston. He died.'

His smile melted. He opened his mouth to speak, and I quickly put my hand up, as if to shield my eyes from his sympathy. 'Don't!' I said, staring straight ahead, my hand blocking him from view. 'If you look at me like that I … I won't be able to keep going.'

There was a small moment of stillness; then he stuck his hand down into my line of vision. He was offering to help me stand. I glanced at him as he pulled me to my feet, and his face was carefully neutral.

'I'm sorry, son,' he said softly. I nodded and avoided his eyes, looking around me for the first time. He stood quietly, taking his lead from me.

We were in a long, deep trench cut into the earth and I recognised it instantly. 'This is Black Paddy's Trench,' I said in my strange new voice. 'This is where Lorry died – where he was sucked into the mud.'

James nodded mutely and his eyes wandered up the clay walls to a thin ribbon of brazen sky.

I looked down the endless, unpopulated length of the duckboards, first one way, then the other. 'It's very different to how I dreamt it.'

He nodded again. It *was* very different. It was silent, for one thing. No breath of wind stirred; not a fly buzzed. And it was dry, so dry that the mud had baked beyond hard and was now soft and crumbling beneath our feet. Everything was yellow, or tinged yellow: the clay, the strange cloudless sky, the bleached wood of the duckboards and the ladders. Even the leaning sign that still faintly read 'Black Paddy Rules' had a yellow cast beneath the beating sun. There was no sign of human life. All the equipment and paraphernalia of war was gone, except for the unusual piles of rope that stood in silent coils all over the duckboards and hung in motionless loops and swags from every convenient outcrop.

'Nan sent me here,' I said. 'She said Lorry wanted us to come here. There must be something …'

Without thinking too much about it, I leapt from the boards and scrambled up the nearest ladder, causing an avalanche of mud-dust and rubble as I went. I pulled myself over the top and stood up into open, breathless air, scanning the horizon. 'It's all empty,' I said, my voice flattened under the weight of the dead air. 'There's nothing to see for miles.'

Everything felt so real. The taste of the yellow mud-dust on my lips, the feel of the crumbling clay beneath my boots, the hot air in my nostrils; it all felt absolutely real, but far, far away. And I realised that

Dom was an ache in my chest that had been with me for years. It was as though I'd buried him long ago. Mourned him and missed him and buried him. He was nothing but a tragic, manageable memory. I didn't like that – it was all wrong – but it was better than the crippling terror of before. At least like this, I could function. Like this, I could get things done.

Shamie stood in the trench, shielding his eyes, looking up at me. I offered him my hand, but he seemed reluctant to climb up. 'I never want to go over the top again, son.'

I understood. I remembered everything now, and after those dreams – that terrible rain of fire and mud, Lorry's awful death – I absolutely understood. But we couldn't just stay here. 'Nan says Francis is stuck, Mr Hueston.'

His face kind of froze, and he waited for me to clarify.

'Inside Dom's body,' I said. James's eyelids fluttered at that, and he lifted a hand as if to push the thought away. 'Nan says that he can still hear and feel, and everything. But he's stuck. Nan says …' The full horror of it struck me. 'Nan says they'll bury him like that. They'll put him in a coffin and bury him. I'm not going to let that happen, Mr Hueston.'

I turned and looked around, slowly scanning the horizon. The barren landscape shimmered under the blank sky. 'But what are we meant to do?' I whispered.

'Lorry must have brought us here for a reason,' said James, squinting up at me.

I knew without discussing it that he was right; Lorry had brought us here. He had been bringing us here all along, trying to tell us something or show us something. 'But this is different,' I whispered.

'I hate to dream about here,' muttered James, down in the depths of the pit. 'Why would he do this to me? Make me dream this again and again? It's like he's tormenting me. I can't stand it.'

I shook my head. 'But this is different, isn't it, Mr Hueston? It's not ...' I turned again, dust rising from my boots. The landscape was a painful shimmer all around us, the trench a silent, listening presence running in a straight line all the way to either horizon. I spun in a slow circle, taking it all in. 'This isn't a memory,' I said.

James Hueston stopped glancing fretfully about him and stared up at me, his pale-blue eyes startled in his grubby young face. 'This is more like a place,' he said.

We met each other's eyes, and I knew he was right. Lorry had brought us to a place: constructed it from his past, given it form and substance by his will, donated us bodies made from his memories. I lifted my hand and stared at it – it was not my hand. It was not my hand. I was suddenly terrified. Where was my real body? Had Lorry cast me out from it, in the same way Fran had Dom?

'Are we dead?' I cried. 'Is this The Grey?'

James shook his head, fear widening his eyes despite his denial. 'We can't be,' he whispered. 'Why ... why would Lorry do that to us?'

I thought of the dream that I'd had before waking here – Lorry's memory. I remembered the reason he had turned back: the voice that had called him from the threshold of heaven. 'He's looking for Fran. He's been looking for him all this time.'

'But poor Fran isn't here!' cried Shamie. 'Lorry isn't here. Your poor brother isn't even here! What are we meant to do with all this?'

The thought of Dom brought a brief and distant tug of sorrow. It had been so long since I'd lost him. I could barely remember his voice. But I knew that if it had been Dom lost out there, trapped and alone and terrified, I'd have done anything to find him. I'd have turned my back on heaven if he'd needed me to. I'd have spent my years searching, and I'd never have given up. The heat pressed down around us, dead and laden, and I knew I had to do something to help Lorry save Francis.

'FRAN!' I shouted. 'FRAN! ARE YOU HERE?'

My voice rang out against the brazen sky and beat up from the iron ground. Down in the trench Shamie winced and made a shushing gesture, as if afraid I'd call something down on us. I waited, my eyes fixed on the shimmering horizon. Nothing. No breath of wind. No sigh of dust crossing the lifeless plane.

'LORRY!' I cried. 'WHAT THE HELL ARE WE DOING HERE?'

'Son,' whispered Shamie. 'Please don't.'

And then, in that breathless place, the sound of creaking came soft and barely audible – the sound of something swinging lightly in a gentle breeze. 'Can you hear that?' I whispered. Shamie, his fingers pressed to his lips, shook his head. I crouched down low, listening. It was coming from the trench.

'That creaking noise,' I insisted. 'Shamie, why can't you hear it?'

Suddenly I flung myself over the side. I didn't even bother with a ladder or footholds; I simply threw myself over the edge, sprawled-legged and loose, out into midair and let the dream catch me. I should have fallen straight down, ten, maybe twelve feet. But I slid instead, impossibly easy, down the sheer wall of clay. It was as if the sides of the trench swelled out and caught me and eased me to the ground – as if they'd been waiting for me to do this all along. I slithered to a halt at the bottom, lying on my back looking up at Shamie's wide-eyed face.

'Wow,' I said. 'That was cool.'

He offered me his hand, and I got to my feet. 'I think we're meant to be down here,' I said. 'I could hear a sound up there, real faint, like as if …'

But James wasn't listening. He was staring over my shoulder with a reluctant mix of wonder and terror. 'What in the name of Jesus?' he whispered.

I turned to follow his gaze, and my mouth dropped open.

James gripped my shoulder as if to hold on to himself. His voice was a tiny scratching in my ear. 'Call me mad, boy, but didn't this trench used to just go on forever, without bend or break?'

'Yeah,' I said. 'It did.'

He stepped to my side, and the two of us eyed the trench ahead. It no longer marched relentlessly on towards the horizon. Oh no. It stopped about four or five yards from where we stood. Just came to an end, faced off with a blank wall cut into the clay. The duckboards continued to three or four feet from the base of this wall, then turned right, leading around a sharp corner and disappearing from view. A broken stake jutted from the ground at the corner. A helmet hung from it, swinging gently in a breeze that did not exist, its leather strap creaking softly as if to say *here, here, here.*

A sign hung on the blank yellow face of the clay wall. It pointed to the right, guiding us round the corner. It was just a rough plank-sign; a bit of torn-up duckboard from the looks of it. Someone had scrawled on it in charcoal, and the wood and the letters were tinted the same sulphurous yellow as everything else. It read: This Way to The Grey.

21. Step over to Grey

The Grey. James, standing in front of it, was dwarfed by its immensity. For the first time in this sepia-toned world, I noticed the greens of his uniform, and the sandy olive-drab of his hair. Muted and worn as these colours were, James stood out as a technicoloured marvel against the great wall of dirty, shifting nothingness that made The Grey. It filled the sky like a universe-sized cinema screen, and cut the trench neatly off at the edges. James, ant-like, craned his neck back and looked up, up, up, trying to see the top.

I backed away, and kept going 'til I stood pressed against the far wall of the trench. I had been out there before, when I was Lorry. I had already felt that terrible silence battering my ears. I had already been buffeted by its malicious turbulence. I didn't want to go back.

The helmet creaked discreetly beside me, and I knew at once that this was Lorry's helmet, the one he'd lost the night he died. I looked from it, to The Grey. Lorry needed us to go out there. But why? To find him? So that we could help him rescue Francis? Or release him back to heaven? Or what? To do what? To find what? So many questions and no hope of an answer. Not here, anyway.

Not here.

I nodded, took a deep breath and pushed myself from the wall. Charging forward, bull-headed, I passed the sign. I leapt a pile of rope. I passed James. He yelled something to me and reached out. I batted his hand away. The hollow sound of the duckboards beneath my boots gave way to hard, resonance-free ground. Colour left me as if it had never existed and I crossed over into The Grey.

Silence grabbed me, and squeezed my skull so that I had to slap my hands to my ears and grit my teeth. My grief for Dom surged fresh within me. Raw and bloody, it blew a hole right through me, and I couldn't bear it. I couldn't. It was too big for me to survive. I immediately spun, trying to find my way out. The trench lay about fifteen feet away, a wavering door of smoky-orange flame where James stood watching. I staggered towards it, but the door retreated from me, keeping its distance as I stumbled to catch it up. I could see James bobbing just out of my reach, screaming my name, and I put a hand out to reach for him. The silence surged gleefully in, and I had to clap my hands back to my head, hunching over at the pain of it against my eardrums.

Someone grabbed my shoulders. I jerked back in fear, but it was only James, smoky and pale-faced in the ashy light of The Grey. He had come in here for me! I grabbed his jacket, so grateful not to be alone. Then my eyes slid past him, and I realised with horror that the door was closing behind him. The Grey was shutting down, sealing itself like a hole in mud. James seemed to register the terror in my eyes, and I think he was about to turn, but we didn't have the time; the orange rectangle of light was already half its original size. The trench-light was fading as it passed behind the cloudy curtain of The Grey.

I didn't think, and I'm sure that's what saved him. I just took my hands from my ears and punched James in the chest. He staggered backwards into the trench, and the door snapped back full-size, its light a vivid fire through the fog once more. James landed on his arse in the dry, yellow clay, a cloud of mud-dust puffing up around him. I held my hand up to stop him coming back for me.

The door continued to drift one step back for every one of my shambling steps forward, and I began to panic. I was stuck.

I ran. My hands glued to my ears, my heart hammering, I ran as fast as I could, but I got nowhere. The door danced and bobbed, always feet ahead of me, James framed within it, a horrified witness to my increasingly desperate flight towards him.

Suddenly he flung his arms up and turned away. At the same time, I tripped and fell flat onto my stomach, my legs flying out behind me. The air pounced on me like a big dog and I curled into a ball, my arms wrapped around my head. *I'm trapped*, I thought, *I'm trapped. I'm trapped.*

Then something slapped across my back. Heavy and slithering, it uncurled itself along my backbone and ran along my shoulders to lay a snaky coil across the nape of my neck. Terror jolted me, and I tried to skitter out from under its grasp. As I rolled away, just before the heavy thing slithered from my back, I caught a brief flare of James's voice, loud and clear in my head.

… *let this work, Hail Mary Mother of God pray for us now and at the hour of our dea—*

I flopped onto my belly and groped, wide-eyed, for what I suddenly realised had been a rope. James had thrown me a rope! Without my hands to protect my ears, the silence tried to liquefy my brain – a head melting *thudDUM thudDUM.* I was just about to slap my hands back into place and roll into a ball once more when my fingers brushed the frayed end of the rope and James's thoughts replaced the agony.

… look up! Why don't you look up? YES! Hold on, boy! Our Father who art in heaven hallowed be thy name, thy kingdom come …

James's frantic recitation of the 'Our Father' continued in my head as I was pulled in jerky fits and starts to the threshold of The Grey and then dragged over into the sulphurous calm of the trench.

I stayed curled in a ball, the rope coiled around my arms, my head cradled in my hands. James fell onto his knees beside me, and he wrapped me in too tight a hug. His thoughts were all a jumble in my head and they blended into a frenzied kind of buzz.

… is that what it's like? Don't let me die, don't, I never want to die if that's what it's like. Is he still alive? Can he breathe? Oh. Is that what it's like, though? Forever? God help us. Our Father who art …

And his praying started again, which was a relief because the monotonous incantation was much better than his panic.

'James,' I croaked. He didn't seem to notice, because he just kept rocking me and panting shivery little sobs into my shoulder. 'James!' I insisted, batting at his shoulder. 'Leggo.'

He released me, and I pushed the rest of the way out of his arms, gulping in air. 'Squashing me!' I managed at last.

He hugged his knees to his chest and gave The Grey a long, haunted sideways glance.

'That's not what dying's like, James. I know, 'cause Laurence showed me.'

He gaped at me, horrified. *Can you read my thoughts?*

I nodded. *Started off when you threw that rope.*

He looked down at the innocent coil at his feet and kicked it away with a look of alarm that almost made me laugh. I sat up and waited for my head to settle a little, then glanced at him again.

'It's nice,' I promised. 'Once you've crossed over. It's peaceful and nice. Laurence was happy, even though he'd been terrified the moment before.'

James frowned at me without comprehension.

'I was Laurence,' I explained. 'In a dream. I was him when he died.'

He drew away from me in sympathy and horror, and I put my hand on his arm, because there were tears in his eyes. *It was okay, James. Once he'd died. It was really nice. There's no need to be afraid.* And, saying it, I realised the same thing went for Dom; Dom would have gone there, too. I thought about that for a moment; Dom would be in heaven. He'd have gone to that gentle place, the place Laurence had lost. I wasn't sure what to do with this thought, but it comforted me.

'What's that, then?' James whispered, jerking a thumb in the direction of the murky shadow-wall. I looked into its strange depths and licked my lips.

I think that's what it's like to be a ghost. Comprehension dawned on him, and he turned to peer into The Grey. We sat like that for a moment, watching the shadows race and flow in that silent, hammering void, both of us thinking the same thing.

'Fran stayed there all that time, looking for Lorry,' whispered James.

And Lorry got lost, looking for Fran.

'We need to rescue them,' I said, looking into James's eyes. I knew he felt the same way.

22. A Shining Bridge

It was very strange and comforting to know that no matter how far I walked, I could turn and find James ten feet behind me. We did a few tentative experiments, and discovered three things for certain: firstly, the person in The Grey couldn't just walk back through the door — they had to be dragged unresisting across the threshold; secondly, only one of us could be there at a time — well, this was an assumption on our part, and there was no way we would risk testing it again because one shot of that door sealing itself shut was enough for both of us; and thirdly, neither of us could stand being in The Grey for very long.

Hard as it was to keep track of time, we figured the longest either of us had lasted was fifteen minutes before we flopped to the ground with our hands clasped to our ears, our eyes turned beseechingly to the door. How Lorry and Francis had survived for so long in that awful place was a mystery to me; but I no longer wondered why both of them were a little cracked in the head.

The landscape within The Grey never changed; no figures came out of the fog; no sounds reached us, no message more definite than that palpitating sense of horror. It was a mindless forward slog, with no end. We were getting nowhere. What did Laurence want from us?

We were soon too tired to talk, and even the buzz of our thoughts through the telegraph wire of the rope became nothing but an exhausted drizzle of sound. I had no idea what my thoughts sounded like to James, but I hoped they gave him comfort, because when it was my turn out in The Grey, his unending round of 'Hail Mary' and 'Our Father' and 'Glory Be' kept me going.

During my turns in the relative tranquillity of the trench, holding the lifeline as James trudged on, I tried to think things through. I thought, in a dim, unfocused kind of way, about Lorry and Francis and their seventy-year hunt through The Grey. Two terrified ghosts, desperate to find each other. I thought of James and myself, anchored by our living bodies to the world: ghosts but not ghosts, trying to do the same.

Ghosts, but not ghosts.

I tried to catch this thought − to make sense of it − but James's thoughts kept drumming away in my head, soothing me, lulling me, making it hard to think. I felt like my brain was wrapped in cotton-wool, like I was sleepwalking on a treadmill, slogging on with no purpose. Getting nowhere.

My eyes snapped open and my hands tightened around the rough coils of the rope. I stared at James's toiling back. We *were* like sleepwalkers; we really were. We were keeping each other too calm and too protected. Connected by the rope, we found The Grey horrible, almost unbearable. Without the rope, it was shattering; it was a deadly, shattering torture. But it was focused. It was real.

We were real.

I suddenly understood. We were keeping each other *safe* out there, but we were also keeping each other *dim*. We were trudging along, shadows in the shadows, when we should have been out there shouting – the only living souls in the world of the dead, screaming our heads off, glowing like torches, making ourselves known.

I swallowed. I couldn't ask James to do that. He hadn't asked for any of this. I was the one who'd taken the sleeping pills. I was the one who'd started this bloody dream. He'd just fallen asleep, poor bastard, and now here he was, keeping me safe, taking my place.

James, I thought. *Stop.*

He lurched to a halt, hunched and wary. *What is it?* Even his thoughts were a whisper. *What do you see?*

It's okay. I don't see anything. I just want you to come back.

He ducked his head around to look at me, his face distorted with the effort of staying in that place. *Are you alright?*

I'm fine.

I can stay a good bit longer. I think I'm getting used to it.

I had to smile at that. I could feel just how not used to it he was. *I know you can. But I have an idea. I need to go out there now.*

Our eyes met, and he frowned. I wasn't sure how well he could read me; my thoughts were such a jumble when compared to his orderly prayers. Hopefully they made no sense to him.

It's alright, Mr Hueston, I'm not going to do anything stupid.

He looked away for a moment, into the distorted non-depths. I could see him jerking, shifting his weight under the unending assault of the air. For a moment, he lifted his hands from his ears, and I knew then that he had some small inkling of what I was at. He let The Grey rush in at him. He opened himself to it.

His jaw tightened immediately and his eyes narrowed. I tried to keep my own thoughts low and unobtrusive. His pain burnt up the rope to me, and I ground my teeth at the electric strength of it. He barely lasted a minute before ducking his head and slapping his hands back into place.

Jesuuus Chriiist.

You … you okay, Mr Hueston?

He didn't answer, just kept cursing in that painful whisper. *Jesuuuus. Jesus, Mary and Joseph.*

Mr Hueston?

I'm … I'm fine.

Did you hear anything?

But he didn't answer me. He just dropped to the ground like a broken doll and curled around the pain, waiting for me to pull him in. He didn't even grip the rope the way we'd both got into the habit of; he just let the slack tighten against the loop that was knotted around his shoulder and lay like a dead weight as I heaved him over the threshold.

I knelt down beside him and put my hand on his shoulder. He flopped onto his back, gaping like a fish. 'Mr Hueston? Mr Hueston? You okay?'

He closed his eyes and nodded, put his hand on my arm, squeezed reassuringly, and sat up.

'No,' he said, his eyes still shut tight.

'Huh?'

'No. You're *not* doing it.'

He began to stand, and I shook off his hand and got to my feet at the same time. When he finally let go of his head and raised his eyes to mine, I had already backed to the threshold, my face set like stone.

His expression fell at the sight of me. He lowered his hands as if in slow motion.

'Boy?' he whispered, looking me up and down. 'What …?'

I looked down, expecting to see Lorry's grubby uniform, his dusty army boots. But instead I saw my new brown cords, my runners, my cream poloneck jumper. It was with dreamlike astonishment that I held my own two hands in front of my face. My own hands, not Lorry's! I looked back at James. He was still the same, still young Shamie and I knew now that it was because of Lorry. That's how Lorry saw him and that's how James would remain, as long as he was here in Lorry's dream-place. But me, I was myself again. I was acting for myself.

'What did you hear out there?' I asked, gentle now, because I knew that James was going to let me go.

'Lorry,' he said quietly. 'I heard Lorry. Screaming my name. And the artillery shells – the bloody Jack Johnsons – trying to drown him out as usual. But it was him. And I *felt* him. *Here!*' He thumped his chest and there were tears in his eyes again, shivering but not falling, on the curve of his bottom lid. 'It were as though I only lost him yesterday. The pain … the *pain* of it …'

'Like a hole blown through you,' I whispered, and he nodded.

We've been doing this all wrong, James. We've been thinking like people. But we're not just people here, are we? We're living ghosts. We're living memories. We're the bridge between then and now – the signal that will guide them home.

What are you going to do?

I shrugged. 'I'm just going to wait,' I said. 'Wait and see what happens. I think we've tried too hard, Mr Hueston. I think … I think

I'm just going to stand still and shout.'

He looked out at The Grey. *But it's awful out there.*

I think it's much worse than we've been letting ourselves feel. I held up the rope. *This has been sheltering us from it, I think. I think it unfocuses us.*

James's eyes widened in comprehension, and he reached for me. I stepped into The Grey before he could touch me, and he became a shimmering watcher once more. The Grey pressed around me. My grief for Dom swamped me in a crippling tide and I bent, my hands pressed to my temples. Through squinted eyes, I saw James flounder as he dealt with his terror. Then he took a deep breath and seemed to pull himself together. He stooped and picked up the rope.

I'm with you, son, he thought. *I'm with you.*

It took me a moment to recover enough to lift my head and force my hands away from my ears. James's face fell as I lifted the loop of rope from my shoulders.

What are you doing? NO!

It's alright, I thought, as I laid the coil on the ground. *Don't worry.*

Just before I let go, I heard him shout, *You're burning! You're burning like fire!*

23. An Unexpected Find

An Unexpected Find

I forced myself to stand upright against the hammering air and knotted my fists in the fabric of my jumper, trying to keep my feet as The Grey battered and shoved me. I would not plug my ears. I would not grab the rope. I would not beg James to drag me to safety.

I heard it at once – loud and clear now that I'd opened myself to listen – a series of vast, dull *BOOM*s moving through the fog. This was Lorry's sound, the big artillery shells that James called Jack Johnsons. Though coming from very far away, each *BOOM* shook the ground, slamming through the soles of my boots and through my chest, right to the top of my head. There was a random feel to them, as though they were wandering around out there, searching, and I knew it was Lorry, looking for me. It was his way of calling.

I wondered if I gave off my own sound, some signal for him to follow through this cloying void?

I figured I should try. *I AM HERE*, I thought. *I'M OVER HERE*.

The Grey seemed to inhale. There was a long moment of listening. It made me want to hide.

Instead, I gathered myself and put more force into it. *OVER HERE! I'M HERE!*

The moment Lorry finally worked out where I was, I felt it. I felt it like a punch to my chest. My body did a series of strange wrenching jerks – *pop, pop, pow* – and particles of me shot off into The Grey like sparks. Oh God, it hurt. It hurt like nettles. It hurt like electric shock. I was a sparkler; I was a Catherine wheel, sending molecules of light and power out into The Grey. I had become a beacon: the mortal boy blazing bright in the colourless world of ghosts. I had become Lorry's guide.

The sound of shelling began to advance through the fog.

I slit my eyes open. It was hard to concentrate, because with every approaching *BOOM* of artillery shell, a surge of power would whip out from my feet, snapping my spine straight. A wave of light would pulse from me each time, and I could see that The Grey was shifting; it was pulling back. Each wave of light was stronger than the one before, and each one pushed The Grey further from me, leaving behind … solidity, definition, reality.

Lorry and I were building a space, a clear space in The Grey – a place where we could meet.

BOOM! Another shell went off, another pulse of light coursed through me, and I was standing on a circle of floorboards, The Grey a blank tube of mist around me.

BOOM! Again, and Lorry was so close now. So close. He had nearly found me; I had nearly guided him to me. But it hurt so badly. I wanted it to stop.

BOOM! My head dropped back and my mouth opened wide. *BOOM!* A swarm of buzzing sparks shot from my mouth. I was a column of fire. I was a pillar of pain. Still I kept calling with all my might, *I am here. I am here. I am here.*

BOOM! BOOM! BOOM! The explosions were unending now, and I was a fountain of agonised light. I was losing myself. I was getting hollow. I was pushing out. The geyser of sparks shooting from my mouth was emptying me of everything. I was so close to being gone.

Around me now were walls, windows, a door – a room constructed from me, made accessible by me, by the energy Lorry was taking from me. A ceiling, a dressing table, a battered bunk all came into view.

But I was unravelling. I was slipping between. I was becoming space. I screamed, terrified now that I could never stop; that Lorry would never stop; that I would be gone.

STOP! I screamed. *STOP! PLEASE!*

Silence. Everything ceased.

I staggered as if I'd been running, though I'd never taken one step.

I still burned – a cold, iron fire hissing out into the void – but all around me, everything had changed. The Grey had gone and I was looking down at two crumbled figures huddled against the wall of a colourless room. I was looking down at myself, Dom's body cradled in my arms, his head tucked into my neck. We were a sprawl of legs and arms on the floor of our bedroom. Our dark curls tumbled together, our identical faces snowy white and expressionless in the moonlight.

A young man exploded from the wall beside our bodies. Passing through the brick and plaster as if it were mist, he tumbled backwards as if he'd been kicked, and rolled in a flurry of army coat and flying limbs across the floor to come to a halt under the window. He was on his feet almost immediately, glaring back at the blank wall. Then he ran, disappearing into the featureless surface once more.

LORRY! I thought. I lifted my hand to pull him back and, as if my attention were a spotlight turned up to full blast, the wall blared a sudden blinding white. The reflected brilliance hurt my eyes, and I turned my head away, squinting.

That was me, I thought. *I did that, just by concentrating on it.*

Lorry returned instantly, struggling backwards and falling again as he broke through the threshold of the wall. He was dragging someone with him. A boy! The boy struggled and flailed, as if terrified. As I watched, he broke away from Lorry and scrambled on all fours back towards the wall. Lorry lurched to his knees. The white light emanating from me made cardboard cut-outs of them both as their struggling shadows darted and flared across the blinding walls. They were nothing but stark highlights and blackness, and I could make out no details, just the warring outline of their shapes.

FRANCIS, I screamed, certain the boy was him. *STOP! IT'S US!*

Panic flared from the boy. It crackled outwards like static electricity, charging the air with a dancing radiance that hurt my skin and raised the hair on my arms and head.

IT'S OKAY, FRANCIS! REMEMBER? IT'S US!

The boy scrabbled away, his desperation increasing as he dived, once again, for the wall. Lorry flung himself forward, grabbing the boy's foot. He pulled Francis towards him, earning a kick in the face that snapped his head back. He retaliated with an elbow to the stomach that winded the boy and allowed Lorry to drag him in and hold him tight.

Then Lorry turned to me, pleading, determined. He could hardly open his eyes against my flaring brilliance, but he twisted his body, pulling the struggling boy around and offered him to me. The boy flung up his hands and ducked his head, blinded and terrified by my searing light. I stepped forward and, as I reached, I saw the matted curls, the slanting cheekbones, the wide-spaced eyes of my own face.

Not Francis! *Not Francis at all!* Dominick! Laurence had found Dominick, and he was offering him to me, even as my brother flailed to get away. At the sight of Dom, I was suffused with an unnatural calm; it just settled down over me like something physical, a kind of serene blanket; a sense of *right*. I reached my burning arms for him. Dom's mouth opened in silent terror, and the sound of the sea filled the room, just as James had described it, a heavy pounding surf grinding the air. So this was Dom's sound.

He fought. He bucked. He tried to thrash free. But Laurence held him steady, offering him up to me as best he could, and I closed my arms around him, swallowing Dom in violent, static brilliance.

As soon as we touched, their voices filled my head: the familiar, throaty rasp I recognised as Laurence; the inarticulate, fear-stricken screams that belonged to my brother.

Laurence was pleading with me. *Take him. Take him, for God's sake. You're burning me. I can't stand it.*

Dom, his thoughts worn thin from the constant strain of fear, made no sense. There was no rhyme or reason to his words, just horror, and everything, everything about him screaming, *Get away, get away.*

I wrapped him in my new-found calm; I tried to share it with him. *It's okay, Dom. It's me. It's Patrick. Can't you hear me? It's Patrick. I'm here.* I pulled him to me and he beat against my chest, rigid with panic. *It's me, Dom. It's Patrick. It's me.*

He held still, his mind a frantic fluttering bird. But some part of him, some small portion, listened.

It's Patrick, Dom. Can't you hear me? It's alright. I'm here.

His hand, a cold solidity against the fizzing energy of my chest, curled into my jumper and he turned his face to rest his forehead against the crook of my neck. He grappled the serpent of his panic and pinned it momentarily, his fear for me overcoming his blinding sense of self-preservation.

Get away, he whispered, *the man is here.*

I pushed my fingers through the knotted curls at the back of his head and held him close to me. I watched as Lorry scrambled across the room and crouched by our physical bodies which were still slumped against the wall. His coat pooled around him, a liquid shadow on the floor as he knelt and looked into Dom's slack face. He put his hand on Dom's inert chest, and I saw his face soften as he whispered something gentle to the boy trapped within my brother's body. At last – under the most appalling of circumstances – Francis could no longer run, and Lorry could assure him that he didn't have to.

In my arms, Dom was beginning to fight me again, his heart and his breathing rapidly spiralling into a frenzy. I pulled him tighter, my eyes on Lorry, waiting for a sign. Dom's thoughts were a hectic rising tide within him, and he pushed against me.

It's alright, Dom, I thought. *I'm here. Hold on. Hold on, Dom. I'm here.*

Lorry glared at me suddenly and pointed to the floor behind me. I glanced down; the rope lay at my feet. I looked back at Lorry. *What?* He slapped the floorboards with angry impatience and pointed again. The rope. He pointed past me to where James must still be watching, cocooned in the yellow quiet of the trench.

Dom was bucking in my arms, and I clutched him to me with unnatural strength as he screamed against my shoulder, the sound of waves scouring the air. His thoughts were bees, and he was infecting me with his panic. Still clinging to him, I stepped back and looped the end of the rope around my ankle. James was with me at once, his voice a formless jumble of words and emotions in my mind. But solid. Real. Alive. I stared at Lorry as though he held a starter's pistol. He raised his hand, telling James and me to wait. I heard James, suddenly loud and clear through the chaos of Dom: *Whenever you're ready, pal. Just give me a sign.*

Lorry turned his attention back to Dom's body. His face softened again, infinitely compassionate, and I saw some clue of how he must have been before all the pain and the eternity of anger. He leant down close to my brother's body, his hands on either side of Dom's face. He said something reassuring again, and then he turned his eyes to James and nodded.

I felt the tug on my ankle and a violent jerk as my foot was pulled out from under me. I hadn't even had the presence of mind to kneel down, to get to the floor. I fell, and I dragged Dom with me. I remember no impact with the ground: just a gliding passage over the threshold of The Grey, Dom's incoherent screams a faint background to James's steady voice.

Over we go! Come on, boys!

I clung to Dom, one hand in his hair, the other fisted in his jumper. I would not be letting him go. I couldn't take my eyes from Lorry. As we were pulled, smooth and sure, over to the other side, I turned my head to keep him in sight. He was crouching over Dom's body, his hands sunk into Dom's chest. He was speaking with rapid gentleness. As we crossed over into the heat of the trench, I saw Lorry glance quickly our way, and then heave. A boy rose in his arms, eyes closed, head lolling, pulled like a shadow from my brother's body …

24. Grass, Sky, Horizon

'Wake up.'

I rose to the surface of a refreshing and satisfied sleep, to find myself under a gentle blue sky. Clouds drifted slowly overhead, lemon-tinted with sunrise. The air was warm but scrubbed clean, like the early morning of what would be a hot day by the sea. I was lying on soft grass; birds were singing. I took a deep lungful of the fresh air and basked for a moment in sheer bliss.

I moved my fingers through the neatly cropped grass beneath my hands. It was slightly damp with dew, but I knew that soon the sun would be cresting the roll of the hill and I would be soaked in its heat. I sighed, perfectly content to lie there until kingdom come – I had never been so comfortable in my life. I turned my head. Dom lay beside me, curled on his side, his eyes open and blankly staring.

I jolted to my knees, my heart in my mouth, and knelt over him, not knowing what to do. He didn't react to my sudden movement; his eyelids didn't even flicker.

'Leave him be.'

I recognised this voice as being the one that had called me awake; its soft rasp had become as familiar to me as my own. I turned to see

Lorry sitting on the slope of ground behind me, the rising sun just starting to glow through his hair. He smiled at me. I reached back and put my hand on Dom's chest. My eyes closed in relief at the gentle rise and fall of his breathing, the pumping thud of his heart beneath my palm. I sat back down on the grass, all the strength gone from my legs. I kept my hand on Dom's chest.

Lorry breathed in deep, closing his eyes and tilting his head, tasting the air. He released his breath slowly and looked up at the fleecy clouds. He was clean-shaven and barefoot, dressed in dark trousers, the sleeves of his loose white shirt rolled to the elbow, his throat bare. The wavy tousle of his hair glowed in earnest as the sun broke the horizon, and he smiled.

Lorry? I thought. *Is everything alright now? Is Dom alright? Is Francis free?*

He looked at me and smiled again. I couldn't tell if it was just an expression of his contentment or whether he was telling me that everything would be okay.

Where's James, Lorry? Just the smile again, and I began to feel that I wasn't quite there for him; that we weren't exactly on the same page.

The sound of footsteps pounded the turf, and we both turned to look as a young boy thundered into sight. He came to a sliding halt on the crest of the hill and stood grinning, framed against the beautiful sky just as the sun finally spilled down the grass and washed us all with slanting morning light.

'Lorry! The boats are in!' The boy had two sticks in his hand, and he flung one in a winnowing arc across the air. Laurence caught it with one graceful lift of his arm over his head. They grinned at each other, these blond twins, one an older reflection of the other, and my fingers tightened around the fabric of my brother's shirt. *What about us?*

Francis swished his stick through the air and turned to go. As he turned, he seemed to catch sight of me and paused. He squinted, his hand raised in mid-swing, a little frown between his eyebrows. Then his face cleared and he shook the moment off with a laugh. It was as though he had caught sight of a strange bird or a fleeting shadow, then dismissed it. He turned his grin to Lorry and flourished the stick like a sword in the air.

'Come on!' Francis said. 'Race you to the harbour!' And then he was gone, his footsteps bumping away from us across an unseen lawn.

Lorry got to his feet. He hefted the stick Francis had thrown him, bouncing it in his hand. He smiled again. 'Good stick!' he said to me, and swung it in an extravagant fencing gesture. He turned and casually mounted the slope, ready to follow his brother out of sight. My heart twisted at the thought that he was going to leave me here, but at the crest of the hill he stopped and turned back to me, his green eyes solemn for a moment.

'What's your name?' he asked.

'Patrick.' My voice was barely a whisper, and I was suddenly thirstier than I'd ever been in my life. His eyes dropped to Dom. 'That's Dominick,' I said.

'Is he the one?' he asked, staring at Dom's unmoving face. 'The one that Fran hurt?'

I nodded. More than anything I wanted to know: would Dom be alright? After all of this, could anyone be alright? But I couldn't summon the words, and the regretful quirk of Laurence's mouth made me afraid to try.

Laurence sighed deeply and gave me one last searching look. He walked backwards over the crest of the hill, keeping me in view all the time. Just as he was about to lose sight of me, as he was about to turn and follow Francis, his eyes flicked up and down, taking in my whole face as if determined to remember it.

'Wake up,' he said.

And I did.

25. Desperation

Desperation

I woke up. Again. How many times had I been bumped awake in this one long night? And where was I now? I leapt to attention, my eyes wide and already focused, slapped into reality with nothing to cushion my fall.

I was sitting against the bedroom wall, clear moonlight splitting the room into light and dark. The smell of dust filled my nose, and the night-time cold of the draughty floorboards numbed my arse. I was awake. I was awake. This was real.

I didn't have to search for Dom; my eyes found him immediately. He lay in the middle of the floor, curled into a lazy 'S' shape. His feet were resting comfortably, one under the other. His hands were tucked under his chin. His eyes were shut.

I scurried across the floor, moaning his name over and over. He wasn't moving. I couldn't see him breathe. Perhaps he was dead. I had already told James that Dom was dead; I had already believed it. But not now that I'd found him. Now that I'd hauled him out of that place. Now that I had rested my hand on his chest and felt his beating heart – I couldn't let him be dead. *Please, let him be alive.*

I grabbed him and pulled him up by his shoulders. He was loose-limbed and limp as rags, and so, so cold. Not Francis-cold – normal cold, dead-body cold.

'Dom.' It came out a dry hiss of a word. '*Dom!*' I shook him. 'Come on!'

He opened his eyes and looked up at me – Dom's eyes, clear and chocolate-brown, looking up at me as if I'd asked a surprising question. I choked out a bark of hysterical joy. Then his eyes rolled back, all the way to the whites, and he rolled out of my arms, turned away from me, and vomited all over the floor.

I've never seen so much puke. It stunned me into a kind of motionless awe. Kneeling over him, my hands held up in surprise, I watched as a spectacular amount of the stuff poured out of him and washed across the floorboards. His silence was eerie; he hardly even made a retching noise. His body just kept contracting and releasing, contracting and releasing, and with each painful inward curl, the tide of vomit grew.

It was everything he'd eaten since yesterday, chewed and undigested, a mass of instantly recognisable bits and pieces: the map of all that had gone before. This evening's chicken casserole and the bread-and-butter pudding that had followed; the grease-coated sausage-and-egg-and-rasher breakfast; the chewed bites of toast; the milky wash of numerous cups of tea; even the lumpy remains of last night's bread, butter and cheese and the white gushing tide of an entire bottle of milk.

The green pills of librium were nowhere to be seen. I found myself scanning the vile pool, watching for their vivid colour in the bland confusion of browns and creams, but they never showed up.

He stopped moving. I stared down at him, waiting for what came next.

Nothing. Nothing came next. The last contraction released its hold on him, and his body relaxed into a loose curl. His hands unfurled from under his chin and came to a rest in front of his face. He looked like he'd fallen asleep saying his prayers, except that he was lying with his cheek in a pool of his own vomit, his curls sticking to skin so pale and shiny that it reflected the moon. His eyes were closed.

'DOM!' I snatched him up and dragged him onto my knee again, pushing back with my feet, distancing the two of us from that disgusting puddle. '*DOM!*' I screamed, and when he didn't answer I just began shouting, very loud, very incoherent. I can't to this day remember what exactly I was yelling.

This time, when the door opened, it was Ma. She flew towards us. I offered him up to her. We weren't alone anymore.

My memories of that night are like snapshots: clear and sharp moments of what I know was a much longer time.

They thought it was food poisoning. They thought it was the flu. They very briefly thought it was meningitis. Theory after theory was proposed and discarded in rapid succession. The longer Dom remained unresponsive, the more puzzled their guesses became. The room emptied and then filled, and emptied again, and filled. I was pushed further and further back 'til I was standing against the wall, wedged into the corner by the dressing table.

I remember a doctor, young and stern. He wanted me to leave the room. He kept glancing at me and saying, 'You go on outside now and wait downstairs.' I remember wordlessly shaking my head, my back pressed to the wall, my eyes glued to Dom. I remember the doctor got very angry. Eventually he stood up and flung his stethoscope down onto the bed. It bounced and clattered to the floor just as my ma came in. She gaped at him as he strode past her, and gasped as he grabbed me by the arm.

'Listen to me, you stupid boy!' He was hissing into my face, but I couldn't concentrate on him. My eyes slid past him, and I tilted my head so that I could look at Dom. The doctor shook me. 'If you don't leave this room *now* your brother will die, do you hear me?' He had more to say, but my ma came up behind him and actually whacked him on the head. He dropped my arm like it had burnt him and ducked away from her, a look of absolute shock on his face.

She didn't say a word, just stood there, her eyes glittering, her mouth a quivering line. She stared the doctor down. Then she raised her hand and pointed at the bottom bunk where my brother lay, still and pale in the shadows. The doctor held her eye for a moment, his cheeks two hectic flares of colour, his hand to the back of his head. Then he blushed a deep, deep red and dropped his eyes.

I got to stay in the room.

They panicked when Dom began shivering. He shivered and shook like someone had dragged him from icy water. His hands clawed up into hooks. His knees drew up to his chest. They thought for the longest while that they would never get him warm.

Morning had just started to paint the windows when my dad came running up the stairs and burst into the bedroom. I remember him making a strange sound when he saw Dom, a half wail, half shout. I remember Ma starting to cry once she saw Dad, as if she'd been waiting until he arrived. I remember him spinning suddenly from where he had been kneeling beside Dom and scanning the room with frantic eyes. It took him a long time to see me; I think I had become part of the wall by then, a shadow in the corner. Dad found me, though. His eyes locked on me, and he made a quiet growling noise far back in his throat and leapt to his feet. I don't know why, but I thought he was going to hit me. He didn't – of course he didn't – he grabbed me instead and hugged me tight to him and rocked me like a baby.

They couldn't figure out the damage to Dom's fingers and toes. They thought maybe they were burns. 'If I didn't know better,' the young doctor said, 'I'd say he had frostbite.'

Then they found the damage to my hands and the damage to Dad's hands. They began to wonder if it was some kind of rash. Meningitis came back into the conversation.

I remember the doctor examining the split in Dom's lip. I remember him glancing over at my bruised jaw. I saw his eyes flick to my poor dad, and a look of disgust crossed his face. Thankfully, Dad had his attention fixed on my mother at the time.

There was brief talk of a mystery virus. The word 'quarantine' began to crop up. There was a suggestion of bringing Dom to Cherry Orchard Fever Hospital. My mam asked what they'd do for him there that they couldn't do here. The doctor didn't have a particularly good answer. Dom stayed with us.

I recall another doctor, an older man with dark, kind eyes and a Jewish face, kneeling on the floor in front of me and taking my hand. When had I slid to the floor? I couldn't remember. The doctor wagged my hand from side to side a little, to get my attention. I looked into his eyes. I remember thinking, *That's what Dom's eyes will look like when he's old.* Dad swam into view beside him, and he was staring intently at me. I think it was very early in the morning, but I can't be sure because the room had that aquarium feel to it that things get when you're very tired.

'Patrick,' the doctor said, 'I want you to answer me truthfully now, yes?' He had a strange accent, like a German accent or something.

Dad was looking at me over the doctor's shoulder. He said, 'We won't be annoyed, son. We just need to know.'

I looked blankly at them both.

The doctor squeezed my hand. Normally I wouldn't have liked that. Normally I would have jerked my hand away. But, right then, it was okay that he was holding my hand; it was more than okay, I gently tightened my grip to let him know I was listening. The doctor nodded and smiled his kind smile. 'Did Dominick take anything he shouldn't have? Any kind of drugs?'

I tiredly closed my eyes. Oh.

Dad was talking. '... sometimes curiosity gets the better of people. It's ... everyone makes mistakes, son. We just need to know ...'

I squeezed the doctor's hand again and let go. 'No,' I said. I wanted to say more, but I was so bloody tired. I couldn't, just couldn't, find any more words.

There was a small moment of stillness, then a hand patted my shoulder and the two men were gone. They had a long and whispered consultation on the other side of the door. I heard my ma quite clearly saying, 'You are *not* making that boy leave this room.'

Eventually, I remember Ma taking my hand and pulling me into a standing position. She got me to peel off my cords, and she dragged my jumper up over the top of my head. Between them, she and Dad helped me to bed. I caught a glimpse of Dom as I staggered across to the bunk. He had finally stopped shaking, and he was propped up on a small mountain of pillows. He passed from my sight as Dad helped me up the ladder. I could hardly hold my head up.

I crawled into bed, flopping onto my stomach with a numb and smoky exhaustion. The bunk swayed like a ship; the room revolved slowly around me. My pillow was cold. The blankets were warm. I began to plummet downwards. I was losing my grip on things. I pulled myself back. *No!* I couldn't do that; I couldn't leave Dom.

Something scraped the floor in the corner of the room, and I tiredly turned my head to see. Dad was sitting by the window in a chair he must have brought up from the kitchen. The sky was a hot blue behind him, the window, open against the smell of vomit and disinfectant that had filled the room. It was late morning, maybe later. Dad's face was in shadow, and he was sitting staring at Dom. He must have felt me watching him because he suddenly switched his gaze to me.

'I'm so sorry, Patrick.'

I couldn't keep my eyes open, so I answered him as they were closing. The pillow seemed to be swallowing the right side of my face. 'What for?'

'You told me Dom was sick. I'm sorry I didn't listen.'

I wanted to tell him that there was nothing he could have done, but I was already gone.

26. Six Days Later – A Conversation about Ska

T he record hissed out dead air as the song came to an end; I didn't even have to look as I reached across and flipped the little lever that raised the play-arm and lifted the needle. I let it hover there while I finished the sentence I was writing, then turned and carefully positioned the needle so that it was back at the beginning of the same song. I'd wear a hole in the record if I played it many more times in a row. There was a blast of static as needle hit vinyl, and then the smooth sounds of Toots and the Maytals drifted out to fill the warm air.

Outside the sun was blazing in a clear blue sky, and all the windows were open, a cool breeze sighing in from the sea. The TV was flickering away in the corner, the sound turned down. It sat on the same kitchen chair that Dad had brought up the night Dom had nearly died. Or the night he came back from the dead. I still wasn't sure what way to think of it.

Dad was in Dublin. Justin had had some kind of emergency at the print shop and Dad had had to run up last night. He'd be back tomorrow. Ma was in the kitchen; I could hear her talking to Dee. The old biddies were due any minute now. They were going to take Nan for a walk, and James Hueston had arranged to join them and bring Dee out in her buggy. Pretty soon downstairs would be filled with the twittery sound of old ladies trying to outdo each other in sweetness and concern, and Dee would be squealing and asking questions and bossing everyone about. But for now, it was just the quiet murmur of voices and the warm smell of dinner cooking.

'Sweet and Dandy' worked its summer rhythm on the air, and I caught myself staring out the window, my head bobbing slightly in time to the music. I sighed, looked at the story I was trying to work on and scratched out the line I'd just written. The page on my knee was covered in scratched-out lines. In fact, only one paragraph remained unmarked. I read it over, my pencil clenched between my teeth: 'The green lasers hissed through the damp air, leaving thin trails of steam in their wake. Carlos felt them hit his back. There was no pain, but they flung him from his feet and threw him forward into the shining wall of his ship.'

I scratched it out. I let my pencil drop to the floor and pushed the copybook off my lap, then laid my head back on the mattress and blew a sigh up at the top bunk. I was sitting on the floor, my back to the bed. The floorboards around me were an untidy jumble of records and unread books, pens and pencils and balled-up scraps of paper. 'Sweet and Dandy' was coming to its conclusion. I let it play through and then reached over and lifted the lever. I twisted around and leant my chin on the bed, looking at Dom. He was lying against a small mountain of pillows, watching the TV; that's to say, his eyes were on the flickering shadows of the TV, but there was no comprehension in them. I flicked a glance at the screen; it was an old black-and-white Tarzan film. Johnny Weissmuller was wrestling a crocodile, his knife between his teeth. He was our favourite Tarzan, the only one of them who looked like he could really bring a lion to its knees. I looked back at Dom.

'Hey,' I said, 'you want me to turn the sound up?'

He didn't so much as blink.

I sighed again, and reached over to drop the needle on the Maytals, but something made me hesitate. I looked back at him again. 'Dom,' I said, 'you want me to put the Horslips on?'

Four days after that terrible night, the doctors finally decided that Dom was out of danger. That was the day Dad had brought up the TV. He had puffed and heaved his way up the narrow stairs with it, and spent a good three hours fiddling with coathangers and rabbit's ears trying to get a decent signal for us. Finally the snow had cleared to reveal the evening news: some shite about the IRA, which Dad turned over because there was footy on the other side. He stepped back, really pleased with himself, his hands on his hips. He blew a lock of hair out of his face and grinned around at me. I was sitting in my permanent position on the floor beside the bed.

'There you go, bud. Seeing as how you can't be wedged out of here with a crowbar.' His eyes crinkled up into the first natural smile I'd seen in ages, and then his face did a strange twitch as he realised he'd addressed only me. His eyes flicked to the still, white form of my brother in the bed behind me, and he tried to stop the smile from falling away altogether. It just made him look crazy when he tried to hold on to it like that. I felt like telling him to stop; he wasn't fooling anyone.

There had been a sudden whiff of cigarette smoke and a soft scuffle on the stairs and James had pushed his way through the door, a big grin on his face. 'Hello the house!' he called, and Dad rushed to help him with his burden. It was a square wooden box with a hinged lid – a portable record player. On top was a small stack of LPs.

Dad had run to find an adapter for the two plugs, and James had winked at me as he set the system up.

'These are all my favourites,' he said. 'Extended loan – as long as it takes for our pal here to get back on his feet.' He gave Dom a smile as natural as the one he'd just given me. 'Now,' he said, shuffling through the pile of records, 'I know you won't think these will be to your taste, lad, but give them a chance. Nothing wrong with broadening your horizons.'

He stacked a few albums one on top of the other. The Skatalites, Byron Lee and the Dragonaires, Desmond Dekker. I'd never heard of any of them, and I have to say, I wasn't too pushed to listen. I was dull and musty, as impervious to everyone as Dom was. But I tried my best to look grateful as Dad returned and plugged the player in, setting it close beside me, and James slipped *The Sensational Maytals* from its sleeve and put on side one.

I'd never heard music like it. It was like a blast of fresh air. It made me sit up straight. Don't get me wrong, I liked music, all sorts, whatever I could get a chance to listen to. But from the minute 'It's You' started to play, I felt – I don't know how to put it – I remember thinking, *I'm home! I found home!* That's how much I loved it.

That evening Dad went out and bought two Horslips albums and some Thin Lizzy, Dom's favourites. That night and for all of the next day, I alternated one or the other with the Maytals. But today? Today, I had just played 'Sweet and Dandy' over and over and over. It was like self-hypnosis. I just couldn't stop.

But it was time to put something on for Dom. I waited for him to respond to my question – Horslips? Or maybe Thin Lizzy? There wasn't a chance in hell of an actual answer; still I waited, my chin resting on the blankets, looking up at him without any expectation.

He'd said nothing but 'milk' for six days. Every mealtime, Ma would bring me up a tray of food and she'd kneel down beside Dom, run her hand through his hair and say, 'What would you like to eat, baby?'

Dom would slide his eyes to her and whisper, 'Milk.'

And that's what he'd get. That's all he'd been living on: glasses of milk. Ma would hold the glass for him, and he'd drain it in a couple of swallows and then lay his head back, his thoughts turning inwards again, and nothing else would get any response from him. I don't think he was ignoring us. He just simply didn't notice we were there. Even his rare trips to the bathroom were nothing but expressionless trials of physical endurance, the shuffling journey there and back enough to drain him of what pitiful energy he had.

'Hey!' I pucked him gently through the covers. 'Lizzy or the Lips?' He didn't look at me. I sighed and turned to the player. 'Alright, so, one more listen to 'Sweet and Dandy' and I'll put on 'The Táin'.'

We listened through to the end of the song once more, and I wearily lifted the record from the player. 'Here we go,' I said. 'Let's switch to the sound of a million hairy men stamping their feet.'

I was carefully slipping the record into the dust-sleeve, trying to hold it only by the edges, when a thin, pale hand touched my arm. I jumped and nearly dropped the album. I spent several dodgy seconds juggling it from hand to hand, still trying to hold it only with my fingertips. When I finally got it back in the sleeve and my heart back in my mouth, Dom was almost grinning. Almost. On anyone else, it would have been the merest hint of a smile. On Dom, right then, it was the sun coming out.

I tried not to overreact. For a minute, I just sat there, trying not to let my eyes fill up with tears, trying to think of something okay to say.

I finally decided on, 'Hey.'

He gestured tiredly at the record, the vaguest movement of his hand. 'Like that one,' he whispered. ''S good.'

I held the Maytals up, my eyebrows raised in surprise. 'Yeah? This fella?'

He nodded, ''S good,' he said again.

I jumped enthusiastically to my knees and pulled the record from its sleeve again. Dom hissed at my clumsy pawing of the vinyl.

'Careful!' he whispered.

I rolled my eyes as I slipped it back on the player, side two this time. 'You think the last song was good, listen to this one.' I carefully dropped the needle and '54-46 (That's My Number)' began its jumpy upbeat groove. I grinned at him, my head bobbing in time, willing him to love it. 'Heh? What you think?'

His eyes lost focus as he listened and his head nodded. Gradually the music seemed to infuse him. He began tapping time with his fingers.

'Well?' I said, dropping to my arse, laying my arm casually along the bunk.

''S good,' he said again. It seemed to be the limit of his vocabulary. 'Like it.'

We listened through the song, and then to 'Oh Yeah' for a few minutes. Then I jumped up and put 'Broadway Jungle' on for him.

'This is great,' I said. 'It's not as old; you can hear a real hard edge moving in …' I let him hear a few bars and then just started talking, telling him all the things James had told me about the Rude Boys and ska and the beginnings of reggae. He nodded and made the occasional murmur of interest, but mostly he just bobbed his head and tapped his hand to the music.

I was telling him about the heatwave in 1968 that led to a whole new form of ska, and he was chuckling at the thought of the musicians being just too hot to play as fast as they used to, when I looked up and saw Ma standing in the door. For a minute I couldn't understand what was wrong with her. We'd fallen so deeply back into our usual groove that I couldn't fathom the huge tears in her eyes, the fingers pressed to her lips. And then I realised: I was sitting talking to Dom. I was having a conversation with Dom. I slumped back against the bed, and Mam and I shared a shaky smile of disbelief.

She cleared her throat into the cupped palm of her hand and wiped her sleeve across her eyes.

'Pat,' she said, her voice remarkably steady, 'would you like anything to eat?'

I grinned at her. 'I'd love a boiled egg, Ma. You want a hand?'

'No, love. You're alright.' She looked uncertainly at Dom, hesitant to ask the question that might confound her hopes. 'Dom?' she said, and I saw her swallow down hard when he turned an enquiring face to her. 'Yuh … you want anything to eat, love?'

'Milk?' he rasped. She bit her lip and nodded. She turned to go. 'Ma?' She turned back to him, and he grinned a ghost of a chancer's grin at her. 'Can I 'ave a rasher sandwich?'

I saw her face squeeze up for a moment before she nodded and hightailed it down the stairs.

'Jesus,' I said, staring at the shut door. 'I wouldn't 've minded a rasher sandwich.'

'You should've asked then, you eejit.'

I looked round at him, and we unintentionally locked eyes. I felt suddenly and almost overwhelmingly emotional. I bit down on my lip and once again felt my eyes fill up. Oh Jesus. This was just great. I was such a bloody sop.

'Your nose is running,' he whispered. He was sunk back into his pillows, very tired again, and solemn. I scrubbed my nose on my sleeve and coughed, not sure where to look.

'Hey,' Dom said, 'Put another record on.'

So I did.

27. Surprise

Surprise

Two days after Easter, three days after our miraculous conversation about ska, Dom and I were camped out in the sitting room. We were each of us immersed in our separate activities, both in our own little worlds, paying no heed to anyone. Ma and Dee were out in the front garden with Nan and the two old biddies, sitting in deckchairs and enjoying the unseasonably warm weather.

I was sitting at the table under the window, my pens laid out in orderly rows, my copybooks neatly stacked according to content. I was working on four stories at once, and each had its own set of copies. At the moment Carlos was dragging himself into a cave on some outlaw planet. He was hoping to find shelter from an oncoming meteor storm. I had other plans for him. I rested my chin in my hand and tried to think of another word for 'slime'. Nothing sprang readily to mind.

Dom had commandeered the sofa, his legs covered with Nan's tartan car-blanket, his markers a technicoloured scatter around him. Sheets of neatly executed comic panels were arranged along the top of the sofa-back, and he was bent over his current page with a fierce look. He was paler and skinnier than I'd ever seen him, but that was okay, because he was Dom. Most definitely Dom. He still hadn't spoken to me about The Grey. Hadn't spoken much about anything at all, really, since he'd come back – but that was okay too. I could do the talking for both of us.

He finished whatever minute detail he'd been hunched over and sat up straight, holding the page at arm's length and regarding it with an intense, critical eye. I had to hide a smile into the crook of my hand. His face was covered in multicoloured smudges and fingerprints. Messy git.

He glanced up at me and silently turned the page so I could see it. It was one of his recent, darker pieces. It had one main panel with only a narrow inset at the top. Four small boys were depicted, engaged in bloody battle with a huge and nebulous creature. The creature was made of smoke, and in its centre glowed a fiery eye that could have been a door of orange flames. Its many tentacle-like arms were edged with teeth, long and white, shining in contrast to the creature's smudged body. I flicked my eyes to Dom's face and back to the drawing. The boys were too small for the heavy weapons they carried, and it was obviously an effort for them to hold them up. Still, the blades were dripping with the fiery blood of the creature, and the boys were fierce and determined. The narrow panel that ran along the top of the page was filled with bright blue; it was a sky of some sort, seen through a narrow window, but clever use of a drop-shadow made it seem to be suspended over the other panel, as if not even part of the same narrative. The sky was background to a row of expressionless adult faces, all looking down at the battle, as if viewing it from another world.

I swallowed hard. 'It's brilliant.' I said. 'Wouldn't mind reading that, when it's done.'

He sighed and turned the drawing so he could see it again. He wasn't happy with it, as usual. 'Nearly finished,' he whispered. He draped the page over the back of the sofa with all the others and began ruling out the panel-boxes on a fresh sheet.

I turned back to my story. *Slime*, I wrote. Then, *ooze*. I scratched both of them out, replacing them with *vile green jelly*. Heh. Well, why use one word when three will do? 'Vile green jelly' it would be.

The garden gate rattled and we looked up to see who was coming in. It was the tall old biddy, Jenny. She had to stoop to pass under the apple trees. She was unusually animated, calling out before she'd even come around the corner, 'Boys … boys!' She paused at the door to catch her breath, her normally stern face all pink with excitement. She gasped and waved her hand about for a minute in an attempt to get the words out, and finally she said, 'Your mother … wants you … A surprise!' And she waved us after her as she hurried back out to the front.

I flung an excited glance out the window and threw my stuff together in a haphazard attempt at tidying. I almost ran out of the room before I remembered Dom. He was only now pushing his blanket back, and swinging his legs to the floor. I gripped the table to stop myself from helping as he got to his feet. I matched his hobbling pace to the door.

The day was a blinding glare as we stood in the shade of the apple trees, and we shielded our eyes with our raised hands. Dom caught on before I did and released a soft exclamation of joy. Ma's smiling voice said, 'Your uncle John traded his motorbike for it.'

It was a great big pastel-coloured Volkswagen van. It had huge blue and yellow flowers painted on it, and it seemed to be crammed to the roof with squirming people. The engine shut off, and it was only then that I noticed all the cousins grinning at me from the windows. Aunty Pet and Aunty Breda were wedged tight into the front seat. I could just about see my uncle John, leaning back from the steering wheel and laughing at someone over his shoulder.

The side-door creaked and groaned and finally slid open in a metallic squeal of protest. An improbable number of human beings began to tumble out. Kids were scrambling over each other in an attempt to be first out the door, and I knew by the look on their faces that there was already some mischief afoot. Dom grinned and raised his hand in greeting.

Aunty Breda stuck her head out the window and yelled, 'To hell with the bleedin' bus strike!'

They all cheered.

Dom grinned at me. 'Race yah,' he whispered, and together we ran, neck and neck, out from beneath the shadows of the house and into the clear promise of a magnificent summer.

CITY OF LIMERICK PUBLIC LIBRARY C 99649

OTHER BOOKS BY CELINE KIERNAN

The Moorehawke Trilogy

Since its release, The Moorehawke Trilogy has captured the imagination of readers everywhere, and has seen American, British, Australian, German, Russian and Spanish rights to the book sold amid resounding praise from international publishers.

The Poison Throne – Book 1

A Friend. A Father. A Kingdom. Which would you sacrifice?

A compelling take of court intrigue, adventure and romance set in a fantasy medieval Europe. Wynter is faced with a terrible choice: stay with her dying father and accept the King's ruinous plans or join in the search for the rightful heir to the throne. A stunning debut from an incredible writer.

ISBN 978-1-84717-170-2

The Crowded Shadows – Book 2

New friends. Old enemies. Who can you trust?

The Crowded Shadows follows Wynter Moorehawke as she embarks on a perilous journey to find the missing Prince Alberon and restore peace to her troubled homeland.

ISBN 978-1-84717-111-5

The Rebel Prince – Book 3

United Friends. A Divided Kingdom. Who will prevail?

Alberon is found, but he plans to protect the Kingdom by the use of the 'Bloody Machine' and the recruitment of some dangerous allies, among them the Loup-Garous, the wolf-tribe who have blighted her beloved Christopher's life. In the final battle, who will survive?

ISBN 978-1-84717-112-2

www.obrien.ie